A Great State: The Divide

by

Shelby Gallagher

Prepper Press

Post-Apocalyptic Fiction & Survival Nonfiction

www.PrepperPress.com

A Great State: The Divide

The first book in the *A Great State* trilogy.

ISBN 978-1-939473-82-0

Written by Shelby Gallagher

Printed in the United States of America.

Prepper Press is a division of Kennebec Publishing, LLC

Dear Dad,

As you read these words, you'll recognize yourself very quickly in the character of Floyd. More importantly, I hope you see your lasting legacy in the character of Julie.

Love "Shelby" (the real Julie)

Foreword

It was a cold January morning when I received an email from an aspiring author who was contacting me under her pseudonym, Shelby Gallagher.

"I'm writing a book about a collapse," her email began. "Could you read it and tell me if it's awful? I know you probably get a lot of requests like this but… please just skim it and let me know if it's any good."

Oh goodness, I thought. *Another unsolicited manuscript.*

After publishing my ten-book series, *299 Days*, I began receiving many manuscripts from authors who wanted my feedback or endorsement. It was impossible to keep up with all the submissions, and most often, they were not of a quality that I'd want my name associated with.

Up until I received this email, I did little with the requests I received. Many were the same old end-of-the-world story we've all heard, and nothing unique ever surfaced. Of course, I always felt guilty after telling writers I didn't have the time or interest to be involved with their projects. However, when Shelby contacted me, there was something about her email that got my attention. I told her I'd give the manuscript a scan and be in touch as soon as my schedule allowed.

A few days and three chapters later, I sent her an email. "I'm pacing around my house looking for a hammer," I wrote.

"Why?" she replied.

"Because I'm picking which one I want to use to cave that guy's face in," I said. "I just read the third chapter of your draft and I'm walking around my house looking for a hammer. I want to kill that guy. I mean, literally, murder him. Hammer blows to the face."

Shelby had written a chapter—and its gut-wrenching scene—so well that it had triggered an emotional response in me. It was raw, deep, visceral. Reading it upset my stomach and caused my hands to shake. Never before had I been so moved by something I'd read.

I wondered what the rest of the book was like. Perhaps there was one really good chapter, but the rest was garbage. I certainly had seen that before. I kept reading and found that I couldn't put it down. The rest of the book was fantastic.

It looked at a potential collapse in a way that no one had before, and yet, it also seemed based on real events. The main character's evolution as a person, a single mother, and a prepper while tragic events unfolded was both believable and extraordinary. This was a book that had to be shared with the world, so I called Shelby.

"Want help getting this out there?"

She didn't respond immediately, and I regretted the offer. What if she was a weirdo? I didn't know anything about her. Why had I just volunteered to help a stranger with her book?

"Are you serious?" she finally asked. "You really think I could get this published? I mean, I've never written anything before. The story is based on some things that have happened to me and stuff that I see happening in the country. I'm not really sure how many people really care to hear about my experiences and beliefs."

Behind her apprehension, I could hear excitement in her voice. She reminded me of myself and how I had wanted to write the *299 Days* series to warn people and help them prepare for what's coming, so horrible things wouldn't happen to them.

Shelby's story was particularly unique as it gave a female voice and perspective to how events would unfold for a woman when society started to fall apart. Most end-of-the-world stories — mine included — are male-centric and don't always offer an intimate view of how different the experience would be for a woman. Shelby's book was real — as real as it gets, because, like my *299 Days* series, it was so closely modeled after her own experiences and how they shaped her view of the world.

As a woman who has been victimized in various ways during her life, Shelby understands how vulnerable women would be during a collapse. She understands how government tries hard to get single moms — like her — dependent on government programs. Millions of women have unknowingly bought into this concept and now depend on government funding to provide for them and their children.

Today, the government can freely spend the money to take care of women and children, but what happens when that money runs out? During a collapse, these women and children will have nothing. That's when the old-fashioned pimping will take over. Men will surely take care of women — but at a terrible price. I don't even want to think about what will happen to their kids. Shelby lays all this out in frightening detail.

Of course, the prepper in me really appreciates how the main character develops a survivalist mentality as the story unfolds. She didn't start off as a prepper, and didn't even own a gun. However, as her life circumstances change — along with the world around her — prepping becomes an unavoidable necessity. Doing so is also what allows her to remain independent, unlike many of the single mothers around her.

"Who better to convince women who might be on the fence about prepping," I said during that phone conversation, "than someone like you? If a woman reads your book and isn't convinced of the need to prep and protect herself, then she'll never do it."

"I just want to save some lives," Shelby said.

I thought about all the women I know who hate prepping, and even the idea of protecting themselves. The men in their lives have tried to convince them, but only from a male perspective, and it has rarely worked. Their strong desire to protect and saves their wives is constantly mocked. I know firsthand.

But Shelby can talk to women about taking care of themselves and their kids, cutting costs, and having items on hand to save trips to the store. She doesn't come across as a gun-crazed weirdo with a thousand cans of beans piled up in her basement. Because she's not like that. I can't imagine a woman reading Shelby's books and not at least saying, "Okay, this isn't crazy." I think thousands of men will be able to hand her books to the woman they love and they will prep as a couple.

"When did you write this?" I asked her during that first phone conversation. There were so many predictions in her book that seemed to be coming true that it was uncanny.

"Last year," she said. I could hear a hint of pride creep into her voice. "I guess I predicted some stuff," she said. I could tell that she was smiling.

"Seems that way," I replied.

"I kind of coined the term 'sanctuary state' before it was being used in the media."

I asked her what else she foresaw coming in this country. After a fascinating and detailed conversation, she ended with, "And that's why America will break apart."

There were several more phone calls after that first one. I jumped into helping her with her first book, and the subsequent two in the series. We talked about the plot, details of the collapse, and the male characters. Just as she could see things from a female perspective better than I could, I could offer the male viewpoint. After I helped edit her final draft, I called my publisher who agreed with my assessment and offered her a publishing deal. That's extremely rare.

Just like *299 Days*, Shelby's first book is about the main character and events that have shaped her life while the Collapse unfolds all around her. When I was editing, I tried hard not to turn them into *299 Days* books and Shelby made sure of it.

"This sounds a little like Grant Matson talking," she said a couple of times.

Fair enough. Her books are her books. She's too independent to let anyone take over any aspect of her life. That's a good thing. Enjoy the story. She has poured her heart into it. I've seen her cry over the story. She has done a magnificent job. I am very proud of her.

Now I need to get back to finding that hammer.

Glen Tate
Author of the *299 Days* series

Chapter 1

The Ugly Cry

Julie Atwood was exhausted. It was Friday and she was driving home from work in Eugene, Oregon. As she looked in the rearview mirror before changing lanes, she noticed her reflection and sighed. The stress she had experienced in recent months was starting to make itself known all over her face. Julie was a fit woman in her mid-thirties, with long brown hair, someone she'd even consider fairly attractive under normal circumstances. But stress had taken its toll. The lines on her formerly smooth skin were becoming more prominent along with darkened eyes. It looked like she hadn't slept well in a long time, which was true given what she'd been through.

At least the long week was behind her. She sat in clogged traffic feeling as though she was so close to home, yet so far because car movement was being measured in inches. It felt so unnecessary, sitting in traffic when she could just get out and walk and get home faster. But nothing was simple in her life anymore. It was one of those moments when exhaustion and the weight of the world compounded to a feeling of... despair. Or maybe hopelessness. Was there a difference?

As she sat there with nothing better to do, she reverted to replaying the last three years — and all their nasty conversations — in her head. A divorce. Single parenthood. One income, and a tiny one at that. Tight budget. Insecurity. Fear. Loneliness. Anxiety. She was never going to be happy again. These thoughts had occurred in her head so much they had almost become her mantra. Her very unhealthy and unhelpful mantra.

Her thoughts most often centered on the ugliness of her divorce. Ugliness in the sense of something beautiful being ruined and then broken and ugly. Before the divorce, Julie found her stride just as she entered her thirties and finally felt like a "real" grown up. She was a parent getting back into the workforce and feeling some success. She felt good about her parenting, her marriage, and her job. That was the beauty. She believed she had finally achieved what all modern women want – she had it all.

Then her husband, Steve, said he needed to talk to her. That evening changed the trajectory of her life forever. Steve had found someone else... ten years younger than Julie. Steve was no longer feeling "fulfilled." He felt it was more important for their child, nine-year-old Joel, to know him as a happy parent. He didn't seem to care about an intact home. Steve talked as though the two qualities were mutually exclusive, essentially meaning that the only way he could be happy was if he did not live at home any longer. They could both exist in the same package in Julie's mind, but Steve had already made his decision.

After that difficult conversation, the next few discussions with Steve turned to details of severing the family. It became about "co-parenting," and "what is best for the child," and "division of assets." It seemed that Steve was the only one unaware that a living child was an asset that couldn't be divided. It didn't take long for Julie to conclude that Steve didn't really want Joel around, but felt too guilty to acknowledge that even to himself. Julie could not comprehend this—Joel was her world.

Steve put up a good show about wanting time with their son, but in the end, it was determined that he would see Joel basically on weekends and a couple weeks during the summer. Julie resented this on so many levels. She'd known all along that he was not going to want shared custody. And she knew he was in denial about it and couldn't admit he was that kind of father, so he caused countless unnecessary and painful arguments on the topic until he was finally man enough to acknowledge he only wanted limited visitation.

It was bad enough he was leaving her, but to turn his back on their child… she would never forgive him for that. Everything during this time was all about Steve's feelings. He never once considered the impact his decision was having on Julie and Joel. He dragged the whole ordeal out until he felt good enough to admit what he truly wanted, and then it was settled. Just like that. Julie now realized he was a pathetic excuse for a man. He was a millennial male. Not a man; just a male.

The light turned green again and there were four cars in front of Julie. She missed that light cycle as well. She was stuck. What a metaphor for her life. As she continued idling, her thoughts went back to ruminating on the divorce disaster: meeting Steve's girlfriend.

Her name was Mandy—even her name sounded young and perky. She was youthful and energetic… and twenty-six years old. She had the idealistic outlook of her generation and still had her whole life in front of her. Her vibrancy made it intoxicating to be around her. Of course he fell in love with her. Sadly, Julie saw a younger version of herself in Mandy – she wasn't much different than Julie had been ten years ago. Now, Julie felt so small. Insignificant. Outdated and replaced by a newer model.

As she recalled meeting Mandy, Julie's vision blurred and hot tears poured out of her eyes. She let them flow today and embraced the relief that followed. In the three years since she was junked by her husband, moments of being able to cry in private were precious. The tears needed a voice, and letting them pour out in her little car where no one could see her was better than in front of her beautiful all-American son, Joel, who was now twelve. He was so sweet and innocent, despite the divorce. He hadn't yet learned what it means for a life to go from beautiful to ugly.

So, she cried. She cried the ugly cry and she inched her way home. A few minutes later, she finally pulled into her crappy little house. Although the house was outdated and needed some attention, it was her sanctuary with Joel. It was their place to stand against the rest of the world.

Whenever she thought about how she and Joel were on their own against the whole world, a thought would come to her. *Survival*, it said.

The thought — perhaps it was intuition — told her that she needed to able to take care of herself and Joel because something was coming. She'd had this inkling when Joel was born. It was vague and easy to dismiss back then, and she attributed it to the endless loop of worrying that often plagues new mothers. Now, years later, after the divorce, the inkling returned and was more powerful. It had become a well-developed thought. A concern. A worry. A problem to solve. She wasn't even sure what she was worrying about or what problem needed solving but the feeling nagged her relentlessly.

The divorce showed her that the world was full of Steves — weak, selfish, indecisive males — boys who happened to be in their thirties. The survival thought in her mind told her that she couldn't count on a world full of Steves and she had to rely on herself. To some extent, she knew this well before she even met Steve.

She flashed back in horror to college and what happened there — and that was even worse than Steve. She could not, and absolutely would not, be a victim again. She could never count on someone else — especially worthless males like Steve — to protect her from the vicious world.

"It will get even more vicious," she said out loud, thinking about this pending, but still unknown, future event. She just knew whatever was coming her way — and Joel's way — would make the world even nastier than it had become. And she would be alone, trying to protect herself and Joel.

"I need a plan," she said to herself. As committed as she was to rely-

3

ing on herself as she and Joel faced the world together, she also knew the odds were stacked against her as a single mom. She'd been wrestling with this for too long now, and her ruminations always led her to the familiar feelings of despair and hopelessness that had been haunting her for years.

***

By now, Joel's after-school schedule had settled into a routine. He went to his friend Carson's house after school. The idea was that he and Carson would do homework together until he came home around dinnertime. There would be no homework, or very little, and the rest of the evening was free for dinner and mother/son time. This arrangement sounded good in theory, but didn't always happen. Joel struggled with simply being a boy. He was smart and could do anything well—if it was something he wanted to do. Math and social studies were not things he wanted to do. So, many nights, Julie worked with Joel redoing his homework. She would come home expecting to relax, but it wouldn't happen. It added to her endless exhaustion. She couldn't be mad at Joel, which added to the frustration.

Tonight's evening was typical. She changed out of her work clothes: basic, somewhat frumpy discount department store attire that she wore at her dismal job for an organization that relied entirely on government contracts. She wanted to leave her crappy clothes on the floor of her tiny bedroom, but that would be a bad example to set for Joel, so she mustered the last few ounces of energy she had and put them away.

She put on a smile for Joel, but dreaded what she had to do next. She looked online at Joel's grades and saw two failing quiz scores. Notes from the teachers indicated he could do an extra writing assignment to make up the lost points. What this meant was extra work—for both of them.

Julie looked at Joel. "Honey, do you see that if you had simply reviewed your work at Carson's and studied a little there, you would have a free evening? You're basically doubling your workload. Do you see that?" She tried to speak gently. She felt like such a nag, but she wasn't sure the adolescent understood the consequences of half-assing his homework. He had become so accustomed to always doing extra work and barely getting by. Just like her. And it never ended.

"Mom, I *knowwww*."

Julie dished out the Sloppy Joe meat onto hamburger buns for the both of them, slid their plates on the kitchen table, and sat down, resisting

4

a sigh.

"Grab your social studies book, let's get going on this." And so, the evening began as Joel learned about the Industrial Revolution in early America.

Julie was bothered by what Joel was being taught. The tone of Joel's textbook did not seem factual. It had a whiff of derision. Impressionable young minds like Joel's were being told that laborers in factories worked in squalor because of greedy capitalists. The book made sure to point out that America's industrial growth came at the expense of indigenous people, and that immigrants saved the day and did work Americans wouldn't do. It also went into how racial minorities were routinely terrorized for sport.

Julie knew that it was true that factories during the Industrial Revolution had unsafe and poor working conditions. She also knew that immigrants worked in factories. But America also flourished during this time and set a new standard in the world for production, ingenuity, and prosperity. A person could be born in the poorest of circumstances and, through hard work, prosper beyond belief. That was the American dream, but none of this was in Joel's textbook. Instead, it went on for pages shaming America's history. By the time she finished reading Joel's lessons, Julie felt guilty for being an American.

This only added to — and fed — her general sense of overall despair. Her son was being taught that America, the country she loved and was proud of, was a filthy, immoral place. Even the outside world was against her. Her mind mulled that over and over until eventually she fell asleep.

Chapter 2

Tyranny of the Budget

The budget. It controlled Julie. She lived and breathed by her household budget, which had to be strictly followed or things got really tight, really fast. This felt like just another facet of Julie's life that she could not control.

In the divorce, she got the house. He bought out his half, but that meant she still owed her half. Julie was thankful for having a decent roof over her head, even if that meant having a monthly payment of roughly what rent would be. This monthly payment was a big chunk of her income—about a third of her budget. She couldn't save much money, but she somehow managed to squirrel away a tiny amount, maybe fifty dollars a month.

Never one to follow the latest fad, Julie still managed to find herself trying out the latest craze of couponing. She attended a few local classes on how to maximize couponing. She learned that the extreme couponing reality show where a person walked into a store, gathered twelve shopping carts of food, and paid three dollars for it was, indeed, extreme. It was totally unrealistic.

However, she learned that by setting aside a small amount of income a month to apply toward stockpiling, she could maximize her budget. She had been doing it to a small degree for the last year and the habit actually provided some relief to the budget.

The idea was simple. She bought large quantities of items with a long shelf life, and would do so by maxing out on the quantity allowed by each coupon, and purchasing the items only when they were on sale. Often, she ended up with more than she would need in the immediate future, but the long shelf lives made it practical. At first, it took some planning, but soon became a natural habit.

Barbeque sauce was a good example. The previous summer, she decided to stockpile it as an experiment. Joel thought she was crazy at first. She followed the formula she learned in the class and went on an auction website where she paid two dollars for twenty fifty-cent-off coupons for a name-brand barbecue sauce that Joel loved, which normally cost about three dollars a bottle. A local store had the barbecue sauce on sale for one dollar a bottle around the fourth of July. That same store had a double coupon offer. She bought the one dollar barbecue sauce, applied a fifty-cent-off coupon, and then the store doubled it, making it free. She made multiple runs to the store during the week of the sale. It took some planning and effort, but she ended up with sixty dollars' worth of barbecue sauce—for two dollars. It was a thirty-to-one return on investment, and was for something that stored a long time and she knew they would use.

She managed to find similar kinds of stockpiling deals on toilet paper, cough medicine, canned goods, pasta, salad dressing, and toiletries. The savings slowly added up. She knew it was a minor thing, but couponing gave Julie some hope that she had some control over her destiny.

Chapter 3

Defenseless, the First Time

Julie grew up in Colorado. She went to the University of Colorado when she was eighteen. She was like many young college students her age: a little unsure of the future, fun loving, ambitious, and slightly insecure.

Julie had a fun job in a local army surplus store in Boulder, near the college campus. It was fun because the store attracted a colorful cast of customers. Students loved the store because they could get that hip pair of army boots to go with their edgy ensemble. Local outdoor lovers enjoyed the mountaineering equipment, hiking boots, cold weather gear, and cross-country skis. The store offered a mix of products that were perfect for a hipster, outdoor-loving college town. One day, a man in his late-forties came in.

His name was Roger, and he struck up a conversation like so many other customers did. He wanted a pair of hiking boots for a trip. Julie inquired about the type of hiking he'd be doing, and what size he wore. This was Julie's job and the conversation generally went the same. As Roger tried on hiking boots, and the conversation went into several different directions about his hobbies and interests. He was older and seemed knowledgeable of life. She listened to him talk and felt a strong attraction and, possibly, a connection.

Then, Roger did the unexpected. He invited her to a local outdoor concert later that week with a group of his friends. Julie imagined it would be like so many gatherings in the carefree college town. "Sure," she said, "where should I meet you?"

He smiled slightly. "I'll pick you up. We'll meet the others at the concert. Parking will be difficult, so let's ride together."

"Oh, sure," she said and gave Roger her address, trying to hide her giddiness.

They went to the concert, but there was no group of friends. It ended up being just the two of them. This surprised Julie, and she wondered if he'd known all along there would be no friends joining him. He was incredibly nice at the concert and held Julie's hand, which she thought was a bit forward, but also didn't mind it.

At one point, as she returned from getting sodas, she walked toward Roger who had a half-smile on his face. "My God, you're beautiful," he said in a sexy voice. Julie was flattered. She couldn't remember the last time a man had told her that.

Later, they went to a local place for a late dinner. He told Julie about himself. He was divorced, and he joked that his daughter was slightly younger than Julie, but that Julie was much more adult. Julie was glad that he saw her as a woman and not as a child. He was attracted to her, and she was flattered. He made her feel good, and it was magical.

He took her back to her place and followed her out of her car. She didn't expect that. Usually, when a date would drop her off, they stayed in the car and made sure she got into her door.

Okay, she thought, *he is walking me to the door. What a gentleman.* She got to the door, and turned around to say goodbye. "I had a great time and I hope we can do this again," she said.

He put his foot in the door. "Let's keep talking."

He had a serious, and almost dark, look in his eyes. "I'm enjoying this evening too much for it to end," he said.

She looked up at Roger, a bit surprised though he'd been relatively straightforward all night. His eyes pleaded with hers. She felt it impossible to refuse him.

They sat on her couch, and continued the conversation from the restaurant. Julie noticed he liked to talk about himself quite a bit. She found his stories exciting. As she listened to Roger talk, she realized how young she still was and her life was a blank canvas. She didn't have too many exciting stories to share yet. So, Roger talked. He managed to sprinkle in some compliments and flattery along the way. The conversation was enjoyable.

He was a retired high school teacher, and was a backup coach for various teams at the local school. He also taught woodworking and metal shop. He showed her a few scars on his hands where shop mishaps had occurred.

Julie looked across the room at the digital clock on the stove. It had gotten late, and tomorrow was a long day. She had an early-morning summer class, followed by an eight-hour shift at the store.

She looked at Roger. "I think we need to call it a night. I'm having a great time, but I need to go to bed."

"Okay," Roger said.

But, he didn't stand up to leave. In fact, he didn't move at all. He stared at her without blinking.

Julie felt a pang of fear in her gut. "I need to go to bed, so... umm...

I need you to…"

She knew it was rude to ask someone to leave, and couldn't come up with an easy way to do it. She cleared her throat. "I need to say goodnight. Let's do this again soon. If you want, I can call you after my class tomorrow before I go to work."

She wondered if she'd given enough of a hint. But, he still did not move. His facial expression didn't even change.

Okay, Julie thought, *I need to be a little rude*. "I have to ask you to leave so I can get some sleep," she said firmly. "Thank you so much for inviting me. I would love to do this again…"

Finally, Roger responded. "I'm not leaving." He spoke with conviction, in such a way that Julie's stomach tensed up.

"You can't stay tonight," she said, her voice a bit shaky. "I don't do that with someone I don't know. But, hey…," she said, and was about to say they could have a second date sometime later.

"I'm not leaving," he repeated.

"I need you to leave," she said, trying harder to mask her apprehension over the situation and change in his tone.

"No."

He wore no expression on his face. Julie had no idea what to do. She had a man in her apartment, who was twice her size and age, and who was refusing to leave. She'd told no one about the date, so there were no friends calling to check up on her.

Instinctually, she knew things had changed—and were about to change again—for the worse. She stood up to head toward the door. Her plan was to open it and repeat her demand.

He was right behind her. As she opened it, he reached above her head and slammed the door shut. Then he put his right-hand palm on the right side of her neck and pressed his fingertips into her windpipe.

"I'm not leaving," he snarled into her left ear. "Don't open that door again," he whispered.

He pulled her by the neck back away from the door. She felt like she was being pulled into hell. By the end of the evening, Julie's life had changed. Irreparably. Permanently.

***

The next morning, Julie felt like a discarded, dirty, ragdoll sprawled out on her apartment floor. He had hit her several times with an open hand. The punches—even open-handed ones—from a grown man with coaching and woodworking experience shocked all her senses. She heard them, saw them, felt them, and tasted them.

He had twisted her neck. She knew that if you twist a person's neck to a certain point, the aggressor can render someone unconscious, but with a slight release of the twist bring the person back to consciousness.

The whole time, Julie felt her life could easily be extracted from her. She knew that if Roger decided to twist her neck an eighth of an inch more, he could break her neck. She couldn't fight him, but she didn't cooperate. Fighting could mean the end of her life. She felt it. She was afraid of it.

But, she survived. In the morning light, she laid on the floor looking at her apartment sideways with her bra on the floor two feet from her face. Bits of the assault flashed in her memory. She closed her eyes and tears slid sideways down her face into her ear. Julie stood up cautiously, and instantly felt rays of pain throughout her body. She took a step back to catch her balance.

What do I do now? Call the police? She imagined what that would be like. They would want to come over to her apartment and ask questions. *How long have you known this man? What is his name? How did he know where you live? How did he get in? What is his phone number? Where does he live?*

She realized her answers to those basic questions would be an indictment of her stupidity. Worse yet, all he had to do was deny it by saying it was consensual. It would be another instance of he said, she said. And she knew how those situations often ended.

Thinking back to the evening's conversation, she realized she knew so much about this man, but also knew little. Very little. Any questioning by law enforcement would only highlight her stupidity for inviting an unfamiliar man into her apartment. She knew all about victim-blaming, and she had set herself up for a perfect case of that.

She stood there, unsteady on her feet, crying. Where he'd hit her radiated with pain. *Evidence!* She gingerly stepped in front of her bathroom mirror, bracing herself to see a bruised face. She closed her eyes, preparing herself. Then, she took a deep breath, and slowly opened her eyes. She needed to be prepared for the shock of a bruised and battered face.

But, no! There was nothing! Her cheeks looked swollen and pink, but there were no bruises. It was shocking but for reasons she hadn't even thought of.

How is this possible? He never hit her with a closed fist. That was the difference. *He knew exactly what he was doing.* In fact, she realized, he had done this before.

Her swollen cheeks could simply be written off as a symptom of being emotional and crying. She leaned on the palms of her hands as the reality began to sink in. The tears rolled down her puffy face. Julie squinted and cried.

Oh my God. Rape. The reality of being raped rolled over her like a wave—a stronger and stronger wave of humiliation each time. She couldn't believe what had happened to her. Rape. Something that happens to other people—not her. She stumbled out of the bathroom and thought of her clothes. Surely, he had ripped or broken something. But, no. Summer clothes were loose-fitting and came off easily.

The apartment merely looked like a morning after a couple had spontaneous, passionate sex. It did not look like a crime scene. She would need to convince the police that a crime had occurred but didn't know how. Who would believe her? It would be her word against his. She looked at the clock. It was 6:40 a.m. Class was at 8:00 a.m. She didn't know what to do. She realized if she called the police, they'd probably call her parents. She couldn't risk that—they'd be devastated and ashamed, just like she was.

Julie willed herself to stop crying and exhaled a shaky breath. Realizing she wasn't going to do a damn thing about the previous night, she took a shower, put on clean clothes, and threw away the clothes she wore the night before. She repeatedly brushed her teeth and scrubbed her entire body to get every trace of him off her.

Julie made her class. She worked her shift that day.

Chapter 4

Gluing Back the Broken Pieces

The nightmares came quickly. They crashed into Julie's life like a sledge-hammer. *Nightmare* was too weak of a word to describe the brutally vivid night terrors that replayed her rape. She was terrified to go to sleep and clumsily fought her numbed mind to stay awake. She became sleep deprived. Her speech was slurred and she couldn't concentrate. She became deeply depressed. Her mind was spiraling downward into the same tunnel to hell as when Roger dragged her across the floor.

She needed a change. Everything needed to change. She quit school and looked for another to transfer to. She also quit her job. She couldn't stand being at the store where it all started.

Julie moved to Eugene, Oregon, enrolled at the University of Oregon, and transferred her credits from the University of Colorado. Julie found a job at a bookstore. Her sole focus was finishing school and nothing else. There would be no more dates with mysterious, charming men. All she wanted was a degree and to get on with her life.

Her dad helped her move. It was a good trip. Julie knew her dad sensed something was wrong, but he wasn't one to be nosy, so he didn't ask any questions. And she offered no information.

Julie's mother was crazy. That was the reason why Julie's parents divorced right after Julie finished high school and went off to college. Her mother was manipulative, sharp, mean, and selfish. Nothing could please her mother unless it served her and no one else. She sucked the life out of everyone who crossed her path. The older she became, the fewer people crossed her path. Julie was not only looking for a new start with her move to Oregon, but she also wanted to put miles between herself and that hateful woman.

As Julie and her dad left Colorado, she recalled her junior year of high school. She was driving a friend home from a Friday night football game and hit black ice. The car spun and plowed into a fence. No one was hurt, and the most painful part of that incident was calling her parents. She stood at a payphone at a nearby gas station and dialed the number. Her dad answered. Julie told him the story, which was laden with profuse apologies.

"Oh, Julie," her dad said with relief. "I'm just glad you're okay. Cars can be replaced and repaired." He paused as if he regretted what was coming. "Here's your mom," he said as he handed the phone to her mother.

"Julie!" her mom shrieked. "How many times have I told you to watch your speed? How fast were you going?"

Julie flinched. "I'm not sure," she stammered, "maybe forty."

"That was too fast," her mom hissed. "You're lucky to be alive," she said without a hint of relief that Julie was okay. "I really just can't believe this!"

Julie didn't remember what else her mother barked about. That phone call epitomized the difference between her parents. Julie felt loved and valued by her father. Julie felt like an inconvenience to her mother and like a screw-up who did everything wrong. This was why Julie decided so quickly not to call the police after her rape; she could not imagine her mom yelling at her... for being raped.

As Julie and her dad crossed the state line, she realized that she was traveling with her doting father and escaping her resentful mother. This gave Julie a sense of independence as the worst parts of her past were literally in her rearview mirror.

During the first week of classes at the University of Oregon, Julie found a conveniently located sandwich shop. While she was eating lunch and reading a magazine, a young man came up to her table and asked if he could join her. She looked up and saw seven other chairs at the table. She waved her hand at the man. "Take your pick."

"Hi, I'm Steve," he said and stuck his hand out to shake hers.

Steve had jet black hair, but otherwise wasn't too remarkable. He kept talking, oblivious to her cues that she wasn't particularly interested. She was more focused on her sandwich than him. She tried not to listen as she transitioned from her sandwich back to her magazine. She didn't want to encourage him, but it was becoming harder to ignore him as he continued with friendly banter. Eventually, she gave in and joined him in the conversation.

By the end of the semester, Steve's bubbliness began to soften Julie. He was kind and it chipped away at the rough exterior she'd been working so hard to create. He was upbeat and had a calming effect on Julie, who was still having nightmares and trouble concentrating in class.

Steve gave her inspiration to get through school. She found herself joining in conversation with him. She could handle a conversation with him a few times a week at the sandwich shop. The dark cloud over her head started to disperse. She sensed that she was on the cusp of a true fresh beginning.

After a few months, Steve mentioned an annual local parade happening at the end of the semester. "Would you like to come with me?" he asked. He sounded sheepish, which was not surprising as Julie had still worked hard to keep him at arm's length.

"Oh… no," she responded quickly. "Thank you, though."

"There's no need to worry about anything," Steve assured her kindly. "There's a group of us from my study group going," he continued. "It will just be a handful of people."

"No, really," she replied, suppressing a primal fear that bubbled up in her stomach as soon as he mentioned going out with a group. "Parades aren't my thing. Have fun, though." She meant that sincerely. She wanted him to have fun, but she wouldn't go.

"How about joining us for lunch before the parade?" he asked. "We're planning to all meet here," he said. "You know, before the parade then carpooling to it. You don't need to make the parade, but could join us." He was trying, and for that, a bit of her resistance went down.

The lunch scenario made her feel better. She could meet this group in public and leave anytime she wanted. She thought long and hard, knowing that this would likely be the first invitation of many. She had been telling herself that she would not date for the foreseeable future. However, this wasn't dating. It was eating lunch with a group, in a public place. She couldn't see what would go wrong.

Then she remembered seeing herself in the mirror in Boulder, searching for bruises to prove she'd been raped. She'd been wrong about a "harmless" date once before. She wouldn't make that mistake ever again.

She had to admit that she was craving a new life. She needed to start making some new memories so she could move that mirror and that evening to the back of her mind. Knowing she could bolt from the group lunch at any point, she accepted that this was a safe first step.

"Okay," she said with a shrug, wishing Steve knew how big of a deal this decision really was.

***

The day of the parade arrived. She had been counting it down on her calendar, not because she was excited to go, but because she was anxious to start a new life without fear.

She was nervous as she walked into the sandwich shop. She didn't see Steve or a group of people, so she decided to order a sandwich and wait.

She sat down with her lunch, pulled out her paperback, and started reading. Soon, Steve walked in. He sat down as she read.

"My study group backed out," he said. "It's just me."

Fear and adrenaline pulsed through her. She tried to calm herself down, reasoning that there was no way Steve was following some sort of how-to manual on raping a woman.

"We have a group project that needs to get done," Steve explained. "Several of them are behind," he said. "No fun day for them."

That's the best he can do? she wondered. *If he's in the study group, why does he have free time when the rest of the group apparently doesn't?*

"I know parades aren't your thing," he said with a hint of desperation. "But after lunch here, do you want to walk around campus a bit?"

Julie did a fast calculation in her head. Walking around campus. This would be in public. She would make sure of that. She would not get in a car with him. She would not allow him to take her home. She would not give him anything but some of her time. However, this was an unfamiliar city to her. He could easily walk her to a location and she would be lost, and he would know that. Plus, there was a swift current river in Eugene—a great place to dump a body.

So, is this how it's going to be? Worrying about being dumped in every nearby river? She was frustrated by her fears, irrational yet justified.

She told herself to toughen up. She could not let the story of her life be about the fear of being dumped in a river. She was tired of being unable to relax and engage with people and have fun experiences.

So, she asked herself, *which is it? Complete safety or some fun experiences? What the hell,* she thought. If she was going to end up in that river, then she was ready to get it over with.

"Okay," she said.

***

Julie quickly learned that Steve wanted to date Julie, not rape her. After their walk along the river, they started to see each other more and more. As they grew closer and more comfortable with one another, Julie's fear grew. It wasn't the usual fear of getting close to someone. No, it was something much worse. She would need to be honest and tell him about her experience, which she'd told no one about. She increasingly felt dis-

16

honest by keeping it from him. But, she was also increasingly scared that he'd run away from her when he found out she was damaged goods. She liked Steve, but she kind of hoped they'd break up so she wouldn't have to tell him. She knew that was ridiculous.

The schoolyear progressed and they became more comfortable with one another, but she harbored her secret nonetheless. As her final semester approached, they began to talk about marriage. Avoidance was no longer an option.

She and Steve still hadn't had sex. She was terrified that she couldn't do it because of what had happened to her. She didn't want to relive it, and she didn't want to be bad at it for Steve. Sex was a terrible thing.

Julie was a Christian. Steve seemed like he was, too. They talked about sex in their relationship. She made it clear that she wouldn't do that until she was married. Her Christianity turned out to be quite convenient in this regard. And, by the time they were married, he'd be far less likely to run out on her when he found out she was so messed up. She hated being so calculating, but it made sense to her.

One Saturday, as they had yet another discussion of their future and the possibility of marriage, Julie realized that she couldn't avoid the topic any longer. She sat Steve down and composed herself.

"I need to tell you something." Her voice and hands shook.

He adored her. Why, she had no idea, but he thought she was perfect. She loved him for being kind, sensitive, smart, and steady. He had a calming and comforting effect on her. She wasn't sure that was a reason to marry someone, but his ability to soothe her seemed like as good as any reason to marry him. After the rape, her self-esteem was not the highest and her trust in men couldn't get any lower.

Steve was attentive and patient as she worked up the nerve to tell him. Too many times, she'd stammer over her words, stop, and apologize to him for wasting his time. It took her almost an hour to get it out. Steve's patience was a testament to his feelings for her and his character.

"What is it?" he pleaded after she stood up to make another pot of coffee.

"When I was in Boulder...," she started.

The story poured out of her. Violently. Suddenly. Sharply. She cried the same burning tears she remembered crying the day she picked herself up off her apartment floor. Finally, she was done telling the story. Her sobs didn't stop, however. She looked at Steve and he gazed into her eyes

17

with nothing but love coming from his.

He reached his hand out and took her hand. He put her left hand in both of his and stroked her hand. "I love you. Nothing is going to change that. I only wish you'd told me sooner."

And on that day, Julie felt the new page in her life beginning. Her life was redeemable.

Chapter 5

Damaged Goods

Julie and Steve were married and things went well for a few years. She still had nightmares, but Steve helped her through them. He was kind. For a while.

She wasn't sure why, but Steve slowly became dissatisfied with her. She assumed it was the rape, but she wasn't positive that was it. She would obsess about why he was growing increasingly distant. She couldn't help but feel like she had done something wrong. She had been raised that way: whenever something bad happened, like the car accident, her mother would always find a way to make it Julie's fault. So, she owned a bit of his growing distance.

As she watched Steve continue to drift away from her, Julie felt extremely vulnerable. Here was the one person who really knew her and her awful secret, who had seemed to accept her, and yet he was becoming a stranger to her.

After a while, the time between their conversations lengthened. They only discussed things like groceries and the weather. Their lovemaking became a task to be done, not enjoyed or expressed. Despite the infrequency of their sex, Julie became pregnant. Joel's birth put temporary brakes on the growing distance between the pair. During Julie's pregnancy and briefly following Joel's birth, there was a common topic and hope that only the two of them could share. Julie's growing belly invited intimacy by simply snuggling close together, whispering, and watching their unborn child create waves on her belly.

After Joel was born, the closeness continued. Julie decided that the distance their marriage had experienced was merely a bump in the road that she heard people talk about. Creating a family seemed to be the reset button they needed and for a while, the family of three was in a cocoon of peace and happiness. Many evenings were spent with the trio cuddling in bed, and Steve would tell Julie about the dreams he had for Joel, their family, and the future. Julie reveled in the picture he would paint. She easily envisioned Joel growing in the dreams he laid out for her. She saw their marriage and future children in his whispered words. It was comforting to hear his plans. His plans were *her* plans.

Yet, when Joel was a toddler, the familiar distance wedged itself between Steve and Julie again. Maybe it was time for another pregnancy? Joel was two years old, after all. The timing seemed right. Julie yearned for the close intimacy brought on by the arrival of a newborn.

She proposed trying for another pregnancy to Steve. He looked at her with a strange expression on his face. It surprised Julie. He had so enjoyed her pregnancy with Joel.

"I don't think now is a good time."

Julie decided not to press it. Maybe it was too soon for Steve — they had just started sleeping through the night again. But, the feeling persisted and gnawed at Julie for another year. When Joel turned three, she brought it up again with Steve.

"Let's just give it a bit more time."

She tried again soon after Joel turned four. Prepared for another rejection, she told herself this would be the last time she asked.

"Julie, trust that I'll let you know when I feel ready."

That was it. By the time Joel began grade school, Julie had resigned herself that Steve would not want more children. She tried to accept and find peace with the concept, but it was difficult. She felt depressed and a bit lost.

To others, their marriage seemed fine. Two parents raising their kid, with decent jobs, paying their mortgage. They showed up to social events with smiles on their faces. To Julie, their marriage wasn't horrible, but it wasn't what she'd always imagined. And, once she knew there would never be another baby to hold, she felt a new void open inside her. *Life is not a chick flick*, she would tell herself. *People don't live for years in mad, passionate relationships. This is reality, not a movie set.*

Julie worked tirelessly at realigning her expectations for marriage. She had to accept that the reality and the fantasy were light years apart. She settled back into her bland marriage, essentially living with a roommate who helped with Joel. Her husband had grown out of his college exuberance and kind heart into a quiet and distant person. It wasn't ideal, but she knew that things could be worse. They could be much worse. He could leave her. And then what would happen?

***

When he was gone and she was on her own again, she told herself it was just another fresh start. Just like after the rape. However, new beginnings were getting old and she was, too. Was it too much to ask for a life of being loved and respected without any traumas?

As a single mom in her mid-thirties, Julie knew that she was damaged goods and the opportunity to find The One was long gone. She didn't like the idea of being alone for the rest of her life, but the low probability of finding a decent man made the time and energy of a relationship a colossal waste. Julie also realized that another waste of time and energy was feeling like a victim. It was time to change that narrative. It had grown old and hadn't done her any favors.

Her church offered a self-defense class for women, taught by a man from her church. She could do this with someone she knew and maybe learn a few things. Two nights a week for six weeks, Julie learned situational awareness, self-defense moves, how to respond to threats, and how to carry oneself when walking and talking. She learned that she could project a presence of strength by simply having good posture, speaking in an active, not passive, tone and looking people in the eye when talking. It was remarkably simple. Julie recalled asking Roger to leave her apartment. Everything she tried in that conversation was passive and timid. He had known it, too. He had probably picked up on the fact that she carried herself from a posture of timidity, both physically and mentally. She replayed the memory of how she carried herself, unsure and without authority. Then something amazing happened — Julie rewrote her memory.

She started to change her history, substituting what she'd learned for what she'd done. She conquered the memory. It was freeing. It made a few nightmares go away altogether. It was positively therapeutic.

***

Learning to carry herself with confidence was the mental part of the class. There was also a physical part. The class presented real-life scenarios where Julie would be attacked by the instructor, who was dressed in a puffy suit and helmet. Julie was tasked with fighting him off, and she had to be able to do so in three different ways. She could taste the fear in her mouth.

The guy in the suit was a former Marine, and was now a policeman. He wasn't there to let the ladies feel like they can take a few punches and pass the class. He made it clear that he was going to come after each woman and that they might end up on their asses.

"I'm not doing you any favors," he'd say, "by giving you false confidence. I'm going to give you real confidence."

Julie didn't want to be the one who ended up on her ass. Worse yet, she didn't want to be curled up in a fetal position reliving that godawful night. But she swallowed her nerves and pushed through it.

In the first two scenarios, she managed to strike him enough in the face that she escaped. It was almost too easy. She wondered if he really meant it that he was going to go at each of them like a real attacker.

And then the third scenario happened. She pretended she was at an ATM machine and he rushed up to her and wrapped his arms around her in a bear hug and lifted her off the ground. This was the worst scenario and Julie was immediately scared it would mean the end of the class for her. She could not use her arms and her legs when he lifted her off the ground. Kicking was an option, but it wouldn't deliver effective blows. It might make it hard for him to walk, but it wouldn't stop the attack.

He was breathing hard under his helmet and his sweat was gross. It reminded her of the night she was attacked by Roger. In the split second when he had her lifted off the ground, Julie considered her options. She quickly decided what she would do. She looked him in the eye through the helmet and acted decisively.

She head-butted him—hard. She saw stars and felt like she might get a bloody nose, but she was determined to stop this attack. Real or not, it was an attack and she needed her head to be in the game. She was going to do whatever it took.

He dropped her and she ran to her mat that indicated she made her escape. She did it! She bent over and took deep breaths. She did it! The instructor came up behind her and tapped her shoulder. Julie jumped thinking she didn't make it to the correct mat or the scenario wasn't over.

"You okay?" he asked. "Let me see your face."

Julie looked up at him, and he told her that she had a slight cut on her forehead.

"You hit me hard," he said. "Well done. Do that in real life if it happens." He paused. "You got what it takes." He patted her on the shoulder and walked away.

Julie felt a wave of pride and confidence for the first time in years. She had done it! Despite her insecurity, she succeeded! A little cut on the forehead was worth it.

In that moment, she knew she'd no longer let herself feel like a victim and would not let herself become a crime victim ever again. She made a personal pledge to herself: never again would she choose not to fight back. She would fight back or die trying. Living as a victim was not an

22

option anymore.

***

Julie also made a personal pledge to no longer be passive. She learned how to carry herself. She walked with confidence, regardless of whether she felt confident. She spoke with confidence, even if she didn't feel confident. She soon discovered that using decisive words, making direct eye contact, and avoiding using filler words while speaking, made people treat her differently. It seemed like they took her more seriously. Julie was surprised to learn that some people didn't like her new confidence. Insecure people felt threatened by her. But, confident people were drawn to her.

After the self-defense course, Julie slept better and was less edgy. She didn't get as alarmed when she met strangers. She conducted herself with confidence and knew how to tactically work herself through a situation. Julie knew that no situation was completely safe, but she felt like she increased her odds considerably. More importantly, she was recovering. She was redeemable. Julie was finally creating the interesting life story she had always wanted to have. She might be a little late to the game, but she was doing it.

"It's not too late for me," she told herself. She had her future ahead of her. She was hopeful.

Chapter 6

Outside Forces

While Julie was finally hitting her stride, the rest of the world started to fall apart. America elected a left-leaning president. The new president rewarded states and municipalities with federal grants for giving safe harbor to America's illegal immigrants, some of whom were vicious criminals. Most of the conservative states refused these grants.

However, Oregon and other left-wing states enthusiastically accepted them. Oregon's mostly liberal legislature set legislative agendas based on policy that maximized the various federal money streams. If states signed up so many people on government assistance, they would receive matching federal dollars. If states met benchmarks for environmental policies, they would receive matching federal grant money. If states followed federal mandates for transportation projects, they received federal dollars. Pick the policy, and the administration either expanded the existing grant programs or thought up new ones to entice states to enact policy. The problem was that states needed legislatures to enact such policies. Oregon's legislature was already on the left side of the aisle, but any election cycle could change the make-up of the legislature. It was easy to fix.

Leftist states also made it easy for illegals to register to vote and, presumably, elect the people who just gave them safe harbor and government benefits. Julie's town of Eugene, Oregon was one of municipalities that gladly put out its hand for the "free" federal dollars—and the new crop of thankful voters. Julie didn't really care about politics, but she was smart and saw what was happening.

She could see that a split was forming between the rest of the country and progressive states like Oregon. It was like watching the country break apart in slow motion. Government grants came with political strings attached, of course. State and local politicians who received federal money—and lots of new thankful registered voters—were expected to voice support for the federal authorities. The state and local politicians dutifully talked up the grants, which didn't concern Julie too much. That was normal politics. But the liberal state and local politicians took it much further. They savagely denounced anyone who opposed the sanctuary and grants. It seemed to Julie like the left-wing politicians were trying to outdo each other on how vehemently they could condemn conservatives. It didn't take long to create a poisonous climate.

Another problem Julie noticed was that the grants weren't free. She could see that they would lead to financial ruin. Federal grants were conditioned on the state or local government raising matching funds. So, a federal grant for one hundred million dollars might require the state or municipality to raise a matching twenty-five million. Of course, the states and municipalities didn't have the money. So, they presented a bond at the next election and said the money was for education, or the children, or saving puppies, or whatever. The voters passed the bond, thereby raising the state or local debt even higher. This, in turn, created even more dependence on the federal government.

When states and municipalities were broke, they would ask the federal government for bailouts. The Feds kept a "naughty and nice" list and would bail out the liberal states and local governments. Eugene was a prime example of this. Julie realized her town was bankrupt and completely subservient to the Feds. As local infrastructure crumbled, Eugene politicians begged the government for more money. And the cycle would start all over again. It had been this way as long as Julie had lived in Eugene. What changed under this administration was that speaking out against such policies would bring unwanted attention at work. So, Julie kept her mouth closed. She needed her job.

Eugene was not the only city in such a precarious position. Other progressive, left-leaning cities around the country were in the same situation. It was easy to pick them out. They had severe debt and decades of Democrats in charge. Those same cities also seemed to have frequent riots.

A riot could pop up over a racially charged incident and last for days with deaths, jaw-dropping property damage, severe injuries, and a helpless police force. It didn't help that the president gleefully vilified conservatives and blamed them for the riots. Increasingly, anarchist groups, which were funded by extreme left-wing groups, would destroy anything they could.

Local police forces in these cities were not allowed to wear riot gear; that was too "militaristic." They weren't allowed to carry a rifle because that seemed aggressive. They weren't allowed to confront rioters with a show of force of any kind. They were only allowed to manage the chaos. They were wussified.

In the end, the anarchists and "racial justice" looters knew the local police couldn't do anything. They might get arrested for a few hours, but nothing else. To these groups, being arrested was a badge of honor. Julie noticed that every few months there was a riot in in Portland, Seattle, Los

Angeles, San Francisco, Detroit, and so on.

Julie also realized that Eugene was a prime location for riots. Why was a medium-sized city like Eugene in the same boat as big cities like Seattle? Because Eugene had the same circumstances as the larger Democrat-ruled cities: wussified police, bankruptcy, and dependence on the federal government.

Julie didn't see these riots in states that didn't support the liberal president or where most jobs were in the private sector. But, cities like Eugene and others where most of the population was dependent on the government seemed to have the same problems.

Julie's thoughts would turn from the political to the practical. What if rioters came into her neighborhood? What about Joel? She had learned that she couldn't count on anyone to protect her. She had a lot of experience rewriting memories, but didn't want to rewrite any more if she could help it. The memories she hoped to create involved her standing up against threats, becoming a victor rather than a victim.

***

Internationally, terrorism exploded. Anyone who wouldn't follow the terrorists' deadly religion was at risk. Beheadings were uploaded to YouTube and Twitter on a regular basis. Children were thrown from rooftops. Homosexuals were hunted down, shamed publicly, and pushed off buildings. Women were raped and then beheaded with their husbands forced to watch. The news was horrifying, yet Julie couldn't believe how normal these headlines had become not only to her, but to everyone. While she knew it wasn't a good sign that the headlines were becoming normalized, she also realized it was unavoidable. They were nonstop.

At the same time, the international scene was exploding, the president refused to use the word *terrorists* when talking about the people committing all the atrocities. He called them *refugees* and convinced his minions and the media that they needed refuge after escaping their dangerous countries. He opened the American border to them, and promised to deny federal funds to any city that didn't allow them in.

Europe also allowed these refugees to flow into their cities. Coincidentally, about every three to four months, there seemed to be a frightening incident in Europe. Women were raped in subways. Schools were bombed. No one seemed to care enough to call for an end to the insanity. European leaders would reach out to the refugee communities and make

26

more concessions to them. In the meantime, no one could — or would — stop the terrorists.

Then the mass shootings began, and quickly happened with regularity. A shooter would yell a hallmark statement before opening fire in a densely-populated area, killing dozens of innocent citizens in a matter of seconds. Blood literally ran in the streets of many European cities.

Julie was appalled at the complete incongruity. During her childhood, if something like this happened, the American president, no matter his politics, would stand behind a podium and declare in no uncertain terms, "Not on our soil, not on my watch."

But not this president. Instead, he would offer *thoughts and prayers* to the victims and their families and vaguely mention that things had to change. Then he would say how America needed to be a country that gives and keeps borders open to these refugees. He would emphasize that guns had no place in the American culture because of such violence. Julie thought that he was an absolute pansy. She also thought that most Americans ate it right up. He was a very convincing speaker and most people didn't think critically. They preferred to be spoon-fed their information. They proved it by re-electing him.

The president had created the perfect storm, mainly by letting terrorists into the United States with no regard for immigration law. Julie acknowledged that they weren't all terrorists, but she also knew that terrorists used these mass movements of people to tactically embed their foot soldiers in local communities. They were doing it in Europe, so of course they were doing it in America.

During all of this, the president aggressively moved toward an executive order to ban guns for Americans. He couldn't say so out loud, but everyone knew it was happening. He didn't deny it, either. Julie was afraid. What if a riot, orchestrated by the progressives and encouraged by the president's leftist policies, happened in her city? What if the rioters approached her house? Joel's school? Her church? The police would be almost helpless to help her, thanks to Eugene being in bed with the president and practice of wussifying and creating dependence.

These thoughts kept Julie awake at night. The best deadbolt in the world on her doors would not stop the storm that was coming.

Chapter 7

The Cabin

Julie spoke with her father, Floyd, often, especially after her divorce. By the time she was divorced, he had been divorced from Julie's mother for about fifteen years, and he'd never seemed happier. Her father had retired as a naval officer and now lived in a retirement community outside of Baltimore. He fiddled around in his garden, visited local farmers' markets, and enjoyed his cable package. Retired life as a bachelor suited him well.

The worst thing her father had to deal with was her brother, Seth. Julie despised Seth for many reasons, but mainly because almost all of Julie's memories of him involved him beating her up during their childhood. He was not a good big brother, and had never tried to redeem himself even as an adult. Ever the optimist, her father held a tremendous amount of hope that Seth would grow up to be a real man someday. Time was running out, however. Julie was in her mid-thirties and Seth was almost forty.

It was a tense subject between Julie and her father. Julie had had nothing to do with Seth for many years, and what she learned about him was based on what her father reported. He would always tell her through rose-colored glasses.

"Seth has a new girlfriend," her father would report. "And she is very nice."

What Julie read between the lines was that Seth was still getting high and mooching off his latest girlfriend. It was the same story as always. Julie would listen, nodding and smiling while waiting for the topic to change.

***

Aside from conversations about Seth, Julie enjoyed all other talks with her father. They could carry on for hours. One of her favorite topics was their family cabin. When she was in second grade, her parents bought a piece of property deep in the Rocky Mountains, just outside of a town called Smoky Flats. Smoky Flats was nothing more than a gas station, dive restaurant, and post office along a state highway surrounded by roads leading into the mountains. It was merely a flat spot in the Rocky Mountains.

At eight thousand feet in elevation, it was a mid-point between the front range cities of Denver and Colorado Springs that were six thousand feet or so, and the high country with fourteen-thousand-foot mountains.

Those mountains were dotted with two sorts of people: vacation property owners and mountain residents who wanted to be left alone to live a solitary life. The highway that ran through Smoky Flats was a vein to both kinds of people.

A few turns off the state highway sat Julie's family small A-frame cabin. It was one of a few dozen cabins located in a development called Western Lakes Association. Julie and her family spent many weekends there exploring the woods, fishing in the lake and streams, watching coyotes walk between the car and the cabin, and countless more adventures. Many of best childhood memories were at the cabin. She was particularly proud of the record-breaking sized German brown trout she caught one summer. Her dad mounted it above the fireplace of the cabin.

Although her father was financially devastated by the divorce, he managed to walk away with the cabin. As the divorce proceeded, many of his personal possessions ended up in the crawl space of the cabin. The crawl space was maybe four feet high and her father maximized every inch of it. He placed wooden pallets on the ground and stuffed in toolboxes, tubs of personal items, and cherished memories. The first time Julie saw it was as a college freshman when the divorce was reaching the finish line. The sight of his personal possessions crammed in the crawl space of the cabin symbolized how torn-apart their family was — and how the cabin warmly greeted them. Instead of being saddened by his possessions being reduced to crawl space filler, it was a place of refuge. When her father first showed her crawl space, he motioned with his finger for her to come closer to him.

"Don't tell a soul," he whispered.

She nodded. "Okay."

"There's something in the crawl space I want to show you."

He proceeded to tell her about the secret space where he had built a double wall with cinder blocks. It was toward the back of the crawl space. Anyone who didn't know about it would simply look in the crawl space and think it was the back wall. He had placed a distressed metal door of some kind to the far corner. It looked like a door to a furnace. If anyone looked at the door, they would simply think it was where the pilot light was located. Instead, it was the entrance to the two-foot-wide space between the new cinder blocks and the actual back wall.

29

"Is this where you hide stuff from mom's divorce lawyer?" she asked.

He smiled and then winked. "Something even more valuable."

He explained that the hidden compartment contained four rifles and four handguns. He told her the kind of guns, even though she didn't know what the calibers meant. They were in protective cases, protected from humidity, and hung on the wall of the crawl space off the floor. The floor of the void had cut up pallet flats on the ground to keep anything from direct contact with the dirt ground. Up there in the Rocky Mountains, soil would be frozen for months. After giving her the tour, he handed her the key to the metal door.

"If anything happens to me, these are yours," he said. "I want these to stay in the family. I want you to have them if you need them. No one knows about these, not your mother, not your brother. This cabin — and its contents — will be left for you in my will. You will have them legally, regardless of who decides to fight over whatever I leave in the rest of my will."

In that moment, Julie was still processing that he had made this vault to think about everything else he was saying. She wondered when he had done it and how long the firearms had been there. Had they been there since she was a second grader? Or had he done this since the divorce? She didn't even know her dad owned guns.

The way she looked at it, and the way her father wanted her to look at it, was that this was his cabin until such a time that it became hers. It wasn't hers to ask about, and she wasn't about to. She just knew that a place of refuge awaited her should she need it.

Her father moved to the Baltimore area the summer after Julie moved to Eugene. He had found a job and wanted to put some distance between himself and Julie's mother. Julie applauded the decision. She was a believer in clean slates and starting over, and saw this as that opportunity for him. Her move to Eugene and his to the East Coast at roughly the same time only deepened their bond. Fresh starts for father and daughter.

The cabin was mostly unoccupied during the years after the moves to Eugene and Baltimore. Julie's dad would visit occasionally but never for more than a week.

Several years later, when Joel was six years old and she was still married to Steve, Julie brought her son to the cabin so he could have some childhood memories there. Steve didn't join them on the trip, which had been a relief to her.

Joel's first trip to the cabin showed a new side of Julie's father — he was now also a grandfather. She enjoyed watching him treat Joel the same way he had treated her as a young child; he even talked the same way he had all those years ago.

"Hey, Joel," he would say, "As the sun goes down, let's go drown some bait."

It was an invitation to go fishing during prime trout feeding time. The expression brought back fond childhood memories of when Julie would "drown bait" with her father. She stood on the porch and drew in the fresh Rocky Mountain air, and felt good. She felt relaxed. Carefree. Worry free.

It was on that summer trip that her father showed Julie something new about the crawl space. He asked her to give him a hand with something in there. As they crawled along the floor of the space, he turned around and smiled at her. It was a playful, devilish grin. And then Julie noticed what he was showing her. The crawl space now contained four ten gallon buckets of freeze-dried meals. She read the labels, which said the meals were for survival or camping situations. Each bucket had seven hundred servings. And there were four buckets! She did the math. These four buckets could feed Julie, Joel, and her dad for months if it ever came to that.

She wasn't shocked by the fact that her dad had some extra food in the cabin. After all, it was the Rocky Mountains, and getting snowed in for weeks at a time was not unheard of. The shocking thing about the food in the crawl space was that her dad was planning for something bigger and more disastrous than being snowed in. She had never seen this side of her mild-mannered dad. He was not a doomsday kind of person.

"If anything ever happens," he said in a hushed tone, "and it could be any number of things, and you need these, they are here."

"Dad, this is great," Julie whispered. "In Oregon, there is always discussion about the coming of a big earthquake. If that ever happened, it is comforting to know that Joel and I could come here and have food and shelter. Thank you."

"It could be an earthquake," her father agreed, "or a divorce, or something else."

"Who knows?"

"I'm not sure Steve is up to what it'll take during a crisis," he said. He spoke with hesitation. Julie knew he was trying to be gentle in his delivery, but it didn't make his words any easier to digest. Hearing the truth stung.

Julie knew her dad was right about an impending crisis and that Steve probably wouldn't be able to help her, but she couldn't outwardly agree with him. Not yet. It would take time. This was three years before the divorce eventually came.

***

Their summer trip ended too soon. Before long, Julie and Joel were on a plane, making their way home. Joel's heavy head rested on her shoulder as he slept. The visit had been good for them.

Julie thought about how her dad had given her a gift by showing her the contents of the crawl space. It was much more than a gift of physical property. It was the gift of peace of mind.

***

Years later and post-divorce, Julie's fond memories of the cabin trip with Joel felt a million miles away from what confronted her now in her crappy little home.

Julie was a problem solver. She didn't wallow in emotion; she got things done. She felt comfort in coming up with a plan and executing it. That took the worry out. The more action, the less worry.

On Saturday, she woke up, still reeling from her long week. She had Joel every other weekend. He was at Steve's this Saturday morning, which meant that it was Julie Time. Was it a bubble bath or a shopping trip to the mall? Not at all. It was couponing. This was how she took control of her bad situation and turned it into the best outcome possible. It was how she problem-solved.

Her Saturday morning routine consisted of perusing couponing websites for the following week. It also listed which coupons from which newspaper could be matched up to the sale prices, using a doubled coupon deal, to get maximum savings. Then she got four copies of the Sunday edition of the newspaper on Saturday — most papers did this — for the bonanza of coupon inserts stuffed in there.

She put the four coupon inserts in a large envelope. She would mark the date on the outside of the envelop and file it in a milk crate under her desk in the bedroom. When she would pull up the couponing website on Saturday morning, the site might say that a certain breakfast cereal was on sale at a particular grocery store. The helpful site would recommend that she use the newspaper coupon plus a coupon doubler from the site, and then it would calculate the final price she'd pay. It was so easy.

But this Saturday morning, Julie took couponing one step further. Normally, she looked for items that she and Joel used every day. Today, she was looking for items that could be stored for long term—like the freeze-dried food in the cabin crawl space. It's great to have a food supply, why not add other needed items? Cheaply?

She paid attention to things like top ramen, cans of tuna, canned soup, and pasta. She did not usually bother with these items because she rarely used them. But now she was looking at the possibilities of how to prepare for a disaster—and it offered a whole new worldview as she looked at the list of coupon deals. These were all things that could be bought with coupon deals for next to nothing and could be stored almost indefinitely for an emergency, ultimately making them priceless. Julie was choosing her destiny. It was easy—and liberating.

Julie's coworkers had noticed the uptick in her couponing. She went out on her lunch hour to grocery stores to make her big purchases. Sometimes she'd get caught when they saw her in the parking lot and noticed the back of her beater car was full of toilet paper and boxes of oatmeal.

"Julie, my goodness, are you getting ready for the zombies?" one of her co-workers joked.

At first Julie wasn't sure what to say. "We can all agree that toilet paper is a necessity," she offered. But she could sense her co-workers were trying to figure out what she was up to.

None of her colleagues saw the inevitable as clearly as she did. At election time, they would vote for the municipal bonds, higher taxes, and the "correct" politicians who seemed to get re-elected all the time. Water cooler talk often centered on how mean the police were to whichever rioters decided to destroy a city that week. It was easy to have these bland, common, and safe opinions. It didn't require any thought on their part. They just went with the flow.

At the same time, Julie could tell that her co-workers were slightly nervous about the situation. On some level, they knew that they were dependent on the government for their livelihood and government couldn't keep growing. But, the comfort and ease of being politically correct overrode the doubts about the system that they were trying to suppress. Some of them channeled the doubt into reinforced efforts to mock anyone who seemed to be preparing.

"I'm getting ready for rioting to come to Eugene," Julie wanted to say. "I'm preparing to have a food supply for when grocery stores are burned down from rioters." These were words that couldn't be said. She was afraid she'd be ostracized at her office, which could put her job in jeopardy. She could not allow that to happen. She couldn't last a month without that paycheck. She and her son would be homeless. Given that the truth was off limits at her office, she had to come up with something else to say so that she could continue couponing and stockpiling at lunch time. Every six months or so, the local news would run a story that the Eugene area was on a major earthquake fault line, like many of the cities on the West Coast. The area was long overdue for a major disaster—hundreds of years overdue.

"It's not a matter of *if*," the newscasters would always say. "It's a matter of *when*."

The story would always end with a reminder that every family should have an emergency preparedness kit of batteries, water, and a sleeping bag. It was the government saying so, not some crazy prepper, so it *had* to be right. Julie rolled her eyes every time she heard this story. She would marvel at the need to keep retreading this scary story when the regular news pipeline was a little dry—especially since the regular news was scary enough. She also couldn't believe that the government would advise to stockpile a few days' worth of items—just what would be needed until order and services would be restored. She felt bad for those who believed it'd be that quick and simple.

Despite finding the earthquake story laughable, it made for a good alibi when she got caught in the parking lot at work with a carload of prepping supplies. As soon as the parking lot teasing started, she would brush them off and tell them to watch the news. She'd tell them they should consider readying themselves and their families for the earthquake, which was only a matter of time.

They would all nod. They wouldn't argue with anyone doing what the government said.

She found it hilarious—and sad—that preparing for an earthquake was acceptable with her progressive coworkers, but doing the exact same thing before a potential riot would be considered crazy.

Chapter 8

The Castle

After her divorce, Julie tried to take one or two self-defense classes a year. Before long, she realized that she was learning the same moves over and over again. She stayed in shape by exercising, which kept her confident in her ability to execute any self-defense moves, but she felt like she should do more.

During one of her Saturday morning couponing internet searches, she came across a coupon for a firearms self-defense class taught by women for women. Women teaching firearms? She always associated guns with men. She had never seen or even heard of a woman carrying a gun.

Years ago, when she was still married to Steve, she had a fleeting thought that it would be interesting to learn how to shoot. She went to a gun store and asked if they had classes. A military-looking man who seemed to ooze testosterone started off by calling her "little lady" and proceeded to ask her about calibers, holsters, and other things she knew nothing about.

"I don't know," she said. "I'm here to learn those things."

He smirked. She walked out.

The coupon that Saturday morning was for Pink Ladies. It was a one-time conceal carry class that included range time. It was exactly what she wanted. Julie wanted to learn the basics, try it out, and go from there.

The class was on a Sunday morning, so she arranged for Joel to hang out with Carson and a few other neighbor kids that afternoon. The class was in a conference room which was connected to a gun store. She made her way through a maze of guns, gear, safes, and gadgetry. It was a bit overwhelming; she had no idea what she was looking at. She had no idea what to expect when she entered the conference room. What does a gun girl look like? Are there even such people? She saw the instructor right away, a goth-looking young woman with jet black hair and matching lipstick. She wore a black tank top, which showed off the rose tattoos that trailed down her arms. Her name tag said *Ash.*

Julie assumed it was short for Ashley. This woman fit right into the Goth culture in downtown Eugene. No one would even guess she was armed if they saw her. They surely would never guess she was an NRA-certified instructor. Ash instantly destroyed Julie's stereotyped image of women who carry firearms.

The class turned out to be just what Julie needed. She learned the four laws of gun safety. Ash had them printed on a laminated card for Julie to put in her purse. Julie learned the definitions of caliber, sight lines, and center mass. She learned how to handle a .22 handgun, following the four rules. Julie racked a slide, and loaded and unloaded a magazine using snap caps. She was invigorated and started to feel empowered right away. The previously mysterious world of guns was being stripped down. A gun was just a tool and with some basic knowledge, it was safe to use.

Julie looked around the classroom. There was a grandmother and her college-aged granddaughter at the table behind her. There was a corporate executive with perfectly manicured nails and perfect hair at the table across from Julie. Two other twenty-somethings in hipster jeans and scrunched stocking caps who could blend right into downtown Eugene without anyone even guessing they were concealing a handgun sat in the room. Apparently, women of all kinds needed to be safe.

Ash mentioned that the class qualified the women to get their concealed handgun license, which she called a *CHL*. Julie had never thought about actually carrying a gun; she just wanted to learn how to use one. She had envisioned having a gun at her house to stop a burglar or rioters. Or a rapist.

The mindset shift happened easily and quickly. For the first time in her life, Julie could see herself carrying a gun. She learned that handling a gun wasn't hard at all—it was easier than putting on make-up every morning. Ash assigned everyone a .22 semiautomatic pistol and gave them twenty-five rounds of ammunition. She gave everyone a target, and ear and eye protection. Then they headed to the indoor range at the gun store.

There, Ash immediately put the first rule of firearm safety into practice. She checked if the .22 she was using was unloaded, and showed everyone it was—all while pointing the barrel in a safe direction, which was at the targets. Whenever she handed it to someone, they would also check if it was unloaded, even if they had seen that it was a moment ago.

"Treat all guns as if they're loaded," Ash repeated.

Guns aren't so dangerous, Julie thought. *As long as you're smart and safe.*

Next, Ash demonstrated how to grip a pistol, sight a target, stand when firing, and pull the trigger with the pad of one's index finger. It was a lot to take in, but manageable.

Julie spent about ten minutes simply putting together all the pieces she had just learned. Nothing came naturally to her. Standing and leaning forward into a stance, pushing shoulders forward, gripping the butt of the pistol with hard tension. It didn't make sense, and yet here she was.

It all made sense, however, when she watched others pull the trigger. The entire reason for all the tension in hands, shoulders, legs, and even the stance were to counteract the recoil. She watched as the other women shot. The recoil from the .22 was much less than she had expected it to be, nearly nonexistent.

Soon, it was Julie's turn. She got ready to fire her very first shot. Some nervousness lingered. Even though everything she'd learned today showed her that guns weren't dangerous, she couldn't easily erase the years of conditioning she'd had. There had been too many horror stories. But she knew that the time had come for her to learn firsthand. She was startled when she fired her first shot. It wasn't as jarring as she'd always envisioned, but it was still foreign. It was also a bit fun and exhilarating. She looked downrange at the target. She had nicked the upper border of the most outer ring of the target.

"At least I hit somewhere on the target," she said to Ash.

"Nicely done."

Julie was determined to improve. She lined up her sights better, stepped her left leg forward in her stance, and placed most of her weight on that leg. She half-closed her left eye to allow her dominant eye to do its work. She did it repeatedly until her twenty-five rounds ran out.

Ash hit the switch for the target to be reeled back. Julie winced as the target approached, hoping all the holes were right on the bullseye... or at least somewhere on the target. Finally, the target was brought close enough to her. All twenty-five holes, except for her first shot on the outer ring, were within the inner two rings.

Ash looked at the target. "Not half bad for your first time. Nice job."

Julie was excited, and she was hooked. She needed to do this more often. At the end of the class, as everyone was picking up their belongings to leave, Julie asked Ash about more classes.

Ash smiled. "I get that question a lot after the first class. We have a Pink Ladies ongoing club that meets once a month," she said. "We have a class time for the first hour, followed by an hour of range time. Members can use the range time for practice using their own handgun, or if you don't have one, you can rent one."

"Where can I sign up?" Julie asked with a smile.

"You just did," Ash winked. "I'll see you the last Monday of the month, here at six in the evening."

The following week, Julie saw a local news story where a single woman came home with her two kids to discover a man hiding in her house. She felt threatened and shot him. It turned out he had a long criminal history, including multiple rapes. The news story cut to an interview with a local anti-gun politician who said guns lead to violence. He threw in the obligatory commentary about being glad that she was safe, but then went straight back into a diatribe on how dangerous guns were. The rapist probably agreed with him.

The next part of the news story surprised Julie. She assumed that if a person killed someone, they'd go to jail. That was one of the reasons she had previously thought it was dangerous to carry a gun. She was surprised to learn that the woman would not be charged. The law in liberal Oregon actually allowed a person to protect themselves in their home when they felt like they were in imminent danger, and this was a perfect example.

Julie envisioned the same principle with rioters. Not that Julie ever wanted be in a position of choosing to shoot someone, ever. But that would not necessarily be for her to choose. Criminals sought victims, not the other way around. Julie wanted to make sure that if a criminal chose her or Joel, that she did everything possibly to protect them. Julie was done being a victim. She would show her son how to protect himself. They would choose their destiny.

For the next several months, Julie attended Pink Ladies and learned a lot about conceal carry laws, holsters, safes, situational awareness, and much more. She used her range time to rent and try various handguns. Julie wanted to buy one, and renting them so she could get a good sampling was the perfect way to do that.

Julie liked how Ash described choosing a handgun. "It's like trying on jeans," Ash would say. "A pair might fit you and flatter you, but the same pair could make me look fat." It varied from person to person, and no one could choose the right gun for you.

"Pick a firearm that you're incredibly comfortable with," she advised, "one that you practice with every chance you get, and can use immediately."

She told Julie to not start carrying a gun until she knew which holster fit the best. "Women typically need several holsters they can carry with since we have a different wardrobe than men," she said.

Ash was right. Women's curvy bodies made wearing holsters tricky. Every woman's body was unique, so the market offered many different options.

Julie borrowed a few of Ash's holsters and eventually settled on a compression waist holster that she could wear under dress pants, shorts, or jeans. She could wear it with about eighty percent of her wardrobe, and that was good enough for now.

Julie also settled on a basic safe that she could put on a closet shelf and bolt down. It locked with a combination. She preferred a biometric safe that opened instantly by fingerprint recognition, but those were three times the price. Combination lock it would be.

Julie's CHL permit arrived soon after she purchased the safe. She needed to decide on a firearm. After renting several different kinds at the Pink Ladies class, she settled on a Ruger LCP in .380 auto. Ash assured her that an LCP was reliable. It was small, concealable, comfortable for her to fire, and less expensive than most of the others.

Julie needed to save what she could for a few months in order to make the purchase, and she did. She directed her coupon savings to a gun and all the things that came with it, like magazines and ammunition. It was money well spent as far as she was concerned.

At first, she was a little reluctant to carry her LCP with a round in the chamber. While watching movies, she noticed that people seemed to rack the slide after pulling out a gun. Ash quickly told her that was only in the movies.

"Carry a round in the chamber or don't carry," Ash said. "Taking the time to rack a round just gives an attacker more time and a much better chance of victimizing you."

That was all Julie needed to hear. She carried with a round in the chamber. Julie made a point to have her firearm on her at all times. At work or at home, her gun was there. She ignored the rule that was buried in the three-hundred page HR policy, which strongly advised against carrying a gun at her office. Criminals certainly ignored those rules. She had seven rounds in her gun and was fully trained. Julie was ready to protect her castle.

Chapter 9

Raising a Warrior

Julie took on a tremendous amount of ammo stockpiling and firearms training. She knew she couldn't keep it from Joel for long. He was twelve and had just started middle school. He was getting taller and starting to notice girls. He was smart, but bored with school. After reading his politicized textbooks, she didn't blame him.

Julie was determined to not raise another pansy like Steve. The world needed young warriors. Especially for what was coming.

"Joel, what do you think about hunting?" she asked him one day.

"Like what? Shooting an animal kind of hunting?"

"Yes. Learning to use a firearm, getting a license, going out in the woods, hunting for food, and cooking it for dinner."

"I never thought of it," he said. "I see that on TV with reality shows and stuff, but to actually do it?" He paused, deliberating for a moment. "Sure, I guess it's okay," he said halfheartedly.

It wasn't the response Julie was hoping for. "How would you feel about taking a hunter's safety course and see what you think then?" she suggested.

"Mom! That would be awesome!"

Julie had no idea where that enthusiasm came from. She was befuddled. "I just asked the same question two different ways, and you gave me two different answers. What's up with that?"

"I've always wanted to learn how to shoot a gun. I'm just not so sure I want to gut an animal."

"Fair enough," Julie replied.

The following weekend, on one of Julie's weekends with Joel, they went to a local gun show. Not that long ago, Julie would have been confused by all of the hardware and accessories. That was no longer the case. She understood that all the gear had a purpose. Of course, Joel loved it.

They found a booth that had information about hunter's safety courses for youth and adults. Adults were encouraged to participate in the courses with their kids. *Perfect,* Julie thought as she folded a flyer and tucked it in her purse.

As they meandered through the exhibitions and looked at all the slings, stands, holsters, and cleaning supplies, Julie found a booth with conceal carry purses. Ash had advised against using them. "Keep it close to your heart. Imagine if your purse is stolen," she cautioned.

Julie still wanted to look. As she perused the purses, a man approached her and struck up a conversation.

"What do you carry?" he asked.

Julie chuckled at his conversation starter. "A .380," she answered.

"If you're going to carry a gun, *then carry a gun*," he scolded. "A .380 is not a gun."

"And, you are who to tell me what to carry?" she shot back.

"I'm a former police officer," he said.

He then told her about a time when he was in the position of having to use deadly force against a criminal and that the only reason why he was standing there now was because he used a Glock in 9mm.

Julie was in no mood to hear unsolicited advice. "Sir, I'm not a police officer," she said. "I'm not going to seek out the bad guy. The law says if I carry, I must have it concealed. I can guarantee you that there is no way in hell any Glock is going to be concealed on my body without tipping me over. Take your unsolicited advice and please leave me alone," Julie said sharply.

She felt her neck getting hot. She'd come a long way since her days of being a mild and meek woman, but it was still a bit unsettling to talk to a man so abruptly. However, it was this type of macho arrogance that kept Julie from wanting to approach the idea of firearms to begin with. She knew that it was generally a male-dominated culture. She was all set with that.

The man looked her in the eye and paused. His face softened and she heard him inhale deeply. "I'm sorry," he said.

Julie sensed it was sincere and felt a little bad about how she spoke to him.

"You're right," he continued. "You're absolutely right. I was in officer mode. Can I at least give some friendly advice?"

Julie rolled her eyes and wondered why she was still in this conversation, though he seemed humbled. "Sure," she said.

"Upgrade to at least a 9mm," he said. "Any kind that you can conceal comfortably. For the sheer stopping power, that is what I would recommend," he said.

That was a reasonable explanation that Julie could accept. "Got it," Julie replied stoically.

"Hey, is there any chance you'd like to get a cup of coffee with me?" he asked.

"No," Julie said, feeling her exasperation return to her voice.

"Well, can't say I didn't try," he said with a shrug and then walked away.

***

The conversation with the police officer about 9mms got Julie thinking. Later that day, she called her father.

"Dad, can I ask you a question?" Julie asked.

"Sure, what's up?"

"What kind of guns are at the cabin?"

It was weird, but it felt taboo to talk out loud about the guns at the cabin. She approached the topic like an unspeakable family secret. But, in this case, it was secret for good reason. She hoped she wasn't asking an unwanted question. Julie and her dad hadn't discussed the cabin guns since the day he told her about them.

"What brings this up?" he asked.

"Well, uhh…," she said, trying to decide if she could tell him the answer. She realized that of course she could. "I've been taking classes on firearms. Even bought my own handgun for protection for Joel and me. Now that I have a better idea of what I'm doing, I realized I have no idea what is stored at the cabin, and I probably should."

"Good for you!" he said, sounding like the proudest father.

He went on to explain the four long guns. There were two shotguns—one 12 gauge and one 20 gauge. There were two rifles, one of which was an antique. It was a Browning 1918 that her dad said was called a BAR.

"It's the semi-automatic version," he said, "so it's legal."

Julie asked where the BAR came from.

"It's a family heirloom." He went on to explain that it used .30-06 ammunition, which could still be found. The gun hadn't been fired in decades, however. "So be careful," he cautioned.

The fourth long gun was a standard Ruger 10/22 rifle, which used the .22 ammunition Julie shot in Ash's class. The next revelation was the one that surprised Julie.

"A fifth rifle has been added out there since I showed you the others," he said. He paused. "I put an AR-15 in the cabin, too."

"What?!" Julie exclaimed. All she'd ever heard about AR-15s was that they were dangerous assault rifles, and that they should be banned. She also realized that the same people who made those claims had been wrong about everything else related to guns. If her father had purchased one, that was good enough for her.

"I got a good deal on one. I couldn't pass it up," he said.

He spoke as though he had found a good deal on milk and bought extra. For him to purchase an AR-15 and then store it in the cabin took effort and planning. It also meant he was still looking out for her and wanted to provide as much safety to Julie and Joel as possible.

"Julie, what about Joel?" he asked. "Is he learning any of what you're learning?"

Julie sensed some hesitation in her father's voice and wasn't certain why these sorts of conversations were fraught with caution.

"Joel is taking a hunter's safety course and will learn how to use my pistol safely and effectively," she answered. "I want to know what guns are at the cabin so we can both practice on the same or similar rifles. The day may come when he and I will need to use them," she explained.

"I agree. Joel will need to use the cabin and the guns soon," he said solemnly. "With the way things are going these days, you'll either need them to hunt for food or to defend yourselves. Or both. I don't want things to ever get to that point, but I cannot tell you how happy I am to hear you're on your way to being prepared for that potential."

Her father went on to tell Julie a story about her childhood that she had not previously heard. Her father had grown up on a farm and knew how to use guns. When he married Julie's mother, she made it crystal clear that guns were not permitted in her home. They had a few fierce verbal fights over the issue. He wanted his children to be familiar with guns, not afraid of them. He offered to teach Julie and her brother gun safety and keep them locked up. Julie's mother said all guns were unsafe and they were frightening to her. She absolutely forbade guns in their house. He could never convince her. Julie was saddened to hear this. Had she known how to use a gun, she may not have been victimized all those years ago. It was a gut punch to realize that truth.

Her father went on to say he was in a bit of a quandary when his father passed away and left him the antique rifles. Where to keep them? Julie remembered that her grandfather had passed when she was about twelve, and that was the summer when her dad started "storing tools" in the crawl space. She realized he was working on the secret storage place for the rifles. Her father explained he did a bit of the excavation for the vault, but that he hired a nearby contractor for laying the cinderblock and installing the fireproof door.

"Julie, the contractor's name is Ned," he said. "He lives on the back road of Western Lakes. He's a good guy. While he never saw the firearms that I put in there, he's no dummy. He knew what he was building and let me know what a great idea that was. That was over twenty years ago. Ned still lives in the house and his kids are almost grown. If something ever happens and I can't be there, you go over to his place and tell him you're my daughter. You'll have an ally."

Julie had met very few of the neighbors. The residents of the subdivision were separated by swaths of land, not fences or hedges. She didn't remember anyone named Ned. Her father must have heard her thoughts.

"You'll find his address and phone number in a little notepad in the dresser," he said. "I put everyone's name and phone number nearby in the Western Lakes Association that would be helpful if either of us needed to stay at the cabin for an extended time for any reason."

She couldn't believe how much time and effort her father had spent preparing for whatever may come their way, and for making sure that she and Joel would be just fine. She couldn't recall the last time she'd felt so cared for.

"Julie," he continued in a tone of fatherly advice, "not everyone will be helpful. Be wise. Be mindful. Don't trust anyone who hasn't earned it."

"Okay, Dad," she said. Goosebumps traveled down her arms.

Suddenly, Joel was by her side. She had been so wrapped up in the conversation that she didn't even notice her son enter the room. He wanted to talk to his grandpa. Julie listened to the conversation.

"Hey, Grandpa!" Joel gushed. "Did Mom tell you? I'm almost done with my hunter's safety course."

Joel was usually a person of few words, like most pre-teens and men Julie knew. He also did not show his emotions very often. To hear him talk to his grandfather with such excitement made Julie realize how important this was to her son. She'd had no idea. She beamed with pride and satisfaction.

"For Christmas," Joel said, "I would like a .22 and a centerfire rifle. One for targets and small animals, the other for hunting large game. But, Mom says I might need to get a job for those," he said excitedly.

He is turning into a man before my very eyes, Julie thought. She also couldn't believe he was now interested in hunting game.

"I saw on the news how a guy shot one of the largest wild boars in

Texas history with an AR-15, and he has a lifetime of bacon from that hunt. Isn't that cool?" Joel continued.

Julie wondered if Joel realized that hunters also had to gut the five-hundred-pound creature and butcher it. Regardless, it was interesting to hear him explain his newfound world to his grandpa. She knew that her dad was glowing with pride on the other end, just as she was.

Chapter 10

Orders from Above

The president continued to push gun control laws through Congress. Colorado passed a law banning the sale of standard-capacity magazines. Other states were considering the same. Julie was worried that she wouldn't be able to purchase some of the guns she wanted. She wanted to get the 9mm that the nimrod at the gun show had recommended. Ash from Pink Ladies recommended it as well.

Julie researched the guns her dad said were at the cabin. She liked the idea of having a shotgun for home defense as well as hunting. An AR-15 was a good all-around centerfire rifle for defense and hunting. A .22 would be good for Joel to learn on and for target practice. Julie, always on a budget, prioritized her gun purchases. She got the shotgun first and then the AR.

The gun control scares followed by the prospect of the current president's gun-hating protégé as the next president led to record gun sales. Stores ran out of once-plentiful guns. Prices went through the roof. There was no way a single mom could afford guns at those prices. Prices eventually leveled out. When prices were down, Julie began to plan. A decent, base model AR-15 was around five or six hundred dollars. A good American-made pump action shotgun was under three hundred. A thousand dollars would get her the start to her long gun collection. *Easy*, she thought, *put away a hundred bucks a month for the next year or so and watch for sales*. She got a little bit of ammunition but wouldn't stock up on it. She'd budget for the long guns first and get the bulk ammo the next year. It would take longer than she'd like, but it was getting done. And that was what mattered. She felt relieved that she had an achievable plan.

Julie worried about Oregon politicians restricting guns, and then Oregon's left-wing dingbat governor announced new gun restrictions.

***

It was the end of October and the holidays were right around the corner. One afternoon, as Julie left the final Pink Ladies class for the year, Ash caught up with her.

"Julie, I know you're a bargain shopper. Make sure you watch Black

Friday deals!"

"For guns?" Julie asked. She'd never heard of guns on sale.

"Rumor has it that there are some good Black Friday deals from some of the local gun dealers," Ash said. She told Julie how to sign up for the local stores' email blasts so she could stay on top of the deals.

Ash did not disappoint. Sure enough, the week before Thanksgiving, a local gun store advertised a basic Smith & Wesson AR-15. Another gun store had a Mossberg 12 gauge shotgun with interchangeable barrels — one for hunting and one for tactical use — on sale. She used the money she had been saving every month to get the shotgun and AR-15 on Black Friday. She couldn't get the .22 rifle and Ruger LCP 9mm and stay in her budget. They would have to wait. She was still quite satisfied with her purchases, though.

With a young son at home, Julie knew that finding a way to lock up her guns was necessary. She was able to find a wall lock on sale as well. With it, she could mount the firearms to a rack on a wall in her closet and lock them down. She knew it wasn't as secure as a safe, but the guns would be secure this way.

When she pulled into her driveway after a long day of Black Friday shopping, she realized she needed Joel to help her. She could carry the boxes of guns by herself, but she knew that her nosy, liberal neighbors would see her unloading rifle-sized boxes emblazoned with *Smith & Wesson* and *Mossberg* in big lettering and know that she had guns. Julie backed the car into the driveway near the house and Joel got towels to put over the boxes. She knew that she was probably being a little paranoid, but she also knew there was a true reason for the paranoia.

Joel was beyond excited. They took the guns out and gave them a once over. Julie kept the manuals to read later. Joel grabbed the drill and they installed the wall lock in her closet and locked them all down.

As she clicked the lock, Julie said, "Merry Christmas to me."

Julie also knew that part of the gun control agenda — a big part — was limiting the number of rounds a magazine could hold. Standard-capacity magazines simply allowed rifles to fire multiple rounds without constantly reloading, which is important when protecting one's self from a crowd of rioters. A standard AR-15 magazine held thirty rounds. Gun control advocates thought it was *too much*. In their opinions, a gun should only hold a handful of rounds; odd because most of them had never fired a gun.

"Why does anyone need enough bullets to turn Bambi into soup?" one of Julie's co-workers had asked. The implication was that guns were only for hunting deer. Julie knew that most progressives had lived safe and comfortable lives; they didn't know what it was like to be attacked and have nothing to use for self-defense. They were naïve to the point of oblivion. Most voters in Julie's state had the Bambi mindset, so a magazine ban wasn't out of the question. As she continued to pinch every penny, she kept her eyes open for magazine deals—not only for her handguns, but especially for her AR-15.

That year, Christmas felt different to Julie. It seemed like the first Christmas where her focus was on preparing for something big. Joel's visitation schedule was structured so that Julie had him for Christmas morning. Later that day, Joel would head to Steve's house until the first of January. Julie always wanted to make Christmas special. She got up early and made cinnamon rolls. As the fresh-baked smell permeated through the house, she relaxed and enjoyed her coffee until Joel's sleepy face appeared in the kitchen doorway.

"Merry Christmas, Mom," Joel said softly as he rubbed his eyes.

"Good morning and Merry Christmas, Joel. I love you," Julie said into his forehead as she hugged him. "Let's go take a look under the tree, shall we?" Julie said playfully.

They had a great morning together and enjoyed exchanging a handful of gifts. Joel gave Julie an ornament he made in class that said *#1 Mom*. She knew that Joel or her father had teamed up on the next gift, which was a bracelet with personalized charms. There were two charms in particular that Julie knew Joel had picked. One was a revolver, and the other was a 9mm casing.

Julie beamed. The things that were important to her were starting to be important to him. A surge of love of pride caused her to almost tear up, but she didn't want to get sappy with her adolescent son. And she knew he didn't want to start getting sentimental!

Joel took down the stockings and handed Julie hers. Julie knew Joel had a handful of candy in his, and was a bit surprised to feel a small box in hers. She shot a questioning smile to Joel.

"What have you been up to?" she asked as she pulled out the box.

"I have one, too," Joel said. "Grandpa sent these and told me to put them in the stockings."

"On the count of three…," Julie challenged "One, two, three…,"

Frantically, they tore through the Christmas wrapping paper, and opened small tin boxes, which contained the same thing. Joel's jaw dropped. Her father had given them each a five-hundred-dollar gift certificate to a local gun store. This would make her gun purchase wishes a reality. She could barely believe it.

"Joel, what do you want to get with yours?" Julie asked, a little breathless at her father's generosity.

"The 10/22," Joel answered without skipping a beat. "What do you want with yours?"

"The 9mm I couldn't get on Black Friday," Julie answered just as fast.

They agreed that they would go shopping soon after Joel spent the rest of the holidays with his dad.

Julie was absolutely astounded. She was already planning to call her dad, but it would have a different tone today, one of deep gratitude. Julie's dad was taking care of her yet again, and she understood what he was doing. He was also improving Joel's future. It was about more than her father contributing to Joel's physical safety. It was also her father's way of encouraging Joel's interest in firearms, which would likely give him joy the rest of his life.

***

While Joel was still at his dad's, Julie decided to go to the gun store and start figuring out how to spend the gift certificates. After looking at the prices, she realized that they would have enough to buy several large capacity magazines in addition to the two firearms. Whatever was left would buy ammunition. Quite a bit of it.

This reminded Julie that this would be the year to start stocking up on ammunition. She realized that the worst was over in terms of cost. The large firearm purchases she wanted to make would be done once she and Joel went shopping. Now, the focus would be magazines, and maybe save up a bit for boxes or cases of ammunition. She would be able to purchase these items before the ban on AR-15s and high capacity magazines would happen. Everything was coming together nicely.

Chapter 11

One in Three

It was one of the long weekends Joel had with his dad. On these weekends, Julie tried to run the errands that she couldn't get done easily with Joel at home—oil change, trip to Costco, a little coupon deal shopping, and the list went on.

This particular Saturday morning, she had walked to a local farmer's market. After walking several blocks, she passed by a park. Then it happened. Suddenly, her head was jerked back and Julie saw the sky. She took a hard step backwards and almost fell. She twisted her head around in a bent-over position to see a man immediately behind her pulling her hair and pulling at her left shoulder. Only then did the pain of her hair being pulled register with her.

"Leave me alone, you sonofabitch!" she screamed as she struggled to stay on her feet while being yanked by her hair.

"Fuck you, bitch!"

Her instincts kicked in and Julie's training immediately came to her. *Don't go to the ground,* she remembered. *You're stronger standing. Throw the attacker off balance.* She kept her feet under her, which was not easy since he was yanking her by her head and she was bent over. She got her feet squared and pulled back—*hard*—on her hair using her leg muscles. That caught the attacker by surprise and he was thrown off balance. She pulled him toward her again.

Julie was now on the offense and he was on the defense, but he wasn't giving up. Between the two hair yanks that Julie gave, she had reached with her right hand to free her 9mm holstered on her left hip. As she pulled it out, she flipped the safety off. The attacker apparently didn't see or hear her do this because he yanked again.

"Stop moving, you shit. I need a good target!" Julie commanded.

He saw Julie's gun in her hand and instantly let go of her. She stood up, took her firing stance and put his chest in her pistol sights. He took a step back with pure terror in his eyes.

"I said leave... me… ALONE!" she screamed. She had a healthy dose of crazy and unpredictable in her voice; this was not the sound of a woman who was joking around. "Did I stutter, you sonofabitch?!" Julie yelled, with her eyes locked on his, and her arms straight out in a perfect stance, finger on the trigger. He froze.

"Your move! Choose!" Julie yelled.

It truly was his choice. If he took one step toward her, she knew what she would do. If he ran away from her, she knew what she would do. She had a plan for any circumstance in this fight.

In a split second, he ran away from her. Julie lowered her firearm and swept the area in a 360-degree circle. She remembered Ash's words from training. *Criminals travel in packs.* She knew she couldn't fixate on one of them; that was tunnel vision, in which people in a fight tend to focus only on the threat in front of them. She looked around to make sure there weren't others. She moved away, holding her pistol lowered but ready to bring to a ready position. It was bizarrely quiet. No one was around her.

Once she was sure no threats remained, she kept her pistol in her right hand and used her left hand to call the police on her cell phone. As she waited for the police to arrive, she cried. They were not tears of sadness; they were tears of relief. They were tears of recognition of what could have happened. They were tears of victory. Her thoughts were gathered, her pistol holstered, and her tears were dried by the time the police cruiser pulled up.

***

One in three women is a victim of sexual assault. Julie had heard this statistic in just about every class she had taken. She was once, but not a second time. In the days following the attempted assault, Julie played out in her mind the difference between being a victim and not being one. She felt like no one could understand without having experienced both outcomes.

Julie's firearms training and self-defense classes had proved priceless. She had never countered a hair pull in training, but the same principles applied. That was the part of the attack she replayed and felt most proud of. Her training had become second nature, and it was effective.

The police officer took her report, which included her physical description of the attacker. Again, her training taught her how to be a good witness. Always register the color of clothes, eyes, hair, height, distinguishing features, tattoos, marks, and so on. She knew that he was in his twenties about six feet tall, a Caucasian with dirty, shoulder-length brown hair. Typical hipster looks. Blue eyes. Expanded ears lobes with whatever it is that people put in them to make them huge. Pierced right eyebrow.

Red plaid jacket. Black pants, not jeans. Tattoos on his right wrist, a small twisty image. The police officer was impressed by the detail she provided.

The officer said they would look for him and that there had been some violent car jackings and muggings in the area of the park where other victims' valuables had been taken. The stolen items ranged from a purse or wallet to a car. Julie's description matched the previous incidents.

"Would you recognize him if you saw him again?" the officer asked.

"Yes," Julie said firmly.

"You'd be the first," he said. "The other victims weren't in a position to take in details. We'll be in touch. If we find him, we'll ask you to identify him. You okay to do that?" he asked.

"You bet," Julie said, hearing her own confidence.

Julie went home and slept well that night.

***

Julie decided not to tell Joel about the attack. He was becoming a man, but she didn't want him scared that his mom was in danger. She needed to tell someone though, so she called her dad. She felt different telling it to him. He would worry about her, but knew that she had taken steps to protect herself—and the steps had worked. He would be proud of his daughter.

She told him the facts and kept the emotions out of it. She didn't want him to worry. Showing him how tough she was by taking the emotion out of it would reassure him.

He was stunned that someone would attack his girl. "Julie, crap…," he said. "Well done. You could have ended up in the hospital, or worse."

"Thanks," she said. "It felt good to walk away from that. He ran away, probably peed his pants."

"That's my girl. I'm proud of you."

A small tear ran down her cheek. So many things from this attack reminded her of the situation from years earlier. But it wasn't painful. It was healing to tell her father the story about today's attack. She wished she could tell him the other story, but she would never trouble him with that. It would cause him too much pain and she had already dealt with it. She was just fine.

***

Later that month, Julie reached out to Ash and asked her if they could chat before the Pink Ladies meeting. Ash agreed, so Julie arrived at the classroom about an hour early. Julie told the story about the latest attack.

"Oh my word, Julie!" Ash shrieked. "That is great! Well, not great it happened, but great that you won. I'm not surprised, though. You're the whole reason why we teach the skills we teach. Well done!" She gave Julie a hug.

"Are you okay, though?" Ash asked "You able to sleep? Having any flashbacks or strange symptoms?"

"No, thankfully," Julie answered. "Ash...," Julie continued, "you should probably know. There was another incident in my past where the outcome wasn't so great." Julie then told Ash the story of the rape. It was only the second time she had ever told the story. For some reason, Julie felt like she could tell Ash more of the details of what happened. She still didn't fully describe everything; even after all these years it was still too painful.

"And that's what happened," Julie said in conclusion.

Ash was silent. She took a moment and then deeply inhaled. Finally, she spoke. "Julie. You're still standing." She paused. "That guy has taken enough from you. You need to make the decision that he has taken enough. Once you make that decision, then you start reclaiming what he has taken."

She spoke with authority, as if she had been through this, too. "You did that by winning the recent attack," she continued, pointing her finger at Julie for emphasis. "You took back things deep inside that were stolen. It feels strange to you to take back stolen things in your soul because it's the first time you've gotten them back. Keep inventorying yourself. When you find yourself hesitating because of that monster from the past, don't hesitate. Press forward. Don't give him any space in your life. In time, he'll get a full eviction notice."

Julie was stunned at Ash's insight and wondered where it came from. She knew that Ash had a story and while she wouldn't ask about it, she would be ready to listen if Ash revealed it. Stories like that were sacred. Julie wouldn't press just to satisfy her curiosity.

"I needed someone to tell," Julie said. "Thank you for letting me unload."

"Anytime, and I mean that," Ash said as she hugged Julie.

Julie wasn't used to girlfriend talk like this. That night on the ride home from Pink Ladies, Julie replayed the conversation with Ash. Julie realized she had spent so much of her life either maintaining a failing marriage, raising a son, working, couponing, stocking, or simply being busy that she didn't have any girlfriends. Forget close friends, just simply a friend. Ash was a good candidate for that, Julie concluded.

Another thought crossed Julie's mind on the ride home. Talking to Ash had closed one chapter of the rape's aftermath—the question of whether Julie could fight back and win. She wouldn't have to reread that chapter. Her brain could now turn off on that topic. There were more chapters, but that one had been closed. It felt good.

Chapter 12

The Back Road

Ned's phone rang. It was an old 80s landline, beige with a curled cord that had faded after a couple decades in the sun. A modern phone was not a priority in his modest Colorado ranch house.

"Ned here," he said.

"Hey, Ned, this is Floyd. How the hell are you?"

"Holy cow, Floyd," Ned said. "I'm great. It's good to hear your voice! Good Lord, how long has it been? Twenty or so? I did that work in your crawl space."

"I think you're about right," Floyd answered. "Maybe a few more, but let's not do that math."

"It's great to hear from ya," Ned said. Back in the day, he'd really liked Floyd. "What can I do for you these days? You got another home improvement project on your mind?"

"Well, sort of," Floyd said. "You remember my daughter, Julie, right?"

"I do," Ned said, remembering her as a gangly high school girl. "Smart girl," he said. "She loved fishing with you. What she up to these days?"

"She's changed a heck of a lot since you last saw her," Floyd said. "That high schooler with braces is now a lovely woman."

"No surprises there."

"She's a single mom," Floyd said. "Divorced from a shithead who traded her in for a younger model. Grass-is-greener kind of thing. She's finding her place and getting on her feet again. Her son, my grandson, is twelve and is great kid. They live in Eugene, Oregon."

Ned tried to picture that little high schooler as a mom with a twelve-year-old. "Eugene is nice," he finally said.

"I disagree, my friend," Floyd said. "Eugene is a mini version of Portland or Seattle. The thought of her and Joel living in that Left Coast shithole scares me," Floyd said.

"How so?" Ned assumed most places in the west were pretty much like Colorado.

"Have you had a chance to watch some of the news these days?" Floyd asked. "Every time someone decides they're offended, some corporation needs to be protested. It happens in progressive cities. Portland, Seattle, Berkeley."

"Oh, ya," Ned said. He vaguely recalled hearing something about flare ups in those cities.

"Eugene has been lucky so far," Floyd continued. "It hasn't had a big one, but I think a big one is coming to her city soon." He started to unload his fears to Ned. "I've talked to Julie and she worries about the same. I've let her know that the cabin has been willed to her... and everything in it, Ned. *Everything* in it," Floyd emphasized.

Ned instantly understood. He'd had his own thoughts about how the country seemed to be splitting apart—and how things would get violent, especially as city people flooded into rural areas like Smoky Flats. Nearby Denver had its own issues that mirrored what Floyd described in Seattle, Portland, and other places.

Ned was a level-headed, practical person who shied away from doomsday thinking, but he knew Floyd's fears about a collapse of the country were well-founded and that a single mom like Julie would be in grave danger. "You're a good father, Floyd."

"I don't want to seem to be one of those 'the sky is falling' people," Floyd said with a laugh. "I don't want to sound morbid. I'm not planning on dying anytime soon. I'm enjoying my retirement too much. But I want to let Julie know that if she needs to bug out of Eugene she can head to the cabin. If that happens, would you mind just kind of keeping an eye on her. Make sure she knows where the breaker box is... that sort of thing."

Ned knew what Floyd was saying. The breaker box meant Floyd trusted Ned with his daughter's life. It was humbling. Ned would have looked after Julie anyway, but for Floyd to call and ask made it that much more important.

"You'd better not kick off anytime soon," Ned said. "Floyd, it is humbling for you to ask about me looking after Julie. Yet you know you don't have to. Of course, if they come, I'll make sure to help out any way I can."

"And that is why I asked you," Floyd said.

"If you find out that they're on their way," Ned said, "give me the heads up. I don't have TV here. I have a wicked set of rabbit ears and I can usually get a news station out of Cheyenne. I kind of have the internet, but I go into town and use the internet at the library."

Ned essentially lived off the grid. He consumed only the information he wanted to consume for a short period at a time. Typically, it was the evening news from Cheyenne, the weather forecast, and maybe a few sports scores. The latest sitcom, celebrity gossip and 24-hour news channels were not part of Ned's day, and he preferred it that way.

He made an income as a caretaker for the numerous cabins in Western Lakes. He preferred spending his day tinkering around cabins, visiting neighbors, hunting and fishing, machining tools in his shed, tending his high elevation garden, berry picking, or maybe making a batch of chokecherry wine. It was a simple life.

"I'll let you know by calling you on this line," Floyd said. "I knew I could count on you."

"You bet," Ned said.

They exchanged goodbyes and hung up.

***

The conversation with Floyd got Ned thinking. His oldest daughter, Rachel, was going to college in Cheyenne. It had one of the few programs in the country that specialized in wildlife management. Rachel had about one year left until she graduated. The last time Ned talked to her she still loved the program and was getting excited about gradating.

Ned's youngest, Johnny, was a senior in high school. He was overly involved in sports, and Ned was fine with that. A teenage boy with time on his hands was a teenager up to no good. Johnny played football in the fall, had a few overlapping weeks of football and basketball, and then played baseball in the spring. He was good at all three sports.

Ned hoped he'd get a scholarship somewhere, but his grades needed to be better. Ned couldn't complain about Johnny's C average. Johnny kept his grades high enough to stay in sports. The kid never stopped moving and was either eating, sleeping, in class, in practice, or at a game. Studying and schoolwork was done, but usually as he nodded off to sleep.

Ned's wife left him when Johnny was in second grade. Ned realized that Floyd may not know that she had left. When Ned helped Floyd all those years ago, Barbara was still his wife. When she left, she moved to Denver because she'd had enough of living off the grid.

She wanted to have friends to visit with, malls to shop in, streets with sidewalks, and neighbors ten feet away. An isolated, self-sufficient lifestyle was not for her. When she left, the kids did not want to leave behind their school and friends. They didn't want to move away to some unknown city that sounded vastly different from where they were being

57

raised. Barbara understood and didn't create a custody battle. They stayed with Ned as their primary caregiver; however, they spent several weeks in the summer with their mother, and would visit on other occasions from time to time.

Denver. Just thinking about the place made Ned roll his eyes. What a colossal mess that city had become. Just a few years ago, it was a city of job growth, technical marvels and thriving industry, instant access to the Rocky Mountains, and a flourishing agricultural side. Now it had all the problems of New York City: drugs, crime, and general social decay. Denver was now just like any big American city except that it was plopped down in beautiful Colorado.

In 2008, Denver took its final plunge into big-city living and jettisoned its Colorado roots. During that year's election season, progressives decided they wanted to take Colorado from the Republicans and turn it into a Democrat stronghold. It was covert, organized, and orchestrated not by Colorado residents, but by well-funded leftist groups who wanted to extend their reach.

Half of Colorado was in the Rockies, where rugged mountain folk lived, but there were only a few thousand of them. Colorado Springs with five hundred thousand people was home to several huge military bases and was generally conservative. But Denver and its suburbs had five times that many residents, and many of them had recently moved in from California and the East Coast. Most of them brought their politics with them.

The progressive experiment worked. The sheer number of Denver voters with all the new transplants, coupled with the millions of dollars of outside money, resulted in Colorado voting for a liberal president and, for the first time in decades, a Democrat governor.

The new governor was entirely out of touch with Coloradans who lived outside of liberal Denver. The first thing he did to reward the people who got him into office was pass gun control laws—severe ones. He talked about confiscating 30-round magazines. This shocked life-long Coloradans.

Colorado's sudden lurch to the left baffled Ned. Didn't the governor know that people in half of the state hunted and defended themselves and their livestock and pets from predators? Yes, but all the mountain people in the state equaled the votes of one Denver neighborhood.

Ned lived far from Denver, and he liked it that way. He acquired his guns and magazines long before the bans went into effect. Most of his guns were handed down to him from family members or purchased through untraceable private sales. He owned them legally, and no one knew. That was fine with him.

The new ban on standard capacity magazines, like 30-round AR-15 magazines, really bothered Ned. When black bears were in mating season or bear calf season, walking outside could be dangerous—especially after dark. Having just six rounds in a lever-action 30-30 was not enough. The time it took to try to reload from loose cartridges in a pocket could be the difference between living and dying.

***

Rachel and Johnny both seemed to like living off the grid. The Rocky Mountains were an amazing backyard for kids: hiking, fishing, hunting, and hanging out with other country kids. Rachel and Johnny also liked spending their summers with Barbara in Denver. However, when they returned, they seemed relieved. City living stressed them out. It was obvious to Ned. They needed a week or so to decompress and shake off the city and then they'd be back to normal.

Ned went into the closest town about once a month. It was two miles away. The closest medium-sized city was ninety minutes away. He took a trip there every six months and stocked up on nonperishable staples. He'd always be sure to buy dried milk in fifty-pound bags. Buying fresh milk would mean going to the store every three days and paying way too much for it. His kids were so used to dried milk that they thought fresh milk tasted strange.

On his trips to the city, he might also buy batteries, lightbulbs, toilet paper, large bags of flour, canned goods, and maybe some hardware items. He didn't need many things. The simple life suited him fine.

Before Barbara left him, he'd take her to the local store on those trips so she could purchase clothes for each family member. He wasn't stingy; he knew she liked feeling good about herself and said nothing about her purchasing feminine, pretty items. Ned never denied her what she wanted to buy. She would get makeup, hair clips, salon shampoo, dresses, and dress shoes. There were times he would wonder who she would wear these things for, but he didn't ask. She wore them when she would head to the town council meeting or church. She looked nice, so he couldn't argue.

Barbara was naturally beautiful. Ned loved watching her stand at the edge of the lake, talking to the kids, with her hair blowing across her face. When she looked up at him, with a playful gleam in her eyes, it was as if time stood still.

Ned loved her flowing black hair. He loved to run his fingers through it while they talked in bed at night. He would prop up on his elbow with Barbara on her back next to him. They would talk for hours about anything and everything. He loved touching her and talking with her. Those were special moments.

As the kids grew older, her beautiful hair started to change color to another beautiful color: silver. Those strands of silver framed her face perfectly. Ned felt like a blessed man.

One evening, after a long trip to town, Barbara's hair no longer had strands of silver. She noticed the quizzical look on Ned's face and shrugged. No explanation. Ned was surprised by how hurt he was when Barbara colored her hair. He couldn't figure out if it was because she did it without telling him. *It's her hair. She can do whatever she wants with it*, he reasoned. *She knows how much I loved it… did she care?* He never wanted to know the answer to that possibility.

Looking back, Ned realized that the first sign that Barbara hated her off-the-grid life was the colored hair. She didn't want to grow old in a mountain home. She wanted to go to the big city and be "normal."

She was the love of his life. He never thought in a million years she would leave. He changed when she did. He withdrew, became quiet. He wouldn't let himself dream. He poured his heart into working. He became a stoic mountain man. A lonely one.

Chapter 13

Tiny Spaces

Julie realized that her father's generous gift certificates freed up the monthly installments she had been setting aside for firearms. Not having to sock that much away each month offered some much-needed relief to the budget. The breathing room gave her more options when it came to prepping. She could buy bigger batches of supplies and save even more. She could also branch out and buy things other than tuna and ramen noodles.

One Saturday morning after her couponing session, Julie took an inventory of her stockpile. She had over a hundred cans of various canned goods. Mostly vegetables, soups, and refried beans. Sometimes she used them, but usually not. She definitely bought them at a faster pace than they were consumed.

She also had a large amount of paper towels and toilet paper. The problem with those items was that they took up a lot of physical space, and it quickly became a challenge to stash them. She and Joel certainly used them, but again, she purchased them faster than they were consumed. Those items were being stacked in her bedroom and it was becoming comical to walk in and see a wall of paper products.

Julie decided she would revisit paper products. There had to be a solution. Toiletries. She had over a hundred bottles of their preferred shampoos. That was a lot. Batteries, cereal, top ramen, instant soup, pasta, and more. Her pantry was full to the point that things were stacked on the floor going into the small room off the kitchen. Some of this had to be put elsewhere.

There was an unfinished attic space in her house. Julie pulled open the small door to the attic and took in the space. Could she store things here? It would get hot in here in the summer, so anything that couldn't take a fluctuation in temperature would not work. Maybe the paper products? She went into the disaster known as the basement. It was an unfinished basement where the laundry machines were along with all the Christmas decorations, luggage, and a lot of things she hadn't opened in years. Steve had grabbed quite a bit of things out of the basement and Julie hadn't even taken the time to ask what he took.

It was time to rethink the basement. It was the solution to her storage problem. Julie decided now was good a time as any. She sorted everything in the basement into three piles. One for trash, one for donations, one for keeping. The idea was to get rid of anything she hasn't seen or used in over a year. That was most of it.

Oh, the junk! Notes from college classes, some of Joel's baby toys, Julie's high school diploma, and so much more. Julie spent the rest of the weekend, and two more, cleaning out the basement. It felt so good. It was long overdue.

On the fourth weekend, Julie knew exactly what she was going to do. She had been scouring Craigslist and local garage sales. She wanted shelving, and it didn't need to be perfect. It needed to be functional. It also needed to be cheap but sturdy enough to hold some weight. Canned goods were heavy.

At a garage sale nearby, a man was selling two sturdy shelves from his shop. They were perfect. She asked if she could offer him a few extra dollars to deliver them to her house. He took one look at her little car and knew she couldn't haul them herself. He was a nice guy and agreed to haul them to her house.

Those shelves made all the difference. Joel came home from Steve's on a Sunday evening.

"Look!" she said with pride. The shelves in the formerly messy basement were organized by type of food and easy to get to. Joel was impressed. She also showed him the upstairs pantry that used to be overflowing with a landslide of food. Now it was organized and uncluttered.

"This is great, mom," Joel said. "It's like we have a real house, not some crazy-hoarder-lady house." They both laughed.

They agreed they would eat items out of the pantry first. They would replenish items from the basement shelves and then replenish the basement with her prepping purchases. The empty spaces on the basement shelves allowed her to know what needed to be purchased and made it easy to rotate stock.

The pantry had a door. Julie liked the idea that all their supplies were out of sight. No one would come into their house and see that they had an overflowing pantry. No one could look into the windows and see their stash either. Looters struck stores, but they also struck houses. She didn't need to make her home a target for looting. She wanted to look as unprepared as possible to anyone looking in the window.

During the reorganization of the basement, Julie realized two things. First, in the past she had only prepared for a short-term disaster like a riot lasting a few days or weeks. Now, with the budget breathing room and the organizational efforts that freed up space, she could have a whole lot more supplies. Now she could weather a mid-length situation like a natural or political disaster that lasted a few weeks or months. She might be without comfort items during that period, but she and Joel would survive without any outside help.

Her second realization was that cleaning out all her pre-divorce junk in the basement led to her being far more prepared for a disaster. It felt good to fill that same space with items that would provide for her and Joel. It was cleansing. The pre-divorce junk trapped her in a bad marriage; the post-divorce basement freed her to be self-sufficient.

Julie evolved into what she called an "urban prepper." To avoid being called a right-wing wacko, she kept up the guise of couponing and preparing for the "big earthquake." She never talked about a long season of lawlessness. She didn't talk to anyone about her stash. People would turn into savages in a crisis. She thought about what happened in Bosnia and Venezuela. People would kill for toilet paper.

She also didn't tell anyone about her new-found love of firearms. To borrow Ash's words, "The 'C' in 'CHL' is there for a reason." She fully concealed her pistol.

***

After one Pink Ladies class, Julie tried to rush out to make a quick stop at a grocery store to use a coupon to get some antibacterial cream. It rarely was ever on sale and she was focusing some of her prepping purchases on first aid supplies.

Ash stopped her and asked, "What has you in a hurry?"

"I need to make a quick stop at the grocery store before it closes," Julie answered.

"Ah," Ash said. "Well, I was wondering if you might be open to sharing your story to our class. The recent story."

Julie was caught off guard. "The recent story meaning the attack at the park, not the thing that happened in college, right?" she asked.

"Yes," Ash said, "the park attack."

"Oh, wow, Ash," Julie said. "I don't know." She paused and said, "I'm no hero. I don't want any sort of limelight on that." She didn't want to try to get sympathy from other women. She didn't need sympathy; she needed to protect herself.

"Oh, no, no," Ash assured her. "I get it. I want you to tell the story to explain the different skills you used. Pulling your hair back to pull him off balance. Yelling aggressively, not passively. I want the women to walk through it with you so they can hear how skills can kick into gear. This is not girlfriend time; this is a time to learn from first-hand experience," Ash explained.

"Can I think about it?" Julie asked.

"Sure. Can I call you in a week or so for an answer? I'd like to have that as our teaching time next month if possible."

"Sounds good. I'll have an answer. Hey, I have to go, walk with me to the parking lot?" Julie said. Ash nodded.

As they walked up to their cars parked next to each other, Ash remarked about the five jumbo sized boxes of tampons Julie had in the back seat.

"Wow! You planning to use those until you're seventy?" Ash marveled.

"Ha! Funny!" Julie said, a little worried that someone had seen her preps, even though she trusted Ash. "No. I'm into the whole couponing thing, and I got those for a deal. I'll stash them away," Julie gave Ash her standard answer.

As Julie unlocked her door and was lowering herself into her driver's seat, Ash looked at Julie with a slight smile and asked, "Are you couponing, stockpiling, or maybe… prepping?" She winked, waved, and started up her engine. Julie knew that Ash was onto her. She looked forward to her call next week.

Chapter 14

The Girlfriend Network

Julie called Ash and agreed to tell her story. Ash wanted to use the story as a springboard to walk through the event so everyone could tactically think through ways to escape. It would be interesting. Julie wasn't sure exactly what Ash was trying to achieve, she just knew she didn't want this to be an hour of sympathy-inducing drama for women. She wanted it to be a practical lesson in how to survive an attack.

Julie and Ash also agreed to meet for coffee on a Saturday morning before the Pink Ladies meeting. Joel was with his dad. Julie had a lot to do that day, but it was nice to sit and relax even if only for an hour.

"So, tell me about your couponing and stockpiling," Ash started right in.

Julie went on to explain her strategy to be prepared for the "big earthquake" and use budgeting and couponing techniques. It was her standard answer she gave anyone to hide her belief that disasters come in many different forms, natural being the only one that is socially acceptable to talk about.

Ash showed her hand first. "You and I know the odds of a natural disaster are much less than other disasters. Look at Detroit. That place looks like a hurricane went through it but that was all man-made. Katrina started out as a natural disaster that became a political disaster. Heck, look at countries in South America. Rich in natural resources that could feed every citizen but political forces are starving them as though they had a typhoon hit. Same for Haiti."

Ash was putting concrete words to the feelings Julie had been carrying around. Political unrest could cause the same, if not worse, disaster scenarios than a category-five hurricane.

"Watch interviews with people who survived the earthquake in California in the 80s," Ash said. "The media left after three weeks. Even today, they would tell that they are still in recovery mode. Ask folks who survived Katrina. Tour the devastated parts of New Orleans. It's as if Katrina happened last summer. Rebuilding?" Ash was on a roll. Julie wasn't sure what her point was.

"I love what you have done in your life to rebuild from your sexual assault," Ash said. "You helped yourself when no one could, and make conscious decisions to not repeat history or live as a victim. I love it. It's inspiring. Can I encourage you to take that same mentality and put it into your emergency preparedness?" Ash asked.

"Not sure what you mean," Julie replied.

"Be strategic," Ash said. "It sounds like you have a lot of supplies, which is great. You're about twenty paces ahead of everyone else if the event—whatever that ends up being—happened right now. Now, take an inventory and ask strategic questions. Ask yourself about medications, water purification, ready-to-make meals, clothing and shelter, batteries, medical supplies—not a first aid kit, but medical supplies. Like wound dressings, stitch kits, and blood coagulating bandages." Ash had obviously thought about this topic. A lot.

Ash continued to talk about being without purified water for an extended period, utilities being down, no communications with far away family members, fuel, and so much more.

It was overwhelming, but Ash was right. Julie realized all the work to supply her home for an emergency might have been a colossal waste of time. Ash also watched Julie's shoulders slump in discouragement as she painted the picture.

"Don't be discouraged," Ash said. "I mean it. You're ahead of the game. Try this…"

Ash went on to give Julie a few resources for prepping, not coupon stockpiling, but prepping. The stockpiling was great, but Ash's approach was much more intentional. Ash encouraged Julie to make a full inventory of what she had and then organize them in a few ways. Items wanted for the immediate needs of her close family and no one else. This would be medications, water purification, food, and ammunition. Luxury items that were not immediately needed, like ten thousand tampons, categorize separately.

"I know from your couponing you have an immense number of feminine products," Ash said.

Julie was amazed that such a young woman could be so wise.

"More than you'll ever use in your lifetime. It's the curse of couponers. Calculate what you use every month, multiply by about five years—yes, five years—and then what is left over becomes a bartering item," Ash described.

Bartering! Of course! "Keep going," Julie said eagerly.

"You and I know that two-thirds of the women in this town buy their tampons monthly and don't think any further in stocking their cabinets beyond next week," Ash said. "When a disaster hits, shelves will be cleared. Think of when Hurricane Sandy hit the northeast. You can take a box of tampons and 'buy' items you need. Those extra tampons become very valuable to those who don't have any. They might have batteries or fuel you need. ATMs will be down most likely. Or if anyone can even get cash, price gouging and empty shelves will render cash fairly useless." So much wisdom in such a young woman, Julie thought again.

Ash went on. "As you inventory, create categories. Medications, tools, and so on. Then step back and ask yourself what you're lacking in. This is really personal. Your immediate needs as a single mother to a teenager will be very different than a middle-aged retired couple or a family of six with small kids."

Julie nodded.

"It sounds to me," Ash said, "like you're lacking in the supplies and tools department. Start looking for deals now that might include water purifications filters, tools, knives, and so on. Not going to lie, the local grocery store doesn't carry most of that. But other discount stores do. Think Walmart, Grocery Outlet, or Big Lots. You don't need to shop at the expensive sporting goods stores for those things. Maybe get good ideas by perusing them, sure. But don't be discouraged by the label or the price. All of us have gaps in our prepping. No one can do it all, but you can prepare for those things that are your priority and barter after that."

"Got it," Julie said. Her head was spinning, but she was no longer overwhelmed. The spinning was her brain firing a dozen great thoughts a minute as she pondered what Ash was saying and how she could apply it to her own life.

"I have to ask," Julie said. "Are you a prepper, too?"

Ash grinned.

Julie headed off to her Saturday errands. As soon as she got home, she opened her laptop and opened a spreadsheet. She printed it out and headed to the basement and started her inventory. She inventoried into the middle of the night. She fell asleep satisfied at the progress she'd made.

Chapter 15

Telling Her Story

Julie was nervous as she walked into the next Pink Ladies meeting. She wasn't as nervous as she thought she'd be, but she was certainly jittery enough. The park attack had become more of a pain in her side in recent weeks. The police had caught the perpetrator. He was charged, arraigned, and released. Julie said she wanted to go to trial, not settle. She knew the prosecutor would give this guy a hundred hours of community service that would never get served. Apparently, there wasn't enough jail space in Eugene. The city spent money on everything else but not on keeping criminals away from peaceful citizens. Priorities.

She had no idea of what the attacker actually intended to do with her that day, but considering he was trying to pull her away and never once demanded her purse told her he meant to harm her. That would get lost in the paperwork; she was warming up to the idea of telling her story. If she didn't tell it, no one would ever hear it. It's not like a jury would ever hear it. Her story was currently limited to the pages of a police report that no one would ever read.

Under some old victim's-rights law, Julie's decision to press charges meant the prosecutor had to set a trial date. It was rescheduled twice. The latest trial date was fast approaching with no word from the prosecutor. All communication from the DA came by mail. No phone calls, no meetings, nothing. She knew a third rescheduling was coming soon. She now realized why people don't bother pressing charges. This explained, in part, why violent thugs pulled women by the hair in parks and did go-dawful things.

Julie walked into the classroom and greeted her classmates. There were about six that evening. Ash started right on time.

"You all know Julie," Ash began. "I asked Julie to share with us an incident that happened recently. She was targeted by an attacker. Because Julie has spent quite a bit of time and energy learning various defensive techniques, she walked away from the situation unharmed. It could have had a very different outcome. I want her to tell her story. Afterwards, I want us to walk through a few of the key points in the exchange she had with this dick, and think through various options, possibilities, and outcomes. This is not a support group for Julie. She wouldn't have agreed to talk if it were." Ash pointed her finger in the air for emphasis. "Instead, this is for you ladies to learn how to use her story to put more tools in each of your toolboxes."

Julie told the story step by step. The attacker surprised her from behind and pulled her off balance. Julie managed to keep her balance and use her hair to pull him off balance. That gave her time to unholster her firearm and switch off the safety. This turned him from offense to defense. He let her go when he saw the firearm. Julie used aggressive words and took charge. The guy ran like a bug when the lights were turned on.

"Let's take a five-minute break," Ash said. "I want each of you to do two things while on break. Think of a what if. For example, what if he pulled on her hair hard enough to pull her to the ground? What could she do next? What could she have done differently? The reason I ask this is not to assign value to her choices, but to think through *all* the choices we have in an attack. If she pulled back on her hair and it didn't work, she would need another option, right? Let's think them all through. I want to pick this apart for all of us. When this happens, we don't realize that we have so many choices that can get us to safety. Start thinking, we have a lot to discuss."

The discussion after the break was incredible. What if she had landed on her ass from the first yank of hair? From that point, what if he did or didn't let go of her hair. Everyone agreed he had an advantage by having her hair. It's very easy to control someone by yanking hair. You can keep someone physically off balance, in pain, control where they walk, and greatly hinder their line of sight simply by grabbing hair and not letting go.

The group also discussed that Julie needed to pay more attention to what she passed as she walked. The guy may or may not have been visible but she was not paying attention like she should have. Julie agreed. Her mind was not present but wondering about what she needed to do that day.

What could she have done from the ground to defend herself? Unholster, yes. But what if she couldn't? A class member asked, "Julie, before I say what I would have done from the ground, firearm unavailable, what would you have done?"

Julie was quick to answer. "Depending on what appendage is available to me, it would have been a direct punch or kick to the groin. Not a pop punch. A full body, swing of my body weight, punching through the target to the other side, blow."

The lady asking the question smiled. "Me too. Good."

The class talked through the language Julie used. It wasn't the soft pleading language glorified by Hollywood. It was aggressive and demanding — and chock full of swear words. One classmate liked Julie's line that the guy should hold still so she could shoot him. It was aggressive, and made her an equal to him in the sense that she was an attacker, too. It also made her sound like she wanted to shoot him, which is something that threw him off.

The questions went on so long that range time didn't happen, and no one minded. It was fascinating to go through the what ifs and rework different ways to escape an attack. At the end of the meeting, Ash had to wrap it up. The conversation could have continued for hours.

"Okay, we gotta stop. I hope you all agree, this was incredibly helpful to walk through and work through. I hope all of you have a different perspective on how to handle and carry yourselves. I hope you all have better tools in your toolboxes. We don't use just one. We use combinations of them. Having firearms training isn't enough. Having self-defense training is only one tool. Having situational awareness alone isn't enough. We must use them in concert, and I think we can all agree Julie did well. Hell, she's still here, isn't she?"

They applauded, and Julie appreciated it. She didn't think she would. Julie wasn't being praised for being a victim and given a pity party. She was being praised for choosing to not be a victim. She gladly accepted that praise. Finally, everyone headed out to the parking lot. Ash hugged Julie. It felt good. It wasn't just a quick hug; it was a hug of appreciation. Julie was really beginning to enjoy Ash's friendship. They were becoming good friends.

"I hope you feel like I do," Ash said. "Tonight went well. The right tone was struck. It wasn't glorifying victimhood. It glorified self-sufficiency and how to get better at it. In my book, you did well, I hope you think so."

"It felt good. Thank you for encouraging me to do this. I don't mind talking about it. I really don't feel any ill effects from it. It felt good that it could be used to help others think through how to be better at self-defense. The Q and A afterwards was helpful. I learned from my own experience. That's kind of crazy," Julie mused.

"That often happens," Ash said. "Hey, I'll see you soon. Would you like to do a Saturday morning coffee again soon?"

"That would be great."

***

One day before the now fourth rescheduled trial date, Julie received a letter from the prosecutor. Her attacker had pleaded guilty and avoided a trial. He would receive a six-month sentence, with credit for time already served. Then he would serve community service. That's right: he would be back in the community. Probably in the park by the farmer's market. And looking for a woman who looked like Julie to exact his revenge on.

Julie was furious. She called the prosecutor's office and got some young intern-type employee. Julie asked for the person who signed her form letter. That person was not available.

"Is that person ever available for calls like mine?" Julie asked.

"I'm not sure what you mean. We get all kinds of calls," replied the confused intern.

"Ah, well, a call from a person who was on the other end of a crime," Julie said, refusing to call herself a victim, "who believes her perpetrator was going to do great harm to her… and he just pleaded guilty and got six months, but will serve maybe four. That kind of call," Julie said, now lowering her voice.

"Oh. Well. Umm… please hold." Elevator music

The intern finally came back on the line. She said, "Hi, Miss… I'm sorry I didn't catch your name. I asked one of our prosecutors about your matter, and I am happy to take down your information and have someone call you back to talk to you about your specific case."

The intern was really good at being unhelpful.

"So, you just spoke to a prosecutor?" Julie asked.

"Yes," the intern said defensively.

"Face to face?" Julie asked.

"Yes."

"And they won't take my call directly right now?" Julie asked.

"No."

"Don't you think that is a little strange? Maybe even a little chicken shit? I'm just asking because that is how I see it," Julie said very evenly without emotion.

"I'm sorry. What is your name? I have your number here; I'll make sure someone calls you back by the end of the day."

No one from the prosecutor's office called Julie back. Ever.

Chapter 16

New Outlook

Julie eagerly implemented Ash's suggestions about inventorying the prepping items she had. Julie started by categorizing them. The first category was what she called "normal food." These were essentially things she could get at a grocery store and used regularly.

She divided this category into those that would keep for a long time and didn't necessarily need to be rotated out and those that needed to be rotated out over time. The category of things that would keep for a long time included canned goods, some grains, and bottled items with a lot of preservatives. The category of things that would be rotated out was food items that needed to be used within a year, and generally were. Those were primarily cereal, snack items, and flour.

Another category was paper products and toiletries. These wouldn't spoil certainly, but she wanted to categorize this by how often it would be used, if at all. There were paper towels and toilet paper. Of course, Julie would always buy those because they always needed them. But then there were things like shampoo, toothpaste, and soap. Those items would never spoil, aren't used quite as much, and would be highly desired when the store shelves were bare.

Julie concluded that she had adequate supplies of the first two categories. There were a few gaps, and maybe a few wants, but nothing major. The next category was what she called survival gear. These were medications, tools, water purification, fuel and fuel alternatives, and so on. Julie quickly realized she had almost none of these. The final category was emergency food. This was ultra-long-term food that, unlike normal food, didn't require a full kitchen to prepare. It was also easy to pick up and move if Julie needed to relocate to a new place. Emergency food was essentially food that only required hot water. An example would be beans and rice with spices that simply needed hot water. It wasn't necessarily freeze-dried food but rather any long-term prepared food. It wouldn't be rotated out; it was truly for emergencies only.

While she knew that her father had freeze-dried meals in the crawl space of the cabin, that resource was not in her basement and she didn't have the money to buy more and put them in her home. Looking at her inventory of "normal food," Julie realized that she had the makings for a lot of prepackaged emergency food. For example, she had beans, rice, and spices to make just-add-hot-water jambalaya. She also had flour and other baking ingredients to make biscuit or pancake mix. She had the basic ingredients, but how to make them last for years to become emergency food?

Google. Julie started Googling long-term food storage. She found that a food vacuum sealer was the best option. The recipes were plentiful. Toss into a vacuum seal bag; lentils, beans, rice, spices, and dried vegetables flakes; seal, label, and store. She tried out recipes for her and Joel before making multiple batches of them. Some were a bust, many were good. Julie made multiple meals of the favorites.

Her Google research indicated that another advantage to eating the emergency food on occasion was that she and Joel would get used to it and, in a crisis, not have an intestinal reaction that could happen with a sudden change in diet.

Julie also found a mix cookbook on a trip to a thrift store. The idea was that one makes a large batch of a mix. It might be a roll mix that was vacuum sealed. The mix would be the foundation of variations on it if other ingredients were available. Over the next two months, she used the mix cookbook to make pancakes, rolls, dumplings, twisted pretzels, and even cinnamon rolls. Joel loved the variety and never once questioned the flavor. Julie decided to make an incredibly large batch, store it in several vacuum sealed bags, and use it on a regular basis. She had plenty of extra bags for an emergency.

After perfecting her recipes with vacuum seal bags, she graduated to something larger: five-gallon buckets with Gamma Seal lids. Unlike vacuum seal bags, buckets could be opened, a little amount used, and the lid screwed back on.

Julie kept buying food for the buckets and sealed them with the Gamma lids. She built up quite a collection. She inventoried them and labeled them with a Sharpie marker. For the mixes, she used a key ring to attached laminated recipe cards to each bucket with the recipes associated with each bucket. The buckets of roll mix had about a dozen laminated recipes. In an emergency, having those quick references would be handy. If she needed to move the buckets, the recipes would simply travel with the bucket.

Her internet research also suggested sealing other things that needed to be compacted and needed to stay dry—clothing and blankets, for example. The vacuum seal bags for food were too small for these items, but Space Saver bags were large and designed for them. They used a regular vacuum cleaner to suck out the air in the clothing or blankets and then sealed them with a reusable seal. They shrunk the items down and kept them moisture proofed. Space Saver bags worked great on toilet paper, reducing about ninety rolls into one thirty-gallon tub and preserving them for years.

Her hours of internet research produced hundreds of ideas, all of which she wanted to do right away. Sometimes it was overwhelming. But then she realized she needed to just plow through it and get as much done as she could. Then, as she learned more, she became familiar with the topic and it was no longer mysterious. She was a student of prepping, and she was progressing nicely in her studies.

***

One of the topics Julie researched was bugging out — getting out of Eugene when things got dangerous. She prepared a bug out bag with essential supplies for traveling and surviving out of her car until they reached their ultimate destination. The idea was that this bag would have everything in it for the trip, allowing them to leave in a matter of minutes and get a head start on the exodus.

In preparing a bug out plan, she realized she needed to have a destination. The thought didn't stay with her long because she had her father's promise. She could go to the cabin for any reason. The cabin was by far the best place to go: remote, rural, conservative people, and pre-stocked. Unbeatable. However, it was far away. It would be no simple matter getting out of Eugene, Oregon and driving hundreds of miles to Colorado. Depending on the disaster, access to fuel could be a major challenge.

If an EMP fried all the electrical components in the region, then the circuitry in the gas pumps wouldn't work (and neither would the cars). Not much she could do about that. Long-distance travel was off the table in an EMP.

But Julie thought a different kind of disaster was coming. It would be a political upheaval and would unwind relatively slowly, over a matter of days or maybe weeks. She would see the signs earlier than her neighbors who kept their heads in the sand and she would leave long before they figured it out. Under this scenario, there would be fuel along the way. She would be one step ahead of the collapse as she moved inland, away from the epicenter of the riots and chaos.

***

Julie had meaningful conversations with Joel during the time her prepping and bug out plans took off. He appreciated being included and found it fun. He got into vacuum sealing meals, storing them, and putting them away. Julie and Joel had some good conversations during the weekends they worked on prepping projects.

The conversations went many different directions. Joel had some ideas that surprised Julie. She was impressed at how Joel was embracing the idea of being prepared. But Joel took it further and understood that they were doing more than taking steps to deal with a disaster; they were providing for themselves and being as self-sufficient as possible. He understood the freedom and peace of mind that came with being self-sufficient. He didn't want to depend on anyone.

Joel would tell Julie how this prepping made him rethink his history lessons. He was accustomed to learning how the colonists came to North America and decimated and victimized the indigenous people. But, now Joel saw it differently. As they talked about the right to own guns, Joel understood that the Second Amendment was in reaction to the oppression experienced by colonists in England. The only people allowed to own firearms were the king's army, with devastating consequences.

"Mom," Joel said. "So, imagine if the only people who could own guns were the military and the police? Especially in Eugene where the police follow the mayor's orders. I know you would give up your guns because you don't do illegal things," he said and Julie tried not to correct him, "but bad guys already own guns even though it's against the law. Why would they suddenly stop? That means we wouldn't have guns, but they would. They'd come to our door, hurt us, and we would have to wait for the police to come. But the police would have too much on their hands."

Julie was proud her son was thinking beyond the crazy, progressive curriculum he was fed at school. She also suspected he was learning good lessons at the various gun safety courses he was taking.

It was in one of those conversations that she told him about the park attack. She told it matter-of-factly and didn't tell him how frightened she was. Julie went on to tell him the results dealing with the prosecutor, and how the guy got a minimal sentence and she was treated like an annoyance. Joel just rolled his eyes at the outcome.

"Mom, you rock. That's what you do, take care of us. I just try to help," Joel said.

"Hon, I couldn't do all this without you," she said. "I think we each do a great job doing all this. Right?"

Joel nodded. Julie enjoyed these conversations. It gave them something to look forward to after slogging through the weekdays when the focus was on schoolwork and struggling to keep grades up. In a small way, prepping gave something for Joel to strive for and work toward. If he got all his work done by Friday, then he could take a firearms course, help with meals, and vacuum seal umpteen rolls of toilet paper — with his mom.

He also liked feeling like an independent adult in the process. Julie knew she was teaching Joel skills he would never learn in school or from Steve. She was teaching him things that he would need to know someday.

During one of their Sunday projects, Julie asked Joel, "In all of this, we're doing what I want to do, have you ever thought of something we could do? Something to add to the list to prioritize?"

Joel did not hesitate to answer. "Paracord."

"Para what?" Julie asked.

Joel went to his bedroom and brought out his book bag. He showed Julie a short cord that was part of the bag.

"That's paracord," he said. "It's used by hunters, survivalists, and emergency preparedness people. I learned about it in one of my classes. You can make so much with it, but in an emergency you can unravel something you've made with it to use as a cord. You can also pull apart the main strand and use the insides for fire starter." Joel had a huge smile as he described this new topic of paracord.

"Let's go look it up," Julie said as she flipped open her laptop on the kitchen counter. Julie realized why paracord had Joel's attention. By the time she scanned a few websites, she almost believed one could build a house with paracord.

"Okay," Julie said, "I'm convinced. This is something you want to do, so you choose. What do you want to do first with paracord?" Julie asked.

"I want to make water bottle carrier to clip on my book bag. I also want to make a shoulder stock cover for the .22. Oh, how about a wristband with a small fire starter tucked inside. Oh, and a belt. I'm not sure what else, but I will think of more."

"So, you have next weekend with your dad," Julie said. "Before you head to his house, pick the two projects you want to do first. Figure out how much paracord you need and what color. In two weeks, we'll make something. Of course, grades up, caught up, no slacking. Deal?"

"Deal," Joel said with a grin and shook her hand. He acted like Christmas was in two weeks.

***

Steve stood with Julie at her front door while they waited for Joel to gather up his things. It was an uncomfortable moment. Joel was uncharacteristically not ready. He seemed to be scrambling in his room in an excited manner, and Julie wasn't quite sure what was going through his mind.

But she stood there with Steve. Awkwardly. Julie didn't like Steve coming inside. It was too weird. She didn't want him seeing her personal space anymore. Standing outside on the porch didn't give him the opportunity to stay and chat in her personal space.

"How is work?" Steve broke the ice.

"It's work," Julie answered. "You?"

"Same. Pays the bills," Steve answered and then flinched a bit. One of his bills was child support.

"How's Mandy?" Julie thought she send a little dart back.

"Not sure," Steve said.

"Not sure?" Julie repeated.

"She left about a month ago." Steve explained how Mandy decided she wasn't being *fulfilled*—the same term Steve used on Julie.

What comes around, goes around, Julie thought. "She left," Julie repeated.

"Yes. She's in Portland. Found a job." Steve gave a few more details.

"A job. She moved?"

"Yes. Found a place with her sister."

"So, this isn't a temporary thing?"

"No. She told me yesterday to expect a call from an attorney next week. She's planning to file for divorce," Steve said as he jammed his fists in his pockets and shrugged his shoulders. He acted like a sheepish teenager. Julie thought he looked pathetic.

"That sucks, Steve." Julie didn't know what else to say. *What should I say? I told you so? You didn't see this coming? Neener neener? Should I jump*

77

for glee because of the immense vindication I feel? Julie had no idea how to respond. She kept what she was feeling hidden behind her poker face.

"Yes, it sucks," Steve concluded.

"Well, I hope you're able to have a good weekend with Joel. Hang in there," Julie said with a smile.

"Joel! Dude, come on!" Julie called. Joel came bouncing down the stairs with his backpack.

"Sorry, Mom! I wanted to print these out for you so we could do them next weekend. Tell me what you think Sunday night," Joel said breathlessly as he handed her printouts. She saw that they were projects for paracord items he wanted to make.

"Will do. Have fun with your dad." She kissed his forehead.

Lying in bed that night, Julie's head was spinning. Mandy had left Steve. *Why was she not feeling fulfilled? Did it blindside him like it did when he left Julie? Did she find someone else? Or were things bad for a while and Steve never let on?* So many questions!

Then the bigger question popped crept into Julie's thinking... *would she ever consider taking him back? Would he ask her back? Would he approach her with words of apology and remorse?* Julie's heart raced at the thought, and not in a good way. It felt more like she had just been startled.

Thoughts about Steve's news raced through Julie's mind like a firestorm. First, she went through the pros of getting back together with him. Having a two-income household would be a huge relief, although she hated that this was her first thought. Having Steve to share in the parenting, instead of dividing it, would be a huge blessing. She tried hard, but couldn't think of any more pros.

Julie moved on to the cons. Steve cheated on her, and lied. It rocked Julie to the soul after she entrusted so much of who she was to him. She gave herself to him; body, heart and soul. Was it forgivable? Probably. Was it forgettable? No.

Could she be in a relationship with a man who was capable of that kind of behavior? Not just behavior, but character. There was no guarantee he would never cheat again, certainly, but having done it once certainly swung the odds that he could do it again. Julie tossed that question around her head and concluded the answer was no—no, she could not be in a relationship with a man who could cheat and hurt a loved one. She would rather be alone than live with that kind of exhausting doubt.

Could she be intimate with him again? After the cheating, after the lying, after knowing he's been in someone else's bed? There are worse things, Julie concluded. But again, being single was a more attractive option.

Putting aside the infidelity, Julie remembered the emotional distance that seemed so comfortable to Steve. Was that something she wanted? She had to expect that would be the norm again if she took him back. The warm, kind Steve from college hadn't been seen since those days. Julie realized she had the benefit of hindsight, and if Steve wanted her back, she had the choice to be attached to his aloof treatment. The thought was not appealing.

Would Steve be open to the new Julie? The Julie who had found her stride, learned to defend herself and provide for herself in times of calm as well as disaster? Would he discourage this Julie or would he want the "old Julie" he left? Would he simply tolerate the new Julie? She concluded it would be a huge stretch to ask Steve to embrace the new her.

Then there was the sobering conclusion Julie had to digest: the new Julie was probably not attractive to him. He certainly was not attractive to her anymore, especially with his built-in distance. He liked feeling like he was taking care of her, supporting her in her brokenness after being raped, and he liked keeping her in that posture. Steve felt most needed by her in those moments. Their relationship was never given the chance to grow beyond that; to a point of equality as Julie grew out of her past. It might have, but that pathway was blocked when he chose Mandy. Even before that, it was blocked when Steve put distance between them.

But the new Julie didn't need Steve. She was self-sufficient. And loving it. Julie rolled over and looked at the clock. It was 3:19 a.m. She concluded the mental exercise: Steve and Julie could not happen again. Julie grinned as she turned rolled over. She was fine with that.

She thought back to a few weeks earlier when she'd received a text from Steve. He rarely texted her and when he did, it was informational in nature, a "running late" sort of thing.

This text was different. *I'll be near you at lunch today, wanna get a bite with me?*

Julie laughed at her phone. The person in the cubicle across from Julie's looked over her eyeglass rims critically at Julie.

Have lunch plans. No thank you.

Another day?

No thank you, she texted back.

Steve never sent texts inviting her to lunch after that.

Chapter 17

Winds of Change

The presidential primary season began that spring. All fifty states were either conducting primary votes or caucusing for the election in November, and it was nasty. The airwaves were consumed by ads, news, scandals, and the usual horse race analysis of who was up or down that week.

Julie knew she would not vote for someone who would continue the current administration's legacy. She wouldn't vote for state candidates who would continue the feudal serf/lord relationship between Oregon and the Feds.

But why bother? Her tiny vote in a sea of progressives in Oregon was pointless. Democrats ruled Oregon and had for decades, and they had perfected ways to stay in power. Gerrymandering districts, appointing their buddies to judgeships, using unions to turn out thousands of votes. Heck, most races only had one candidate — the one Democrats selected.

Julie could no longer tell the difference between a news story and a political ad. They both screamed things like, "State budget cuts caused a shortfall," or "cutting jobs is not what Oregon needs," or, Julie's favorite phrase, "for our most vulnerable." That was how the media and the politicians were about to pass yet another huge tax increase.

Julie got on the internet and quickly found a small publication from the State Treasurer's Office showing that the budget had not only been fully funded but grown exponentially, especially in the last two election cycles. Where were the cuts that everyone was talking about? No one Julie knew — *no one* — ever asked this question. They just watched TV, drove their kids to a million soccer games, and buried their heads in the sand. Julie felt very alone.

For the presidential election, Julie wasn't sure. By the end of Oregon's primary season, the two parties had put forward their candidate — their worst candidates — and it was ridiculous. Both were very flawed. Both were egomaniacs. One was a liar that seemed to skirt the law. The other was a corporate tycoon who seemed to be a corporate insider. Julie had no idea who to vote for. She put off that decision until November. She also gave herself the option of not voting. There was never any doubt that Oregon's Electoral College votes would go to the Democrat, so why go through the frustration of even voting?

As she debated whether to vote, she watched current events closely. She saw alarming trends. First, mass shootings happened with regularity. Mass shootings that not only involved terrorists that the exiting president referred to as *immigrants*, but disturbing and diabolical school shootings perpetrated by disturbed young men. It concerned Julie how numb the American public was becoming to them. There was no longer gasp and horror—it became normal.

The shootings all had one thing in common—every perpetrator was a mentally ill young man or had ties to terrorism. What was causing mentally ill people to start killing dozens of people? They were all on severe mind-altering mental illness medicines and had fallen through the cracks of what little mental health services were available to them. Julie noticed that every boy in Joel's school who got restless—who acted like a boy—was medicated and the doses kept going up. If a boy quit taking the drugs, he often lashed out violently. She assumed that the huge spike in mental illness medications must have something to do with wave of shootings.

Terrorism really frightened Julie. Not just that they were shooting people, but that the president didn't seem to care. Not once did he speak out against terrorism or terrorists. Each time there was a shooting, there was a call for prayers, vigils and more gun laws, and people agreed with him! It was maddening to watch the uptick in this scenario. Mass shooting, massive loss of American lives, terrorists take credit, the president blames guns, gun laws are presented to legislatures, and some pass. Lather, rinse, repeat.

In cities all over the country, violent protests erupted over ridiculous things. Julie called them what they were: riots. Mobs of thugs rioted over any convenient cause: homelessness, rent prices, banks raising fees, animal rights, forest management, or oil drilling. In each community, police resources were stretched beyond their capacity to respond. While the police were distracted with riots, local crime went unchecked. Resources were tapped, and the rioters conducted their riots to do just that: create unmanageable chaos. It was their game plan. It was the goal of the global progressives funding them. The president's mentor, Saul Alinsky, even wrote a book all about the plan to have rioters strain resources to bring the system down.

The media fueled the process. When local police couldn't handle the riot, then the riot was the police's fault—not the rioters'. Incumbent politicians chimed in with agreement and solidarity for the rioters. The public ate it up. They were handed an explanation for what was going on, relieving them from having to think for themselves. It was the police's fault.

Julie couldn't get over how odd it was to watch public officials side with the rioters. The governor and police chiefs took the rioters' side. It seemed like the government was on the side of violent criminal acts. It seemed like the government was holding back controlling rioters and, at some point, might team up with them. Julie thought she was crazy for even thinking it. But she still felt it.

The riots and associated madness got her thinking long and hard about the future of the country under the reign of either of the two presidential candidates. It got her thinking hard about safety in her own neighborhood.

If the liberal candidate won, government would grow and grow. This would cause more entitlements, and liberal states like Oregon would be even more indebted and intertwined with the federal government. It would mean more gun control. The economy would tank as businesses were suffocated. It would mean Eugene would end up like Detroit. Not only Eugene, but every other city because of the Fed's financial and political control. America would be no more. If the liberal candidate won, then the rioters would absolutely go ballistic with glee.

If the other candidate won, Julie saw one issue that would cause the Left Coast states' big cities across the country to directly confront the federal government: sanctuary city funding. The conservative candidate was promising to pull big chunks of federal money for any sanctuary city or sanctuary state that harbored illegal aliens He wasn't having any of it.

If he won, sanctuary cities like Eugene and Portland—and sanctuary states like Oregon, Washington, and California—would lose billions of federal dollars. Much of those funds were needed for public safety and law enforcement. Those funds came from the same pool of money and resources that were already stretched to capacity. Oregon municipalities needed the constant federal money flowing in. Without it, they'd be broke within a few weeks. Their checks would bounce.

Liberal politicians and the dependent people who voted for them would go insane. They had seen that the police couldn't handle the little riots. They could destroy property and steal and absolutely nothing would happen. The progressive politicians in these states and cities, via their dependable friends in the media, would tell millions of people that their welfare money was being shut off by a mean corporate tycoon. The pre-election violent protests would look like a picnic compared to what was coming if the conservative candidate won.

As Julie pondered this one day, her father called.

"How you doing?" he asked.

"I'm alright," she said slowly, not wanting to share her seemingly crazy worries with her dad. "What's up?"

"This presidential election is nuts."

"Agreed."

"Julie, it worries me where you live. Heck, it worries me where I live. If things get really bad, we might need to make some decisions. Have you thought about what could happen?"

Julie's ears perked up. She and her dad were on the same page. "You mean in an emergency? Or a disaster? Joel and I have been working hard on prepping for over a year now. My basement is full of goods to tie us over if we are cut off from supplies. Why? What are you thinking could happen?"

"These riots have me worried," he said. "You live in a very liberal town. Think about the L.A. riots or Ferguson, Missouri. I think that it is possible if the election doesn't go to the liberal candidate. Liberals will pull out the stops on riots. I want you to think about the ability to bug out. Where you would go, and for how long?"

"The cabin," she said without hesitation.

"You prepared to be there for a long time?"

"I'd always thought about the cabin as a temporary place to be until things calmed down," Julie said. She thought about what was really holding her back from going to the cabin and staying a long time, like a year.

"Dad, if me and Joel went to the cabin, it would be a huge waste. My basement is full of good supplies. If we had to bug out, we would leave behind the supply of items that would be our lifeline. Especially in a bug out situation where we would leave on a moment's notice." Julie felt deflated. She'd thought these things, but there was something concrete about it when she said it out loud.

"Let's think about this," her father said in his supportive way. "Let's each take a trip to the cabin this summer and bring a load of supplies. Maybe you can do this when Joel is with his dad? Or maybe bring him? I don't know. But if you could borrow or rent a large vehicle, we each bring what we can, and stock that place up. Let's exchange lists of things to pool resources. If I know what you have and don't have, I might be able to fill in missing items."

"Dad, that's a fabulous idea!" Julie nearly shouted.

What a relief! A plan to make them safer – and an answer to the worried thoughts in her mind. No more mulling over the many potential outcomes of these riots. Now she could occupy her thoughts with plans for actually doing something.

Over the next few months, they exchanged texts and emails. They traded lists and discussed ideas. It felt good, not only to prep but to interact with her dad, especially on something so important. Julie needed to figure out a way to get ahold of a large vehicle and take it across several states and through several mountain passes. On a budget.

Chapter 18

Summer of Fortification

Julie had vaguely talked to Ash about her summer plans, but didn't reveal the specific details. Ash was the only person Julie told about her prepping, but still Julie didn't tell her everything. Ash didn't know the contents of Julie's home basement, the cabin, the crawl space, or her father. It had become second nature for Julie to keep prepping details hidden from others.

One Saturday morning coffee meeting with Ash that spring, Julie revealed a bit more to Ash. "Ash, this election season is crazy!"

"No kidding! The riots! Jeez! Now, imagine this. If people are willing to riot over the pay at a local discount store, imagine what happens when one of these idiots wins the election. And one of them will. There will be riots. It simply comes down to which side will riot. And it will be the same rioters. They will just have to decide the topic to riot over. Their candidate didn't win or they want more free stuff. How the hell did we get here?"

Ash obviously felt the same as Julie. She didn't hold back.

"My dad and I agree," Julie said, feeling surprisingly comfortable revealing a little more to her. "We are now talking about focusing our preparations for what you just described. We also know the cities where we live, and virtually every other city around the county, will be ground zero for riots. It will be ugly."

"You're smart," Ash said. "I didn't know you were working on this with your dad. Awesome. I've always been a little worried that if things get crazy you would truly be on your own. I'd try to help, but we have our family and resources to consider. When the pipe bombs start flying, it will be every man or woman for themselves."

Ash had two children. They were a little younger than Joel. One boy and one girl, and Julie could never remember their birth order. Ash was divorced but lived with a boyfriend. Julie didn't know his name or what he did, but Ash paid her bills by her partial ownership of the gun store and running firearms classes at the store. Julie was always a little envious; it would be nice to have a second income. Julie wasn't sure how communal Ash's income was with her boyfriend, but just having someone who could pick up a few groceries, pay a bill in a pinch, pitch in for rent... it would be nice.

Julie wished she had some help not just on bills, but with the entire prepping project. Ash's boyfriend was working with her on their own preparations, although Julie didn't know any details. Julie quickly realized when she started prepping alone how great it would be to have a man's help and support. She yearned for a man to vacuum seal bags with her, grab some items on sale, and make the budget a little less tight. Most of all, she wished she had a man to support her "crazy" fears of a collapse. She wanted to do these magnificent prepping things together with a man. A team.

The thought of prepping as a team also made Julie realize that she could not give non-team members, like friends or co-workers who didn't prep, her supplies in a crisis. It was simple. A family unit needs to prepare for the immediate needs of their family. That family unit must protect those resources for the family members they were intended for. Once those immediate needs are taken care of, extras can be considered. Extras for creature comforts or extras for others. Charity was an extra. Helping others was only possible after the family's needs had been taken care. To do otherwise is to jeopardize the family's survival.

It is also unfair to the family to give away supplies so the family's needs go unmet because someone who had every chance to prep chose not to. Why should Joel go without food because someone outside the family chose to spend their time and money on leisure, while the family sacrificed time and money to prepare? It was the ant and the grasshopper fable. Her family was the ant; others were grasshoppers.

This didn't mean others would never be given Julie's supplies. She would consider doing so if the other person agreed to contribute resources or skills to add to the family's well-being. The same applied to community: someone might receive supplies, but was expected to contribute to the community.

At first, Julie thought turning people away who needed help was selfish. The more she thought about, the more she changed her mind. She kept asking herself, *Why does Joel have to go hungry for someone else?* She never had a good answer to that. She was a survivor; she'd already survived terrible things. She wasn't going to put herself or Joel in jeopardy over something as trivial as helping someone who refused to help themselves. Charity was a luxury. It wasn't in her budget.

"So, we're doing what we can to prep, but I'm kinda more into it than him," Ash said. Her words jolted Julie back from her wandering mind.

"Ash, you all set?" Julie said abruptly after having just thought about what will happen to people who were not fully prepared. "I mean seriously, if something happens, are you and your family taken care of?"

"I think so," Ash said with confidence. "My brother and his wife have property in Idaho. It's in the panhandle there, just a few miles from the Canadian border. If we really needed to get out of here, that's where we'd go. We've talked to them about this, and they are cool if we park a camper on their property while things calm down."

"You have a camper?" Julie asked, thinking about her upcoming trip to Colorado to stock up the cabin.

"You could call it that," Ash said. "It's vintage... from the 1970s. It runs and it sleeps a few people. We use it in the summer and pitch tents outside because it's a bit tight inside," Ash showed Julie a picture from her phone. It was a cream color with brown stripes on it. Very 70s. It was a Coachman camper attached to a Chevy van cab. Julie was amazed it was still driveable.

"Where did you get that?"

"I found it a few years ago on Craigslist for cheap. As I began my preparations, I saw the potential. I had the money. We've used it for some fun camping, but it will be full-time shelter if needed. The only bummer, it guzzles gas. If we have to bug out, we have to think through keeping it fueled."

"Can I ask a favor?" Julie said with a tiny hint of pleading in her voice. "And I mean it, feel free to say no. No hurt feelings."

"You bet."

"Could I borrow it this summer?" Julie described the plan to move supplies to the cabin. She didn't disclose the cabin's exact location. By borrowing the camper, Julie could save hundreds of dollars on a rental vehicle and a couple hundred more not having to pay for hotels on the way there and back. She figured she could probably save almost a thousand dollars.

"I would pay for gas," Julie continued, "and take good care of it."

"I'm open to it," Ash said. "Let me run it by my boyfriend, make sure he doesn't have a camping trip planned. I'm happy to help a fellow prepper."

"Thank you," Julie said with a huge smile. "I mean it. If this works, it would save me a lot of money that I can put into more preps. That could save me or Joel. Seriously."

"What are friends for?" Ash asked with a grin.

Chapter 19

Summer Break

By the time summer rolled around, Julie and her father had planned the trip to the cabin down to the smallest of details. Joel would be with his dad for a month. Julie put in for her two-week vacation. Ash loaned the camper to Julie. Julie rented a small trailer to pull behind the camper. She would strap in boxes or buckets on the trailer.

What to pack? Julie knew that if they ever needed to stay a winter at the cabin, they needed warm clothes for a freezing Rocky Mountain winter. Her winter clothes for Oregon—layering a couple of sweatshirt—wouldn't cut it in Colorado. They would need sub-freezing, even sub-zero, winter wear. This would mean boots, coats, gloves, and hats. These cost a fortune at normal outdoor stores.

Julie did some digging. Since it was spring time, many of these items were on clearance. Even clearance prices at outdoor stores were out of the question with her budget. Julie went to the discount stores and used clothing stores Ash recommended. Ash got her retro Goth clothes there, but those stores had boots, coats, gloves, and hats. They even had thick flannel sheets. Even though they were a fraction of full price, these items put a pretty big dent in Julie's monthly prepping budget. But, warm clothes were a must for the cabin.

Julie went online and found army surplus wool blankets. Those were golden. Not only were they warm, they were incredibly durable. She also found wool-lined surplus jackets, wool glove liners, and wool liners for boots. Army surplus was great. It reminded her of the days working at the surplus store. She regretted not grabbing more of those items when she worked there, but she had no idea fifteen years ago that this was in her future. Back then she assumed she'd have a normal suburban life, so why would she need Army surplus stuff?

All the clothing and blanket items were vacuum sealed in large Space Saver bags. They would be worthless if they got wet and were stored that way.

She went into her basement and selected the items to go to the cabin. She took her time and really thought about what should go there. The items had to be necessary for life at the cabin and had to be easy to store.

The main things she'd bring to the cabin were emergency housewares, like sleeping bags, extra sheets, towels, and blankets, and a spare set of cookware. She added extra tools and fishing gear that she had picked up at garage sales.

She'd fill in any remaining space in the camper and trailer with five-gallon buckets of staples like beans and rice, and flour mixes. She also put in tubs of canned good and vacuum sealed pre-made meals. She had a whole tub of spices, which would be invaluable. She put in a few cans of ammunition.

But the main purpose of this trip was to stock the cabin with house-hold items. Having them pre-positioned would free up space in subsequent trips — or, more importantly, during a bug out — to bring food. She stood alone in the basement and looked at the pile of things she was taking to the cabin.

"A household starter pack," she said with a smile. "And a place to take it," she said with an even bigger smile.

***

A few days before the date for the trip to the cabin, Ash brought over the camper and showed Julie everything she needed to know to run the camper. It wasn't difficult.

As Julie stood at the back door looking inside the camper, she started formulating a packing plan. She would fill this thing floor to ceiling, but it couldn't be all the heavy items. Those needed to go in the trailer. She could throw this whole operation off balance by weighing down the camper too much. Especially driving through high-elevation mountain passes.

Julie rented a trailer from U-Haul. It didn't cost as much as she thought it would, about thirty dollars a day. The camper came with a trailer hitch so the U-Haul guy just hooked it right up and she drove home. It wasn't too hard to drive with the trailer hitched to the camper.

Just like the day when she secretly brought home the guns on Black Friday, Julie backed the trailer up to the house. It's one thing for her neighbors to see her load a camper with camping supplies. It's another thing for them to see her load up a camper exclusively with five-gallon buckets and tubs. The neighbors didn't need to see that.

She began to load the camper and trailer — at 11:00 pm when it was dark. She felt like a criminal surreptitiously sneaking loot around in the dark. As she brought the first items out of the basement and to the trailer in the driveway, Julie realized she needed an additional item for the trailer. Her initial plan was to tie down the heavy buckets and tubs with ratchet straps, but someone could steal them easily by simply cutting the straps.

She finished loading the camper, which would be locked, and went to bed at about 2:00 am. She set her alarm for 6:00 a.m. She had a plan.

In the morning, she drove her car to a farm supply store as it opened. She bought about ten yards of barbed wire, twenty yards of light-duty chain, and a lock. She returned in the early morning when none of her neighbors were up and began loading the tubs and buckets. She ran the chain and a strand of barbed wire through all the bucket handles and locked the chain down to the trailer rail. Sure, someone could cut it or break a bucket handle. However, they may not want to unravel all the barbed wire intertwined with the chain. She put a tarp over the load on the trailer and lashed it down with ratchet straps. She threw wire cutters and two pairs of leather gloves into the glove box. She and her dad would cut up the wire and chain when she arrived.

Julie was so focused on getting the camper and trailer loaded she didn't fully pay attention to Joel. He was helping when he could, but many of the buckets and tubs were a little too heavy for him. Julie didn't want Joel to become frustrated so she told him she could do the loading on her own. Joel took off and disappeared for the rest of the day. Julie didn't pay attention to what he was doing.

Toward the end of the day, Julie was sitting on the back porch, dusty and dirty, gazing at the camper and trailer and feeling a bit over-whelmed.

"Hey, Mom, can I put a few things in, too? To have at the cabin?" Joel's voice came out of nowhere and he approached Julie.

"Oh, Joel, yes," Julie said. "What is it? I should have asked you sooner." She put her arm over his shoulder and pulled him close.

"I've made some paracord tools," he said. "I have a water bottle car-rier I want you to give Grandpa when you see him. But I also have four belts and four gun slings. Those can really be used for anything. But the one I want you to have is the woven hammock."

"A hammock?!" Julie asked with shock. "Seriously, a hammock?"

"Yep," Joel answered with a confident smile.

"Who are you and what have you done with my son?" Julie laughed. "Show me this hammock. I can't wrap my mind around this."

Joel had a box at his feet with the paracord items. He got a big ball of paracord out of the box and handed her one end. He gingerly unfolded it and stepped back from Julie. Sure enough, there was a multi-colored hammock. Julie could tell he had made it with pieces of leftover paracord as he finished projects.

"You used a lot of paracord to do this," Julie said as she looked over the hammock. "I don't remember buying you this much."

"Well, true," he said with a devilish smile on his face that Julie rarely saw. "I asked dad to buy me some so I could make stuff, but he didn't have any money. So, Grandpa bought me two big rolls when I told him what I wanted to make. He had them sent to me at Carson's house," Joel explained.

This kid is smart, Julie thought. *And caring*.

"So, this is like a present, from you to me?" Julie asked.

"Yep," Joel answered.

"Come here," Julie said as she stood up and hugged Joel close to her. She kissed his cheek and whispered, "You make me so proud. Thank you." She felt so blessed to have a child like this.

***

The next morning, Julie dropped Joel off at Steve's. She stood at the driver's side of her car door in his driveway as Joel pulled out a suitcase from the trunk. Joel came to her and hugged her.

"You have a fun time, son," Julie said into his head.

"You have fun, too," Joel said. "Tell me all about it, okay?" Julie knew that Joel would rather be with her and Floyd than be with his dad. Going to the cabin would be more fun, but he knew his dad had him for the summer.

"Joel, do me a favor," Julie said, "and don't tell your dad everything we're doing. He doesn't need to know, okay? You can tell him I'm going to spend some time with Grandpa at the cabin but that's it. That is the truth. You wouldn't be lying. But your dad wouldn't understand what we're doing with all the stuff I'm taking there."

Joel looked worried. "I did tell him about the paracord projects," he said. "I hope that was okay."

"Oh, for sure, that's fine. It's all the prepping we're doing and what we have in the basement and the cabin. Does that make sense?"

"Yes," Joel said with a slow nod. "He would think we're weird. I won't say a thing."

"Right on," Julie said. "Enjoy yourself. Text me if you need to. I also

92

have a great idea for what we can work on when you return."

"What?" Joel looked up expectantly.

"I'll text you later," Julie said, enjoying raising his expectations about what was coming. "I need to check some things first to make sure, but I have a cool plan if it works. You're the perfect person for it." Julie hugged her growing son. She would miss him.

After the hug, Joel said begrudgingly, "Gotta go." Julie nodded. Joel pulled his wheeled suitcase up the driveway.

Steve was on the porch. "Hey there, Joel! Ready for a fun summer?" he said as he patted Joel's shoulder and waved to Julie.

Julie knew that in time she would be in Colorado, Joel would seem to grow by years. He was maturing so quickly, though not in his stature. His teenage growth spurt hadn't happened yet, but his thinking was maturing.

As Julie drove home, she realized that over the last year, Joel was managing his time better. He finished his schoolwork more often on time and did it right the first time. Not always, but certainly it was improving. He knew that if he got too far behind, he would miss a gun safety class, or he couldn't work on paracord projects. He was even picking up after himself. Joel was becoming a young man and finding his way.

***

Julie left Steve's apartment and headed to the interstate. She was nervous. She hadn't traveled on a multi-day road trip since… she couldn't remember. She was doing this one by herself. She planned to make this a learning experience. As she traveled east toward the Rockies, she made a note of every exit with a fuel stop. It was tedious. She used her smartphone with word-to-text technology so she wouldn't have to stop each time. By the end of the first day of travel, she had a long list that read "exit 84, exit 164, exit 202." She would edit it later. If the day came when she really needed to bug out and head to the cabin, knowing the fuel stops would get her there.

By end of the first day of driving, she was almost in Idaho. She was in Ontario, Oregon, a few miles from the Idaho border. As she walked into a campground office to arrange to stay the night, she couldn't help but notice what a lovely summer's evening it was.

An older lady sat behind the counter. She was not a delicate little flower. She wasn't rude or gruff. A life of hard work showed on her hands and face. When she smiled, every wrinkle and scar lit up. She was lovely and greeted Julie warmly.

"Evening," the lady said. "What can I do ya for?"

"My name is Julie, and I'm just passing through. Wondering if I can have a spot for the night for myself and my camper out there with the trailer?"

"You bet," the lady said. "Fill this out, we'll get you going. My name is Roberta. Glad to meet ya." Roberta held out her hand to shake Julie's hand. Julie couldn't remember the last time someone shook her hand. She gladly shook Roberta's hand.

A handshake reveals a lot about a person. The grip reveals confidence and strength—or lack thereof. Rough skin reveals a life of hard work. Sweaty palms reveal a bit of nervousness. There is a reason why it is good to learn how to give a good handshake. It is part of how one makes a good first impression.

Julie was worried about what she communicated in her own handshake; it was probably soft and not too confident. But, that handshake told her a lot about Roberta. Hers was firm, almost too firm. It hurt a bit. Her skin was rough, almost dry.

"Got your paperwork," Roberta said. "Now just need to put some money down. I prefer cash. Then I'll take you outside and show you two spots to choose from. Being a weekday, we have choices. On a weekend, you'd get the spot next to the highway. Not the best night's sleep you'll get listening to logging trucks rattlin' down the road all night." Roberta was chatty. Julie liked her.

Julie pulled out her wallet and put down her cash payment. Julie chose a spot closer to the back of the property fairly near the shower house, but not too close. She backed the trailer with Roberta's help. Roberta stood at the back of the camping spot and waved her arms like she was guiding in an airplane. Julie wasn't sure what she would do without Roberta's directions.

Julie hopped out of the cab of the camper and approached Roberta, held out her hand and thanked her. Julie made sure her handshake was better than the last one.

"Roberta, thank you. I don't have enough eyes to back that thing in without a lot of worry. You just saved me a lot of stress and thirty minutes."

"Anytime, honey," Roberta said with a smile. "You let me know if you need anything else. You know where to find me. Enjoy yourself."

94

Roberta waved as she walked toward the office.

Julie stood for a moment and looked around. She couldn't remember the last time she was out of the city. It was quiet. She took a deep breath and smelled earthy, fresh air. It was cleansing.

She needed to figure out her sleeping arrangement. The camper was full — very full. It was packed tight with clothing, blankets, paper products, medications, and some tools. Julie also put in buckets that held pasta.

Julie saw the tub she had specifically for water purification supplies like filters, filtration pitchers, chemical purification tablets, and filtration drinking straws. She even packed six water bladders. If things got really bad, water would be an issue. Despite the beer commercials that made Rocky Mountain seem pure, bacteria called giardia was in every stream. Drinking untreated water with giardia would lead to intestinal discomfort at best. Giardia could lead to death in a person weakened by malnourishment. Untreated water would kill more people than bullets during a collapse.

Water could be treated by boiling it, but that wasn't the best option. Heating the water consumed precious fuel, whether that was propane or firewood. The cabin was served by a well, which provided treated water, but if the power went out — which would not be unheard of — the cabin's water supply was no longer safe. They could get water from a nearby stream, but that would require hauling it and then purifying it. At least with the water bladders and purification items she was bringing they could do this.

They could gather snow in the winter and let it melt without having to purify it. But this didn't produce much water, and wasn't an option for about eight months of the year. Not a solution.

As Julie thought through the details of supplying the cabin with fresh water, she marveled at how almost none of the prepper websites ever mentioned water purification. They would talk about bug out bags at length but never acknowledge that three days without clean water would kill a person.

***

It was time for Julie to start getting ready to sleep. Julie had packed her duffle bag, sleeping bag, and a tent at the very end of the trailer so it would be easy to get to. She felt the warm air. Sleeping in a tent would be nice.

When she hiked as a teenager, she could put a tent up in about ten minutes. It took almost an hour that night. She hadn't done it in a while and, back when she hiked, she had someone helping her. Not tonight. She was frustrated and getting increasingly angry. Finally, the tent was set up. *Finally.*

She threw down her sleeping bag and tied open the tent flaps so she could watch the sunset. She grabbed a sandwich and a bottle of water from the small cooler she had in the cab of the camper. She sat down at the picnic table at her camp site and watched God paint a beautiful sunset for her enjoyment.

Lying in her tent with her arms behind her head, Julie waited for sleep to come. Her brain was busy. So many holes in her preparations, and this trip was exposing them. First, the food she had and that her dad was bringing would feed them and Joel for a few months. Probably. But what if they had to stay at the cabin longer? They needed a secondary food source.

Julie knew they could fish from the lake, and they certainly would. Hunting? She needed to talk to her dad about the possibility of hunting. What were the rules and regulations in Smoky Flats? What about outside of the development? Maybe hunting and fishing rules wouldn't matter if the collapse were bad. Maybe they would. And everyone would probably be hunting, so game might get scarce quickly.

What about gardening? The high elevations of the Rocky Mountains were not hospitable to gardening. The ground was frozen half of the year, and the soil was typically gravelly granite. What passed for soil around the cabin was full of rocks. Relying on gardening in Smoky Flats was not an option.

The high plains of northern Colorado and surrounding states were farmed and could be a source of fruits and vegetables, but people in Smoky Flats would need to barter for these and drive far and use precious fuel. That wasn't a viable option, either.

Could a greenhouse at the cabin work? Potatoes, tomatoes, peas, and beans? These were crops with small plants and high yields. Julie wanted to talk to her dad about that too. Root vegetables were a good option for a short, cold growing season. So maybe they could raise a small amount of food in a greenhouse.

What about small livestock? Julie had been looking at small animals like chickens, goats, or rabbits. Chickens could provide eggs. Goats could provide milk. Rabbits could provide meat.

She had never raised any of these animals. What she read told her that raising them was easy and they could be butchered within a year.

When she was a little girl, she knew there were a few homes in Smoky Flats with cattle. They weren't in the subdivision but private property outside of it. She needed to find out the rules and regulations for owning cattle. The cabin property was not large enough for cattle, but maybe her family could barter with a neighbor who owned cattle. That reminded her that it was important to meet the neighbors and be on good terms with them.

This all sounded great in theory. Only one thing caused her to pause: she had no experience with any of these things. It's one thing to read about it, but there's a steep learning curve to putting these skills into practice.

Preserving meat. That was the next question in Julie's mind as she tried to sleep that beautiful eastern Oregon night in the tent. They could make jerky by dehydrating or smoking it. She knew they could build a smoker or purchase one, but again… she'd never done that.

These were all things that she wanted to talk to her dad about when she saw him.

***

Julie's eyes popped open. The sun filtering through the tent was bright. The air was cool and damp. She stirred in her sleeping bag. Her back was a bit sore. She figured it might be worth it to find inflatable air mattresses. It was time to get going. She made a trip to the shower house, and then made her way to the office to check out.

"Good mornin,' hon," Roberta said cheerfully. "How'd ya sleep?" Roberta was wide awake and chipper. "Grab yourself a cup of coffee if you want some." She motioned to a coffee carafe and paper cups.

"Oh, thank you," Julie said, still a little sleepy and sore. "Perfect. What do you need from me before I head out?" Julie asked.

"Nothing," Roberta said. "I got your payment, and you got your coffee. We're set. Safe travels to you and come back if you can."

Julie stirred her coffee and waved to Roberta. "I'll make sure to come back if I'm through here again."

Julie grabbed two bananas out of her cooler and revved up the camper. She was so glad she had backed this beast into the campsite. She simply put it into drive and steered toward the freeway. Julie wanted to

97

make sure she noted in her log that Roberta's campground was a good place to stop.

About a half mile down the road, Julie filled her gas tank and struck out on the freeway. Soon she would steer toward the mountain pass that would take her to her childhood cabin.

Chapter 20

Safe Spaces

Julie was almost to the cabin. Memories flooded back as she rounded the corner off the mountain highway and onto the road to Smoky Flats. Childhood memories and memories from a few years ago when Joel was with her. The smell of mountain air, the dry midday sun, and the sound of the breeze through the pines and the grasses. So quiet, yet so noisy. Good noises, not city noises.

She turned into the subdivision and rolled up the window. The gravel road was dusty as she made her way to the cabin. She made a right turn at the familiar cattle guard. A few miles later, she turned left and went up the hill.

Then she saw it. The familiar cabin perched on the slope of the hill. Parked at the cabin was the full-sized van and covered trailer her father had rented. He came around the back of the cabin and greeted her as she pulled into the gravel driveway. It felt good to hug him.

"Hello, Dad. You look good," Julie said.

"You look absolutely radiant," he returned with a smile on his face. "You look absolutely happy. Dare I say? Divorce has been a good thing?" he asked with one eyebrow raised.

Julie knew her father was proud of her bravery through the divorce. "You're probably right," she said. "But let's not waste our breath talking about him. We have work to do." She linked her arm in his and started for the cabin.

Since it was getting late in the day, they were limited on how much they could tackle. Her father had been there for a few hours already and had opened windows to air out the musty smell and bring in fresh air. All the curtains that were normally closed for privacy were open. From every location in the cabin there would be a view of the mountain sunset. The front of the A-frame faced the northeast and was a bank of windows. The outdoors was part of the view from any room, except the bathroom and the back room.

Julie stood in the middle of the living room, assessing the cabin through a new set of eyes. How to prepare this place to be home in case of a disaster so they could all live here in some comfort? It's one thing to survive a catastrophe. It's another to live in so much discomfort that you start to wish you hadn't survived.

There was an upstairs exposed loft. Looking up from the living room, you could see into the loft. It had two twin beds. The back bedroom had one double bed. The bathroom was incredibly small: toilet, sink, and stand up shower. The kitchen was no larger than a cheap hotel's kitchenette. However, it had a stove, oven and very old refrigerator. Two upper cabinets, one lower; that's it. No storage.

The back bedroom didn't have a closet. It had a metal wardrobe closet that was moved in to provide closet space. It had a few jackets in it. There was also a dresser in both the back bedroom and loft. Not much storage there either. However, there was a small coat closet as one entered the back of the cabin. More coats and few fishing rods were in it.

Under the stairs was a void of space. It housed the ancient TV that had a full tube and was the size of small desk. Time for that thing to go. If they needed a TV, they could easily find a small, cheap option. But the space a TV would take up was too valuable to simply watch a few football games. A tablet connected to the internet would suffice.

Julie and her father talked through the layout of the cabin almost from the moment they walked in. They agreed that the coat closet needed to have pantry shelving installed; the kitchen cabinets were not enough. The bedroom might need a shelving unit as well.

For now, the strange void under the stairs would store supplies. Their initial thought was to put the medical supplies and tools there.

They went upstairs and made a few observations. The loft was visible from the road. Having tubs of things visible from the road would invite looting or simple robbery. They decided to pull the two beds closer to the rails, stack a few tubs, and then look to see if the beds blocked the view enough to at least put a few tubs upstairs. Tubs with clothes and blankets made the most sense to have in the loft.

Before the sun went down, they decided to open the crawl space. Everything was the same. The hidden compartment was seemingly untouched. Her father went over to the door, unlocked it and peeked in with his flashlight. He gave a thumbs up back at Julie who was on her knees at the crawl space opening.

"Good," Julie said.

While this place was secure, and Ned kept an eye on it, it wasn't monitored one hundred percent of the time. Far from it. Good to know all was where it should be.

The pair discussed how to rearrange the crawl space for maximum space, yet ease of access. It was a pain to come crawling down here on a sunny day. It would be incredibly difficult in cold weather with drifting snow.

They would make sure to carefully label each bucket or bin. Put the food closest to the door that needed to have ease of access or would spoil the soonest. Anything that was stored in the crawl space needed to be freezable. The temperature in the winter would be below freezing for months. That could be a good thing—a good way to preserve meats, but not controllable. What if there was a week of warm temperature in February that raised the temperature unexpectedly? They decided to ask Ned his advice on this. Might as well try to take full advantage of the cold weather.

Julie thought this through. Typically hunting season was in the fall months. Yes, it got cold but irregular enough that it if any unseasonably warm day happened, it could ruin a lot of meat. However, what if they acquired a deep freezer to stock, but also used the outdoor freezing during the winter months to supplement their freezer space?

They crawled out of the crawl space. Her father came to the same conclusions Julie had. They needed more dedicated space for many purposes, but what did that look like? He liked the idea of a dedicated freezer for meat when it wasn't winter. There was absolutely no space in the house for a freezer, though.

They looked at each other and simultaneously said, "A barn." They nodded at the same time and then laughed.

"If we build a barn," Julie said, "we could raise small livestock. And store things."

"I like that idea," her father said. "Especially if we are here for an extended time, say longer than three months."

"If we build a barn," Julie said, "it will need power. The livestock will need heat."

He nodded.

"The barn could have a dedicated room for a freezer," Julie said. "It can also be a pantry. We could stack more tubs there, as well. We need to think through space for not only animals but their roaming space and a place to hold their hay and feed, depending on the animals. The barn would need a water supply, even if it's a simple well pump." She was on a roll.

"I like it. I like it a lot," her father said. He was an understated Midwesterner. "Let's sleep on it. Unload and organize what we have tomorrow. That will give us a good idea of space as well. I'll give Ned a call tomorrow, too. He knows we're coming, but it's always good to check in."

Julie made a couple of sandwiches and broke out a few bottles of water. They sat on the porch in rickety lawn chairs and watched as the sun slipped behind the Rocky Mountains in a fiery display. As they sat on the porch with a beam of soft light from an interior light, Julie decided it would be a good time to give her father the paracord gifts from Joel. She went to the camper, got them, and gave them to her dad. She explained what they were.

He rubbed the woven belts in his fingers. Julie could see that he was getting sentimental. "You've got a treasure in that one, Julie," he whispered.

"Agreed," Julie sighed with a huge proud-mom smile.

Several minutes went by before Julie spoke again. She had been thinking for quite some time about how to approach the next subject.

"Dad," she started. "We need to talk about who can have access to our resources if... something happens."

It had been bothering her to think about her free-loading brother making a simple phone call to her dad and getting a key to the cabin. Then everything they had worked hard to create would be gone. Hell, he sapped resources in normal times—it would be far worse in a crisis.

"I know," her father said with resignation. "What happens if Steve wants to come here?" he asked. "He'll say he has a right to because his son is here."

Julie hadn't thought of that and wasn't prepared to discuss it. "I'll think about how to handle Steve if you make a plan for when Seth calls, and you know he will."

Her father slowly nodded.

"Let's make this agreement," Julie said. "This place is too small to handle more people—and that doesn't even consider supplies for them. There simply isn't enough space to house any others." Julie knew this wasn't completely true. In a pinch, they could people out on the floor, but it would not be optimal. It certainly couldn't be a long-term arrangement.

She continued. "This place can only house you, me, and Joel. Period. The resources we have here are only for the three of us. And no one can know about them. Can we make that deal?"

He nodded slowly again.

"I think we both know there will be difficult conversations in the future," she said. "I'm committed to taking care of mine if you are committed to taking care of yours," Julie stated, though it was more of a question.

Her father looked up. "I agree."

Coming to the agreement was very business-like. Almost like negotiating the purchase of a car, not an understanding between a father and his daughter about which family members would live or die. Keeping it business-like allowed potential emotional conflicts to stay out of it. Julie was unsure how this conversation would start or end. She was hopeful that her father had not told Seth about any of his or her prepping. Seth couldn't know about it because he'd ask to come to the cabin and their father had a hard time saying no to Seth.

Julie realized that her father's concern about Steve was valid, and she hadn't even considered it. When Julie thought about bugging out of Eugene to go the cabin—and she thought about it all the time—she had only imagined plopping Joel in her car and heading straight to the cabin. Steve hadn't even crossed her mind, especially as an obstacle to bringing Joel. She knew that if she assured Steve that she was taking Joel to a safe place, Steve could then demand to come. He had hinted at reconciling with Julie, and heading to the cabin would be the way to do it, in his mind. Steve, who never prepped, would want to be in a safe place. And, Julie had to admit, he had some sort of rights to be with his son. Julie needed to figure this out.

Julie had slept in the loft while her father slept in the back bedroom. It was a quiet, quiet night. Julie hadn't slept that soundly in a long time.

***

Julie awoke to the smell of eggs and coffee. After breakfast, father and daughter got to work. They unloaded their gear. Clothing and blankets went upstairs, tools and medical supplies went under the stairs. Food was stacked on the porch until they could prioritize exact locations for each item.

By midday, they both realized they were not used to the thin air of the Rocky Mountains. They had both been living at sea level for years. Smoky Flats was at eight thousand feet and the air was noticeably thinner during physical exertion. The altitude made every trip up and down the hill to the car feel like ten flights of stairs. They managed, but it slowed down progress.

As midafternoon set in, the vehicles were unloaded and the cabin was looking like hoarders had moved in. Her father used white and gray tubs and he had bright orange buckets. Julie used black tubs with white buckets. They didn't do that intentionally, but it made it easy to tell at glance who brought a particular tub or bucket.

Over a late-afternoon rest break — the fatigue from the thin air was at its peak — they decided to not try to combine the contents of each other's tubs and buckets. They would keep them separate for now.

An identification and inventorying system for the tubs and buckets was crucial. They kept it simple. They used blue tape to number each bucket and label its basic contents. The full list of contents would appear on a spreadsheet. For example, bucket number twelve was labeled *Medical Supplies*. The spreadsheet entry had a number twelve, and then the detailed list of the bucket's contents: ten rolls of gauze, fourteen tubes of antibacterial crème, twelve boxes of Band-Aids, six bottles of rubbing alcohol, six bottles of hydrogen peroxide, etc. All non-liquid items were vacuum sealed. She would email a final copy of the spreadsheet to her father when it was done.

Their numbering system helped prioritize which food buckets and tubs would end up where. The idea was the food items that would be the most used or needed should be closest to the kitchen. So, they needed to be in the back bedroom or unloaded into the coat closet once the shelves were installed.

At the end of the first day, they were exhausted. They were happy with their progress, but realized they had a lot more to do.

Chapter 21

Meet the Neighbors

Right before lunch time, Julie's father insisted that one of the things they do during their time at the cabin was visit Ned. Julie didn't see why it was a big deal, but she was happy for a break in the tub-moving operation. Julie hoped Ned could build the barn since he had already done construction on the property.

The distance to Ned's place was a toss-up between walking and driving. Driving was an option if you wanted to get there quickly or if it were snowing outside. Walking was an option if you wanted to take a walk in the nice weather and time was not a consideration.

They decided to walk. As they walked, Julie tried to remember when the last time she had seen Ned. Twenty years or so? Julie remembered he had a wife and little kids at the time. She couldn't remember his face. If she saw him in public, she would not be able to point him out.

Julie took in Ned's property as they ascended the driveway. Two out buildings. One seemed to be a combination workshop and garage. One side of the building had a double wide garage door and it was open. Looking through the open door, Julie could see the silhouette of equipment.

The second building seemed to be a barn of some kind. It had a traditional barn look to it. It had a traditional barn door and a second story where hay would be stored and tossed to the ground from an opening. However, looking through the open barn door, Julie could see there were no animals or outside animal pens, but she could hear the soft cooing of chickens somewhere.

Julie and her father stepped up on the porch as the front door opened.

"Ned! How the hell are ya? Good to see you!" her father said exuberantly as he thrust his hand out and shook Ned's hand.

"I'm livin' the dream. It is great to see you, old friend," Ned answered, with his own corresponding exuberance.

Julie watched Ned. He was tall, probably over six feet. Even though it was summer, he wore a neat cotton, collared shirt. Julie remembered her father telling her he preferred collared shirts in the summer outside since it protected more of his neck from sunburn. Julie could see from the tan hue of Ned's face that he spent time outdoors. A lot of time.

Ned was a rugged middle-aged mountain man. Julie figured he was around fifty but that was always hard to tell since many Coloradans developed early facial wrinkles due to sun exposure. His hair was salt and pepper; not thick but not thin either. Julie enjoyed watching Ned smile. As he smiled, his eyes lit up. His tan skin was a beautiful contrast to his blue eyes and gray hair. Watching him smile was easy on the eyes. It put Julie at ease.

"Ned, I don't know if you remember my daughter, Julie."

"My goodness, I do," Ned said. "Julie, you certainly don't look how I remember you. Your dad told me you're all grown up, and now I can see for myself."

"Welcome to my home, please come in," Ned greeted her warmly. His gaze lingered on Julie for a split second more than if he were meeting a stranger.

Julie, too, looked at him for a bit longer than she would if meeting any other neighbor. It wasn't a physical attraction as much as it was a curiosity. She found Ned's ruggedness interesting. Out of the ordinary. Not anything like the hipster men-children of Eugene.

"Good to meet you, Ned," Julie finally said. She was so burned out on men that she never really looked at them anymore, but Ned was interesting to her. She couldn't ignore it.

Julie looked around the living room. It was a small, but open space. The living space was to the right; the dining room and kitchen were to the left. Ned was in the middle of a project. The dining room table had newspaper on it with small mechanical parts strewn from edge to edge and what looked like the barrel of a rifle. Several tubes and cans of lubricants were lined up next to a heap of rags.

"Hunting season is coming up. I wanted to get ready," Ned said, as he noticed Julie looking at the project. "Grab a seat," he said diverting her to the couch in the living room.

"Glad you two could take a few and come on over. It's good to see you."

Julie's father smiled. "Thank you, Ned. Hey, Julie and I have some plans we're trying to put in place for the cabin and wanted to float some ideas by you. Who knows? We might need to hire you for a bit of work. Interested?"

"I'm open to that. I think you have a lot of potential to either build up that property to be more for vacationers or for permanent living. What are you thinking?" Ned asked.

Julie's father explained the basics of the plan to make it a bug out location. He didn't hold back any information from Ned, so Julie knew he trusted Ned a great deal. She listened as her father explained that the plan was to make some improvements to the cabin to allow sustainable living. He mentioned the barn idea. Ned listened intently.

"Let's do this," Ned said with enthusiasm. "Let's go look at my out-buildings. The barn came with the property when I bought it, but I have worked on it so much, the foundation is probably the only thing original to it. I built the workshop, and I have a chicken coop I made from a converted shed. You tell me what you think might work, and we'll get some plans on paper."

As they toured the workshop, Julie liked several aspects to it. Ned's truck was on one side of it by an ATV. Off road, an ATV was just about the only way to get around. The other side of the workshop was open space. Ned used it for tools, but Julie could use this sort of space for a deep freezer, tools, stacks of tubs, and buckets. They went to Ned's barn. There wasn't much in there. She looked up and saw some hay in the loft.

"We used to keep goats and chickens here," Ned explained. "I had pens set up and we would breed goats every year, and then send them to Camp Freezer." He was used to using euphemisms like that around his kids.

"You didn't do that this year?" Julie asked.

"Haven't done it in several years. That was something my ex-wife would do. She bred the goats, I'd butcher them. I just don't have it in me to do it all since she left."

"Barbara left?" Julie's father sounded surprised.

"Didn't like living off the grid," Ned said without emotion. "She moved to Denver." Ned shrugged.

"Raising small livestock goes smoothly with an extra set of hands," he explained. "I tried it the first year and realized I had too much work on my hands, and ended up with a lot of meat in my freezer. I had so much that I didn't breed them the next year. Seemed easier to not take on that project after skipping it that year."

"Well, that makes sense," Floyd said. Then he patted Ned on the shoulder and said, "I'm sorry to hear that. We've got our own bachelor club started between the two of us."

Julie decided to add a little levity to this otherwise-heavy conversation. "Are bachelorettes allowed in the club? Otherwise, I'll just go wait outside while you two bond."

"We're a misfit bunch, aren't we?" Ned joked.

Yes, we are, Julie thought. She got back on the topic at hand. "Ned, I am not going to sugar coat. I think eventually, we will need to have this place ready to live in. At the very least, I need a building supplied with power for storage. I'd also like to be able to have small animals. Chickens or rabbits. For sure chickens. If I could dream, goats. I realize that requires storage for the supplies needed for them. I also think we need to keep it to one building. However, I am intrigued by your ATV. The ability to have an alternative form of transportation seems nice, but it also means fuel and costs. I'm kind of rambling here, but that is what I'm thinking."

"When I built my workshop," Ned explained, "I sent away for pre-made plans, changed them a bit, and then ordered the materials. It took me most of the summer to get it all done. The most time-consuming part was waiting for the county to send out a permit guy to approve and sign off on the permits."

"Ned, could you find us a few plans we could choose from? Then let's talk price. If you're open to it, I'd like to hire you to build it for us. What do you think?" Julie appreciated her father's way of cutting straight to the point.

"You bet," Ned said. "I'd like to get the design and permits done by spring so that when the weather breaks, we can build it and be done. Given the best scenario, we can have it done by next summer. We can't get it done this summer," Ned already was calculating a timeline in his head.

"Tell you what, we're here for a few more days. Let's have you come over to dinner before we go, and we'll land on a plan and get the ball rolling before we go back."

"You got it," he said. "I'll finish what I have going on the table today and pull out plans. How 'bout I come over tomorrow night?"

"Sounds good," Julie's father said with a grin.

They all walked out to the driveway. As they got to the end of the driveway, Ned came to a stop. "I know if you decide to move up here, it will be because the shit hit the fan in the cities." He paused, looked at Julie, and said, "Pardon me."

Julie liked to see such old-fashioned manners. But, she didn't want Ned to think she was a prude, either.

"I've heard it before," she said with a wave of the hand. She found it endearing that Ned tried not to swear around women. That was something lacking in every man she'd ever met in Eugene.

"I certainly don't want that to happen," Ned said, "but having great neighbors will make living up here workable and actually enjoyable. Good neighbors make all the difference, and it will be good knowing you're one of them," Ned said as he put out his hand out to Julie's father for a handshake. They shook hands.

He looked at Julie, smiled, and said, "It'll be good know knowing that you're one of them, too."

Julie put her hand out as well. She was used to women acting like men, and shaking hands was something women in Eugene did, just like men. Ned looked surprised as she stuck out her hand to meet his. She realized this was not something that Ned probably saw very often.

"We'll see you tomorrow night around six or so," Julie said, smiling warmly.

Ned put two fingers up to his forehead and dipped his head, like cowboys used to tip their hats, and smiled. Julie hadn't seen a man do that in decades. And, certainly not in Eugene.

***

Ned went back inside with Julie on his mind. He noticed that she didn't have any makeup on but looked great. She was natural and simple, and completely at ease at his modest home. He also noticed Julie's eyes. She looked people in the eye when she spoke and was direct. Yet she was warm and engaging. She was practical and didn't waste words.

Ned remembered when he told Floyd he'd look after Julie if she came to the cabin in a crisis. He had assumed that she'd be high maintenance because she was from the city. He was no longer concerned about that. Julie might be a city girl, but she was resourceful. She wasn't afraid to tackle new challenges. She may not have all the knowledge that a person living in the county might have, but she had the desire to learn and a mindset of independence. The rest could be learned.

Ned chuckled as he dumped the last swallow of cold coffee down the drain. He thought about how Barbara lived there for years and had all the skills, but not the mindset. Julie had never lived in the country but seemed a better fit for living there.

***

Julie and her father rounded the corner toward the cabin. It was getting close to midday. The direct sun was intense. It was time for lunch and a cold beverage. The sun was hot.

"Well that stinks," her father said. "I hadn't realized his wife left."

"He seems to be over it."

"I like his workshop."

"I do, too," Julie said enthusiastically. "I like the idea of doing a workshop, but with some sort of annex for housing chickens. But that is my imagination. I want to see what plans he can find for us. Let's take a walk around our property today to see what we can come up with for a location."

"Let's also think about talking to Ned about pooling resources," her father said. "He has tools, equipment, and skills that honestly, are way beyond what we can provide for ourselves. Let's see if we can barter services with him."

"I like it," Julie concluded. She had thought about bartering in her many hours of thinking about prepping, but now they were applying the principle to a real-life situation.

As the evening approached and the intense sun transitioned into a cool and colorful sunset, they walked the property.

"Dad, here's what I see. Goats are a lot. They need a lot more than we have. We can build a barn that provides for them but it will cost. Ned's barn isn't being used for goats. Let's barter with him. I'd take care of the breeding and butchering of the goats if he lets us use the space. Then we can divide up the harvested meat. That allows us to focus on more of a workshop and chickens here."

"Good thinking, my smart daughter. Knowing Ned, it kills him that his barn is not being used to produce something. He's so practical."

After walking their property, they decided on a spot about twenty feet out the back door of the cabin. It would be accessible by cabin occupants. However, with a little extra grading, the driveway could be extended so a vehicle could be parked in it. Currently, the cabin had no garage. But no one lived there permanently, so it was never considered. Shielding a vehicle from the extreme cold would be nice.

"Let's also talk to Ned about predators," Julie added. "Chickens will be a draw to them, especially in the winter."

"Yep."

Julie continued. "Let's also ask him about hunting regulations around here. This is private property. Everyone here owns a plot of property, but this subdivision abuts state forest. It would be nice to be able to hunt."

Julie felt her father looking at her. She turned to him and saw a huge smile spread across his face. "What?" she asked.

"Oh, nothing… just listening to you talk this way… you make your father very proud."

"Well, I have the best teacher!" Julie said, jabbing her father in the side.

In that moment, Julie knew that no matter what happened to their world, she and her father—and Joel—were going to be just fine.

***

The next day, Julie started planning for dinner with the men. She decided to try an experiment. She would try out one of her premade vacuum sealed soup mixes with a batch of dinner rolls with her roll mix on her father and guest.

Since it was summer, Julie made a vegetable based chicken soup. It was light, but nice in the cool evening. Earlier in the day, she had put out a large jar of sun tea on the back porch. By evening it was brewed and she poured it in a pitcher over ice.

Not a fancy dinner, but it didn't need to be. It was a nice dinner.

Ned came up the driveway at six o'clock sharp. Right on time.

Julie had put a folding table on the deck with a mismatched collection of lawn chairs. It was too nice of an evening to not be outside.

She let the men know to ladle up their soup and to head out to the porch. Utensils, rolls, and drinks were out there. Julie watched as her dad and Ned chatted casually with positive declarations about the meal sprinkled through their banter.

"Julie, the soup smells great. Thank you so much for putting this together," Ned said.

"You're very welcome."

It was so rare for anyone to appreciate her cooking. Then again, she only ever cooked for herself and Joel.

Julie followed them out the sliding door with her own bowl of soup. They were seated as she closed the slider. Both men were hunched over their bowls and had already taken a sip. They were smiling at her.

"What? You bachelors never had chicken soup before?"

Her father looked at Ned and declared with a note of sarcasm, "Soup? Brewed ice tea? I don't know about you Ned, but since the lady

111

left, my meals come out the freezer in a cardboard box. You?"

Ned smiled. "Comes out of the freezer, yes. Not so much in a box. Spices and flavor are a luxury; I don't ever really use them because… well, I'm not sure why. I sure like them, though. Oh, and I haven't used a ladle for about five years. This is nice and tasty, thank you."

Having secured their approval of the tastiness of the meal, Julie then revealed the origins of their meal. It came from the prepped supplies that were already in the cabin. That she made and sealed.

"Dannnnggg," Ned said. "I would never have guessed this great soup came from prepper supplies. This leaves me thinking a zombie apocalypse is something to look forward to."

The results of Julie's experiment worked. If these two can like the same soup and roll mixes that she and Joel liked, this food prepping project was a success.

After dinner, the trio moved inside as dusk turned to dark. They got down to business.

Ned brought out three plans he had found he believed would be helpful. They talked prices. Julie realized she had very little to offer to building such a project. The prices being discussed were higher than she imagined they would be. Her father didn't flinch at the costs as Ned described them.

Julie gave her opinion, though, on which design worked best. As the discussion wound down, they settled on a pre-fab workshop plan that seemed to fit their need the best. It could be customized to add on a shed-like structure for chickens.

"Julie and I like this plan the most. I'll get back to you before I head out for a final okay," her father said. The discussion turned to costs, goats, hunting, and so on.

"Now… regarding goats. We realized after talking yesterday it seems a waste to work this place up for goats when you have a goat-friendly barn but without any goats. Wondering if, when the shit hits the fan, or whatever… when the time comes, can we visit the idea of us using your barn, kind of communally, to raise goats and butcher them. We'd do all the feeding, breeding, all that stuff that was too much for you to do alone. Maybe we split the harvest? What do you think?"

Ned looked impressed with the proposal. "That's a great idea," he said. "Especially if I know you two are heading this way, I'll make a point to purchase some kids," the term for young goats, "from local ranchers and get the herd started. Let's work out the particulars soon, but that is a great idea. It kills me that barn takes up rent-free space on my property."

"Now hunting. What do you know about hunting game on the local state-owned property?"

"Great question," Ned said. "I haven't hunted state land since Johnny was in grade school."

Julie figured that Johnny must be Ned's son. Then Julie remembered Ned was cleaning his rifle and getting ready for hunting season. Why was he starting to hunt again? Was he thinking that a collapse was coming soon? She would need to find out.

"I'm sure the rules have gotten stricter and permits are more expensive for the state land," Ned continued. "I'll check."

"Great," Julie said.

"Speaking of hunting," Ned said, "We should talk about fishing. Now you two know, as property owners and association members of the neighborhood, the lake we have here is privately owned."

Ned explained that the neighborhood association dues paid for the lake to be stocked with fish twice a year. Association members were permitted to fish two, twelve-inch or larger trout a day out of the lake. Each property owner could have two guests fish, as well.

"I have been thinking for a long time that the association board needs to come up with a policy for an emergency," Ned said. He explained that he had two concerns. His first was that residents would over-fish the lake because they were hungry. His second concern was that the resupply of stocked fish might be cut off. In a collapse, government would shut down things like subsidized fish hatcheries that many private lakes, such as Western Lake, paid to stock for recreational fishing.

"I'm going to propose to the board a couple of responses to that kind of crisis," Ned continued. "First, if we can't restock the lake for whatever reason, for the following six months, each association member can only fish one fish a day, and guests no longer have fishing privileges. That would allow the fish in the lake to have a breeding season and allow them to mature instead of being over-fished. It also keeps the eco system of the lake in check. But that's not all." Ned suddenly became very serious. "Outsiders also know this lake is here," Ned said in a hushed voice, "and if food gets really scarce outside of this slice of heaven, we need to think about how to secure this lake. I have some ideas how to do that. People will think I'm being all militant and crazy, but reality is reality."

"What are you picturing to secure the lake?" Julie asked

"There are two entrances by road to this place," Ned said as he pointed in the direction of each entrance. "Each has a gate and they are normally open. We put guards at each closed gate that only allow property owners in. Period. This is private property and the roads are easements to the property. No need for anyone from outside to be here. There are some key high points in the subdivision that overlook the lake as well as key access points. I have identified six points. I would want to put lookouts at each point, they could then radio to a central location if any sort of problems or poaching is spotted."

"Wow," Julie said.

"I also think every person in this subdivision needs to look in their freezer. For Pete's sake, we've all fished out of this lake, gutted and put fish in the freezer. We all have freezer-burnt fish that needs to get put in a stew and eaten—not wasted," Ned said with a little frustration.

"Guilty," Julie said raising her hand. "Jeez, I think there are fish in the freezer here that have been here for twenty years."

"Bottom line is that the lake will become a valuable source of food, not recreation, in a major crisis. We, as an association, need to protect it not only against over-fishing but also with security measures. It can be a rationed food source for the association if we do it right," Ned concluded.

"Agreed," Julie's father said. "You bringing this up to the association at a meeting soon?"

"Yes," Ned answered. "Next one is in the fall. It will be right after Labor Day when the next scheduled lake stocking is happening. It will be a good time to bring it up."

"Do you expect any resistance?"

"A little," Ned answered. "Those who live here year-round will agree with me. They will grumble that they will have to provide security for all the folks who vacation here. Those who live here have more skin in this game. They will also not like that those who use their property for vacationing will now have access to the lake. I have had to point out more than once that they pay their dues just like everyone else. Where the resistance will happen is the vacationers who want to bring in the whole family and over-fish that lake, then leave when the crisis is over. That is why I want to put these policies in place now before we have to fight about it. The vacationers also won't like my ideas regarding guarding the lake, but I am not going to attempt to bring that up at this next meeting. I just want the resolutions for fishing to be put in place. We'll deal with the security issue in a vote later."

"Good. Smart," Julie's father said.

It was getting late and they had accomplished a lot. They said goodnight and Ned walked back to his house.

***

The next morning, Julie and her father got their vehicles ready for the long drive to opposite coasts each had ahead of them. Julie had been texting with Joel regularly during the trip. She told Joel how proud his grandfather was of Joel's paracord projects. From their texts, it was apparent to Julie that Joel wanted to be with her. While she knew things clipped along much faster without having Joel nearby to keep on task, she missed him. It was time to go home.

Packing up the camper. Picking you up in two days. Much to tell you, Julie texted.

Drown some bait for me before you come home.

Julie felt tears burn in her eyes and then she realized that her father was watching her.

"You okay?" he asked, sounding concerned.

"Yeah. Joel told me to go drown some bait with you before heading home."

"I think that is a great idea. Let's do that at sunset tonight. I'll say it again; you have a gem with that one."

"*We* have a gem in that young man," Julie clarified as she put her phone back in her pocket. "We're family, remember. It is no surprise to me that you two are related."

Father and daughter drowned some bait that evening. They also caught two rainbow trout that they tossed them back.

"For another day," Julie said under her breath as she leaned over the edge of the lake and watched the trout slither into the dark water.

Chapter 22

Stormy Times

Julie pulled into Steve's driveway. Her stomach tightened up. She'd been dreading this for several days. There was no particular issue between them at the moment. She just got nervous every time she saw him because he might throw some curveball at her. Maybe it would be him wanting to get back together or adjust child support amounts. Maybe it was paying some bill or maybe it was him whining about Mandy. It would be something, and it would be negative, and she'd get a stress headache for at least a day. He didn't throw an issue at her every time they saw each other. In fact, it wasn't that common. But she was always ready for a battle when she rolled into his driveway. She wished she never had to see him again, but she did so because Joel needed a relationship with his dad. She was sacrificing. Again.

She called it "re-entry," which meant re-entering the world that included Steve. She would happily live her life without him for days and not even thinking about him. Then something would happen, like picking up or dropping off Joel, and she had to re-enter "Steve world," as she called it.

That was happening today. She had arrived back in Eugene two days earlier after a fabulous drive back from the cabin. She visited Roberta on the way back and they had a long conversation about life and love and heartbreak. Julie saw amazing scenery and had hours and hours of silence to think about her life, Joel's life, her dad, and prepping. The two nights she spent in Eugene alone were golden; it was so quiet in her house. She had no schedule. She had no chores. The only errand she ran was returning the trailer to U-Haul and the camper to Ash. During those two days, she fell asleep early and woke up late. She was refreshed for a change.

Before she could take the keys out of the ignition, Joel was at her door. He came running out to her. God, that felt good. She opened the car door and got out, right as Joel starting hugging her. Deeply. Good grief, he must have grown an inch in two weeks!

"Oh, Mom, I missed you!" he said into her chest as they were hugging. He pulled his face back and asked, "How was it? Tell me everything you did!"

"I missed you too, hon," she said. "I'll tell you all about it once we get heading home." She looked at him and winked. He knew what she meant.

"Now where's your dad?" she asked. "Let's get your stuff and see where we're at."

Julie looked up and Steve was on the porch waving. She couldn't tell if something was coming. She started walking up to the porch where she could see Joel's gear.

"I hope you two had a good vacation," Julie said.

"We did," Steve said, disclosing nothing.

"Anything I need to know about?" She might as well get it over with if there was a curveball coming. Julie was wondering about the progress of Steve's split with Mandy.

"Nope," Steve said with a grin.

"Okay. Catch you later," she said with a slight smile, the courteous unemotional kind of smile you give to a co-worker or a grocery store clerk. "Joel, tell your dad goodbye and thank you." He did. They got in Julie's car.

***

"Tell me, tell me, tell me!" Joel said as soon as he got in the car. "What's the surprise?" He was hoping the answer was that they were moving to the cabin to live permanently.

"Remember how I mentioned I had a special project for you after your time with your dad?" She was stretching out the anticipation just for fun. That was a mom prerogative.

"Yesssss," Joel said with expectancy.

Julie handed Joel a gift bag. He pulled out a bright red book entitled *Ham Radio License Manual*. Joel had a quizzical look on his face as he reached into the bag for a second item. Out came *Ham Radio Flashcards*.

"What is this? Ham radio? Like ham? As in bacon?"

Julie laughed. "Think walkie-talkie radios. Think being able to talk to someone on a CB radio but over a long, long distance."

"Okaaaayyyy…"

"Amateur radio operators are regular people. They're not military, law enforcement, or government officials, they're just amateurs and are called ham operators. Ham is kind of a shortened version of the word amateur. It has nothing to do with meat."

"How can I use ham radios?" Joel asked. "I'm just a kid."

"You get a simple license," Julie said. "It's like a driver's license, but way easier to get and you don't need a car." Julie had confirmed in her research that there was no minimum age for a ham license, which surprised her.

"A license, huh? Interesting." Joel sounded like he was warming up to the idea.

"To operate a ham radio, you need to be licensed. You've played with walkie-talkies, right?"

Joel nodded.

"Well, walkie-talkies only reach a short distance, like maybe a block. But ham radios can reach for miles and miles. It would be really handy if one of us had a license," Julie didn't want to finish the whole plan she had in mind. Joel loved this kind of technical stuff and Julie was hoping he would sink his teeth into it like he did paracord.

"Is it hard?"

"There is a written test," she said, knowing that Joel was thinking about school tests, which he didn't like much.

Joel started to speak but Julie cut him off. "It's not like a school test. You can take all the practice tests you want on the internet and then pass the real one easily." She had researched this and found out this was true.

"You can read about ham radios," she said, trying not to sound like she was giving orders. "That's why I got you the book and flashcards." She needed to get his mind off tests, so she switched to the topic that enthralls adolescent boys: adventure.

"Think about the cabin. What if the phone lines go down. Maybe Wi-Fi goes out. We could communicate with other ham operators in Smoky Flats, or town, or even another state. We could call for help, alert others what is happening, or who knows what!" Julie watched the look on Joel's face, hoping for a spark of interest. It came right on cue.

"So, like, I could radio someone in Alaska?" The excitement was clear in his voice.

"Eventually. A basic ham radio license, like the first one you'll get," she said subtly injecting future expectations, "would allow you to talk to people closer, like maybe anywhere in Eugene or Portland."

Joel looked confused.

"After your basic license, you could get a bigger one that would let you talk to people in Alaska or even the space station." She was referring to a more advanced license that allowed the use of frequencies that travelled farther, like over the earth's horizon or even into space.

"Okay."

"You've studied radio waves in science, right?" Julie asked, hoping for some version of a "yes."

"A little," Joel answered, rolling his eyes. The quality of Joel's education was grating on Julie's nerves.

"So, you know how sound waves move," she explained. "Radio waves are pretty much the same thing. They can't go through obstacles like buildings, hills, mountains, or over the earth's horizon. A basic ham license lets you use frequencies—another word for wavelengths—that can go much further, but not through mountains or over the earth's horizon. You'll learn all that as you read and test yourself with the flashcards."

"Okay," Joel said simply and unenthusiastically.

"Can I ask a huge favor?" Julie asked.

"Sure," Joel answered.

"This might be one of those things you may not want to do, though I was hoping you would," she said, talking to him like an adult. "I am still hopeful since you don't know much about it. But in a situation where we have limited communications, and we end up at the cabin, your ability to be able to communicate will be key to our success in living there. Do you understand? I trust you to do an important job. I don't have the time to study for and take this test anytime soon. I need someone in this family to know how to do this. Soon," she said with conviction.

"Okay, I get it."

"Good. Let me know when you feel ready to take the exam. The book has practice exams. There are tons of them online, too. I'll find a test location to take it," Julie offered. "Oh, and hey," she added, "I'll talk to your teacher when school starts about getting you extra credit for passing the test."

Joel smiled. "Okay, Mom. I'm on it."

That was the answer Julie was looking for.

***

After Julie's trip to the cabin, things drastically changed with politics, society, and current events. She worked for a company that, like a huge percentage of companies in liberal Eugene, relied entirely on government contracts. Her company was paid by the government to dole out housing assistance.

At her job, staff meetings and trainings took a different tone. It was

119

all about "access to services" — government handouts. She was getting email invitations to meetings for single mothers who needed services. Educational services for kids, divorce recovery, free college scholarships, and more. She was shocked at all the free government handouts available. But she was even more surprised that the government seemed eager to find people to incentivize recipients to sign up for the "free programs." Wouldn't the government want to save money by encouraging people to only use such programs as a last resort? Why encourage people to sign up? These programs made people dependent on them with no end date. Julie remembered when being on government assistance was shameful, not a prize to aspire to.

Of course! Now she got it. The government was trying to get as many people — single moms in particular — hooked on government so they would be forced to vote to continue the money they now counted on to feed their kids and pay the rent. They would re-elect the politicians who promised to keep the programs funded. In election campaigns, the shiny mailers would say "prioritizing our community's vulnerable," or "open opportunities for access." It also allowed Oregon to demonstrate to the Feds the "need" for funding. After all, so many people were using the programs.

Soon training meetings sounded like an infomercial for signing up for government programs, especially to single moms. She routinely heard phrases like, "More children are born to single parents now than any other time in our history. We have a great opportunity to serve these families and provide much needed services to a vulnerable population." Blah, blah, blah.

Her office was directed by the government to prioritize these families ahead of two parent households. They were trained on what services they would now be expected to provide, the reporting requirements they would be under to receive the extra funding from the state, and even how to persuade reluctant single moms to sign up for services.

Julie was offended. Single moms like her were being treated like helpless waifs. She had seen, especially at her job, that government was terrible at actually helping people. Children routinely died in foster care and Medicaid fraud was rampant. Welfare payment cards called EBT and food stamp benefits called SNAP cards were used as much for drugs and alcohol as they were for groceries and diapers. Her office was quietly told to quit auditing for such abuse. Complaints were taken, not documented, and certainly not followed up on.

Julie wondered how much of all these government services were helping single moms. An entire class was being funded with the money — criminals who then preyed on single moms. Fewer and fewer people coming to Julie's work were of the population espoused in the mission statement that every employee agreed to uphold. Most of her clients were not actually needy. Certainly, they were not high-paid executives, but they made enough to live on. However, the state cooked the books of calculating what being needy looked like on paper so that just about anyone smart enough to know how to report income cleverly could qualify. In fact, other nonprofits showed her clients how to do just that, and then referred them to her office. Anyone who spoke up against such practices was sanctioned and written up for "promoting an environment of hate and denying access of services to the citizens of Eugene."

***

One of Julie's co-workers, Karen, sat at the employee breakroom table and allowed Julie to read a letter of reprimand Karen had been given earlier that morning.

"Denying access to citizens? We don't require proof of citizenship and you and I know our clients couldn't provide any, anyway. Karen, I am so sorry," Julie said as she handed the letter back.

"This is the second one in a month, and if I get another one, I'll be placed on one year of probation. I think if that happens, I'll quit. That year will simply be a year of vultures picking at me for any little infraction," Karen said evenly. "I've been doing this for almost twenty-five years. I have served so many families and helped so many people get on their feet. I have cards and emails telling me so. The rules changed, and I guess I didn't change with them." Karen's eyes turned red.

"I hope that doesn't happen," Julie said rubbing Karen's shoulders. There wasn't much else to say.

***

Julie realized something even more sinister and corrupt was happening. She knew that Oregon was on a trajectory of financial collapse. By aggressively signing up as many single moms and their children for state welfare programs, when that collapse happened — and it would — what would happen to those mothers and children? As tempting as it was as a single

121

parent to enroll one one of the programs, she didn't. She knew it would collapse.

What would happen when those EBT and SNAP cards weren't loaded with credits? What would happen when the rent voucher programs her office administered no longer had money to pay landlords? What would happen when the facilities accepting Medicaid suddenly closed? What would happen when the state-run food banks suddenly ran out of food?

These young moms and children were the most vulnerable in society. They couldn't fend off criminals. To stay alive in a crisis, the women would need to avail themselves and their children to horrible men who would do horrible things. These thoughts haunted Julie and gave her the chills. She was one of the targeted demographics for such programs.

Work was no longer a job to go to, earn a paycheck, and go home. It was now a moral dilemma. It was difficult to go and participate in what she was beginning to see would be a tragedy for hundreds of thousands of women and children in her state. It sent shivers up her spine to think Oregon's leadership was purposely crafting policy and programs targeting vulnerable women and children, all the while knowing that in the not-too-distant future, those programs would be bankrupt.

***

Oregon's dependence on the federal government went deeper than just getting welfare money to hand out. Oregon was dependent on Feds for something no one ever really thought about: wildfires.

Every summer the wildfires burned more and more land in Oregon, California, and Washington State. Usually it was off in some mountainous area no one cared about. In recent years, they started to burn up farms and sparsely populated rural areas. Those were areas not touched by the urban news media in the Portland and Eugene areas. Now, these massive, uncontrollable fires were no longer limited to forests and rural areas. Instead, they burned near towns and, increasingly, cities. Every year, the fires crept closer to Eugene and Portland. Environmentalists started holding work groups to clean up protected watersheds and designated preserves.

"Wish they'd clean up the parking lot at the state park, but I guess a protected turtle population is more important," Julie mused as she watched the news espousing the great work of a local environmental group that had just planted native grasses for a protected wetland devastated by a recent grass fire.

One Saturday morning during her couponing routine, Julie saw a news story about the wildfires. It wasn't the usual story about country people packing up the pick-up and fleeing. It was about the cause of the fires. The story, much to Julie's surprise, described a study done by a property-rights think tank in Oregon (Julie wasn't even sure one existed) about how environmental regulations were fueling the fires.

The story described how the federal government owned or controlled much of the public's land in Oregon. Julie already knew that. Oregon was built on the logging industry when the federal government allowed logging on those lands. Then, back in the 90s, the environmentalists applied a lot of political pressure on both the federal government and state government to stop logging—to preserve some owl. Logging was virtually halted.

As a result, those logging communities, which were signed into effect by Oregon's liberal governor back in the mid-90s, agreed to receive PILT, "payments in lieu of taxes." Former logging communities now received federal subsidies instead of the tax benefits they received from selling locally logged timber.

Several financial problems arose from that. While communities received federal funds to pay for schools and roads, the local communities lost hundreds of thousands of good jobs. It was tragic to drive through the small communities around Eugene, small towns that were now ghost towns since all the jobs were gone. Those were towns that once produced millions of dollars in timber used to build houses all over the world. Now they were run down and empty.

The second problem that arose out of shutting down Oregon's logging industry—so much timber in the federal forests was not being harvested. Hundreds of acres of diseased and decaying forests resulted from the policy enacted in the 90s. They were all susceptible to fires, and every summer for as many years as Julie could remember, there were devastating fires. Fires that burned so hot that forests would take decades to recover since the land left behind was so scorched nothing could grow for years to come.

Logging isn't just cutting down big trees; it involves cutting underbrush and the small tinder that fuels fires. It also involves building roads into the forest, which can be used by firefighters. The logging ban ended the harvest of underbrush and closed forest roads. Logging harvested trees, allowed for replanting, and grew Oregon's economy. All of that burned up every summer because of environmental, liberal policies. The federal regulators' policy to address annual fires was to let nature run its course. The public was banned from managed forests areas. Underbrush grew. Dead trees became drier and drier, awaiting a lightning strike now that they weren't logged and hauled out.

To make matters worse, the liberal administration also prohibited local residents from fighting fires. Officials of the Bureau of Land Management, the hated BLM, arrested locals who tried to trim underbrush near their homes. Hard working farmers of rural Oregon were imprisoned for fighting fires. The headlines were jarring to read. Fire was good; humans living in rural areas were bad. The Feds' philosophy was "let it burn." And it did. Millions of acres of forests burned uncontrollably summer after summer.

However, the Feds provided massive firefighting resources. As with many things, the federal government both created a problem and then spent huge resources combatting the very problem it caused. Wild fires were a perfect example.

The state of Oregon, which was broke, couldn't pay for forest firefighting. Yet again, Oregon depended on federal firefighting resources. The Feds did anything the state asked regarding fire fighting and provided plenty of resources. Oregon was fine—on paper—when it came to the federal government managing Oregon's forest.

Except if the conservative candidate won the upcoming presidential election, Julie realized. He was looking for ways to show sanctuary states that they needed to play ball. Withholding federal firefighting assets would be a perfect way to do just that.

***

Julie headed off to the coffee shop to meet Ash. She really looked forward to these talks with her prepper gun-loving girlfriend.

"Ash, I need your opinion on something," Julie started.

"Sure. I'm always good for an opinion," she said with an edgy smirk.

Julie laid out the new direction she saw state agencies taking and the new focus at her work on targeting single moms for dependence.

"Am I being paranoid?" she asked. "I'm thinking of all the women and children who will be victimized when the state finally acknowledges that is has no money and the programs suddenly end."

"I think you're spot on," Ash said. "I think we have tragic times ahead. What's crazy, you and I see the inevitable and yet we're a little allured by the extra services if we were to sign up for them."

Julie agreed. She hated to admit it, but she'd thought about how all that free government money would make her life better.

"I gotta tell you," Ash continued, "having one of those government cards with a few hundred dollars on it a month would help us a lot." This was the first time Ash had implied things weren't rosy with her boyfriend. "But, hell no am I going to do that," she declared. "I know what happens when that card isn't reloaded because the state finally hit the bottom of the money pit."

Julie sensed that Ash had seen what happens when a woman is in a terrible position. She wanted to change the subject.

"Oh, did I tell you? I tried out of my prepper soup mixes on my dad and Ned. It was a hit. Made my day."

She described the dinner she made for her father and Ned. Ash listened attentively and started to smile more and more. Finally, Ash beamed.

"Why are you smiling?"

"Who is Ned?" Ash asked with a grin.

"Oh wait. No. Stop. Not what you think," Julie said, noticing that she sounded slightly defensive. She told Ash about Ned and omitted any description of his appearance. It wasn't important to her.

"How old is he?" Ash asked with a devilish smile.

"First, this is dumb," Julie said, feeling even more defensive. "Second, I don't know. Mid-fifties? Based on my age, his age, and his kids' ages," Julie answered.

"What does he look like?" Ash said coyly.

"Why? You single suddenly?" Julie retorted.

"No, but you are," Ash countered.

"This. Is. Dumb," Julie said, not annoyed as much as she was surprised that Ash might think she was interested in a man. "I dunno," Julie continued as she searched for the words. "He looks like a lonely, weathered mountain man who doesn't get out often."

"And?" Ash said with that same devilish smile.

"There's nothing there except that we could be neighbors if the big earthquake happens. He's building a barn for us. That's all."

"If you say so," Ash said with a smile as she sipped her coffee.

***

125

The remainder of that summer, Julie and her father had several conversations regarding the outbuilding, which they were now calling the barn. One conversation involved the price estimate they got from Ned.

"Dad, not gonna lie," Julie said. "I was not expecting it to be so much."

"Ned isn't overcharging us," he said.

"It's not that. I don't have nearly enough to even contribute fifty percent to that effort. I *might* have a tenth."

"Julie, don't worry," he said in his reassuring fatherly voice. "I have some savings. Plus, the cabin is paid for. I will take out a line of credit against the equity. I can have it paid off in a year. I'm not worried. At the very worst, I can sell the cabin and the money I would get would be double what we paid for the barn."

"Sell the cabin?" Julie asked.

"Julie, that would be the worst of the worst scenario," he said. "I would sell my property here and move there before I would sell the cabin. I'm just telling you how this is a good investment. If the day were to ever come to sell the place, the barn would more than pay for itself. My point is that we're improving an asset—which we're not going to sell."

"Thank goodness. I wasn't sure where you were going with this. What can I do to help or contribute?"

"I need you to make sure when the day comes that we need it, that you know what you're doing with small livestock," her father said. "I have no idea how to tend to livestock, nor do I have any interest in learning at my age. I am building it for all of us, so you can feed all of us. If you want to put in some of your savings for the down payment, I understand."

"Deal," Julie said. She may not have much money, but she would make sure she had valuable skills. Skills are the best substitute for money. Actually, they're better, Julie realized.

***

As the summer came to an end, the election season grew more and more heated. Julie had never seen an election so nasty. People seemed to be frothing at the mouth, especially in Oregon where denouncing the Republican candidate was getting more and more aggressive. Julie didn't know who would win, but she predicted that riots would take place the day after the election.

Anarchists would riot in progressive cities around the country even if the current president's endorsed candidate won. They would be called "celebrations," but the results would be anarchy, injuries, property damage, and probably some deaths. The local wussified police couldn't stop the "celebrations." Well, they physically could, but the politicians would order them to stand down.

If the Republican won, there would be riots, for sure. The intensity would be greater. More injuries, property damage, and deaths. The local wussified police would be even more unable to stop them.

No matter who won, there would be violence.

***

Ned's phone rang and he knew it was his daughter, Rachel, making their weekly call.

"Hey, Dad!"

"Hey baby, how are you?" He loved his little girl who was such a grown woman now.

"What are you up to?" Rachel asked.

"Funny you should ask. Remember Floyd?" he said. "Well, years ago I did some work on his crawl space. He has a daughter about ten years or so older than you. Her name is Julie. You remember?" Ned asked.

"Oh, barely. I had to be kind of little," Rachel answered.

"It's the one on the upper hill above the east gate. The A-frame," Ned described.

"Ah. I know that one."

"He was here this summer and wants to build an outbuilding on that property," Ned continued in an energized voice. "He came over with his daughter to discuss it. He's going to contract with me to build it. That will give me a project on my hands for the next year. I need to get the permits this winter so that when spring comes, we can put it up quickly."

"Good! That will keep you busy for a year." Rachel smiled.

"Good folks. It was great to see Floyd again, and that last time I saw Julie she was a teenager. She isn't anymore," Ned said.

"Oh? Do I hear something in your voice?" Rachel teased.

"You hear my surprise at how quickly time flies," Ned said, self-conscious about how he seemed to talk a lot about Julie. "I don't get a day older but when I see a person after twenty years, it's a rude reminder that time is precious."

"So be it," Rachel said. She changed the subject. "I talked to Mom last week. Still in Denver. Still doing her thing."

"Good to hear," Ned replied. He was sincere.

"Dad, in your project, don't forget I'm graduating next summer. I would love it if you could make the trip to Cheyenne for my graduation," Rachel reminded.

"Oh, you bet. I wouldn't miss that for the world," Ned answered. "You narrowing down your job offers?"

"I have an offer from Iowa for sure. That one is intriguing to me. There aren't many jobs west of the Rockies. The western states are mostly owned by the Feds and they don't want state wildlife officers. The Feds are only hiring firefighters for the western states. I can find some good wildlife management positions east of the Rockies."

"You go where you need to go. In my dreams you'd be close by, but I'm not a fool, either. You gotta land on your feet somewhere, just don't forget the things I've taught you. Those lessons will serve you well," Ned said nostalgically.

"Of course! I gotta go dad. I'll catch up with you next week, ok?"

"Love you baby, be good."

"Love you, Dad."

***

Julie got a notification on her phone of an email coming in as she got into her car after work. She was about to mark it as spam and start the car. Until she saw the subject line.

Soup recipe

Oh! Julie thought. She read on.

Julie, this is Ned. Your dad gave me your email address. Hope you don't mind. I wanted to thank you again for the hearty dinner earlier this summer. It was quite the surprise to find out a good soup like that was from a prepping recipe. Wondering if you could point me in the direction of the resource you got that from. I am thinking I might put some up for the upcoming Colorado winter. Regards, Ned

Nice, Julie thought. She forwarded him a copy of the recipe as well as the title of the cookbook later that evening.

Ned, Julie here. Glad you liked it. Attached it a copy of the recipe. Please note, I added chicken that night. Otherwise, it's a basic vegetable soup. Below is a link where you can purchase the cookbook online. You'll see on page 12 the mix I premade. I then used this mix to make the dinner rolls on page 45. Not sure you wanted those but just in case. Thank you for all of your help this summer, looking forward to hearing about the finished outbuilding next summer. Blessings, Julie

Ned. There was just something about him. He was intriguing. He surprised her. For a person who spent an incredible amount time alone, he was very personable and warm. Smoky Flats had a selfless servant in Ned. If he were gone, there would be big shoes to fill.

Chapter 23

Elections Have Consequences

The conservative presidential candidate won. One would have thought Armageddon happened. Riots. But not like riots Julie had ever seen in her lifetime.

In Eugene, police closed a freeway at rush hour, to allow rioters to riot. That's right. The police were helping the rioters. Portland had violent riots daily for weeks. Once the public got sick of the election being the reason, the rioters simply switched their cause to rent prices and started rioting all over again. Property damage was in the millions, none of which was covered by insurance. So, what did the progressives do? Protest the insurance companies, of course. They had a right to riot and for someone else to pay for it. Violent riots became normal. They were inconveniences much like rush-hour traffic was an inconvenience.

Julie and Ash discussed the post-election riots during one of their Saturday morning coffee dates.

"I don't think these riots are going to be over any time soon, Julie," Ash said seriously.

"Me neither," Julie said sadly.

"I think when the inauguration draws closer, there will be riots. I also think once the president starts making good on the reforms he promised, there will be riots at every single turn. I also think once he starts pulling the plug on states like Oregon that get tons of federal subsidies, we'll get hit extra hard here. I'm actually afraid."

Ash was uncharacteristically shaken. Nothing shook Ash.

"Remember when I got back from the cabin last summer and I told you about how the big focus at work was to get women dependent on state welfare?" Julie said, trying not to have an "I told you so" tone when it came to tragedy. "Crap, Ash, I hate to say it, but I think it's going to come true. I really think there will be children who starve when the subsidy plug gets pulled. Here's where I'm a weirdo. I think the plug should get pulled! This damn state needs to quit relying on subsidies just like women need to stop being dependent on government programs. Am I awful for saying this?"

"No," Ash said softly. "Oregon will feel it worse than other states because we depend so much on the Feds. California. Washington. Illinois.

And cities like Detroit. And all those sanctuary cites. It will be just as bad as the 'big earthquake.'"

"But Ash, get this," Julie said and then paused. "Think about the wildfires we have here every summer. Because the Feds don't manage the forests we have. Imagine now, if the Feds pull the firefighting support they provide. Eugene bumps up against the Cascade Mountains. A fire there—without federal firefighters—could reach us here. Portland is by the mountains, too. A fire in the Cascade Mountains or Columbia River Gorge could easily reach Portland. Then everyone could try to leave all at once. Clogged highways. People fighting over gas when their Priuses finally run dry." She paused again and said, "Even if the fires are contained in a few days, in the meantime the criminals will have a field day. No law and order. At all. Anywhere."

"I had never even thought about the potential for fires," Ash said. "Riots and wildfires. I need to talk to my boyfriend and make sure we are ready to bug out if we need to."

Julie noticed that she and Ash were whispering and leaning in close during this conversation. They knew they were in downtown Eugene where almost eighty percent of the population voted against the newly elected president. They knew their conversation, if overheard by the wrong person, could cause an unwanted confrontation. They had seen this happen to others.

When she realized that they were whispering, Julie wondered if they lived in America anymore. Was this how it is in countries like Syria? Venezuela? China? Hiding one's true self to avoid attention from those in charge? Is this how it is? Is this how it was going to be from now on?

***

Julie couldn't stop thinking about riots. They were happening in Portland every day and protestors were shutting down parts of Eugene on a regular basis. People were injured and hospitalized. The mayor of Portland had protestors on his front lawn.

Julie, wondering if she was crazy, so she tested the waters with Steve.

"Steve, so these riots have me worried. How are you feeling about them?" Julie asked during a drop-off.

"They're stupid," Steve answered.

Not quite the description Julie was anticipating.

131

"They worry you at all?" Julie pressed.

"A little. Why?"

Julie decided to reveal a little about her prepping. For Joel's sake. "Well," she said, "I've gotten into emergency preparedness in the last couple of years. You know the news always says that's a good thing to do because we're in for the big earthquake," Julie explained. "But," she continued before he could dismiss her, "I also want to have a plan in case things get out of hand and Joel and I need to leave Eugene for a few days. I want to make sure Joel is safe. As his parents, I think we need to have a plan." Julie was trying to play it cool.

"Huh. I see. What's your plan?" Steve asked bluntly.

"I have some feelers out with friends outside of Eugene for a place to stay if we needed to leave for a bit. I'm working at getting the location pinned down. But wanted to see if you had any plan for leaving Eugene if needed."

Julie threw the ball in his court. She was being vague on purpose. She didn't want Steve to know the preparations at the cabin.

"Actually, no, I hadn't thought of it," Steve said. He seemed bored. He also dismissed her concerns as a way to dig at her. So, he truly didn't care about Julie's "apocalypse" craziness, but even if he did, he'd shrug it off just to piss her off.

"Well, let me say this. If we need to leave, I will take Joel for the sake of safety, but will let you know what we are doing and where we are going. I will make sure you know what is happening. I will make sure I keep all lines of communications open. I also would want Joel to be able to know where you are as well. For sure, I don't ever want to have to do any of this. But jeez, these riots are crazy, don't you think?" Julie continued.

"Hmm… can I run this by my attorney? I am wondering if there is any way we can draw up an agreement."

Oh, good grief, why can't Steve make one decision about Joel without consulting an expensive attorney? And what good is a piece of paper during a collapse? Julie thought. But Steve never thought of such things.

"Sure, but please do it soon. In the meantime, can we make a handshake agreement in case something happens sooner rather than later?" Julie pressed. She knew she had Steve a little off his game.

"Fine," he said sarcastically. "If the zombies arrive tonight and we all need to grab our supply of Sterno, batteries, and tents, you can take Joel to an undisclosed location and keep me informed. Sure, Julie. Whatever."

She got the agreement she wanted.

And she kept the promise to her dad about not letting others come to the cabin.

***

Julie had been thinking about the talk on the news and internet about whether the president was about to cut welfare for sanctuary states and cities. She didn't know it, but he had already decided to make some small cuts to welfare in all states. It was a closely guarded secret, but the foreign government — China — that was loaning the U.S. government the money it needed to keep spending, told the president that unless he got welfare costs under control that they wouldn't continue to loan him money. He knew when the other person had leverage and did what they said.

***

Julie was driving Joel to a new club activity. It was a skeet shooting program. Joel was excited. This club was much like Julie's Pink Ladies group. There was class time for the first hour, the second hour was spent on the range, unless the weather was terrible. Joel was very excited.

"Imagine, Mom," he said quickly. "If I get good at this, I could go duck or geese hunting!" He had completed the hunter safety course. Now he was learning how to shoot a target — and a moving one at that. Julie knew she needed to figure out a way to get him out in the woods, but Steve wasn't a resource.

"I know!" Julie said, encouraging Joel. "I have no idea how to cook duck. I need to look that up."

"Or pheasant, or grouse, or geese," Joel said quickly, reeling off the game birds he'd learned about in hunter safety class.

They drove up to the range. Julie let the car idle while Joel retrieved the shotgun from the trunk. He checked that the action was open and didn't have a shell in the chamber. He carried it correctly, always making sure the barrel wasn't pointing toward anyone.

"Be safe. I'll see you in a few hours," Julie called out.

Joel gave her a thumbs-up. With a huge grin.

***

It was Saturday. She and Ash didn't meet for their usual coffee because

133

Julie needed to get some errands done. As she approached the grocery store, she knew something was wrong. She could hear yelling from somewhere and people were gathered around the entrance.

Julie parked at the far end of the parking lot and observed. Most others would have, purely out of habit, tried to find the closest spot and walk right into whatever it was that was causing the commotion. But not Julie.

Julie squinted and focused on the automatic front doors. She could see a group of about twenty people shouting with their arms in the air. They seemed to be blocking the store and maybe protesting, but it was angry protesting, not walking around with signs. *What was going on?*

Two police cars pulled up. One officer got out and the other one stayed in the car.

The loudspeaker on the car with the officer in it boomed, "You have been told to leave. Leave now or face arrest." The crowed hooped and hollered. They were energized that they now had the police after them. Just two of them. No match for the twenty or so angry protestors.

Oh, good grief, Julie thought. *What are they protesting at a grocery store?*

A woman walked in front of Julie's car away from the grocery store. She was in a hurry to get into her car.

"Excuse me," Julie asked, "what is the protest about?"

"The SNAP cards are now limited to only WIC-approved food items," the woman said. WIC items were generally healthy things like baby formula, fruit and vegetables, and milk. Up until then, SNAP money could be used for potato chips, convenience foods—just about anything. "The protestors say their right to food access is being trampled," the lady said, who seemed sympathetic to them. "I tried to get in but decided I didn't want to try." The woman abruptly got in her SUV and drove off.

And, so it begins, thought Julie. She started her car and found another grocery store.

***

That night on the news a spokesperson from the state Department of Social Services reported on the new SNAP policy.

"As we all know, there are changes at the federal level," he said. "The new administration is cutting crucial food assistance. Our priority is to make sure Oregon families are taken care of. To comply with the new mandates, we want families to use their SNAP benefits judiciously, which means buying nutritious food on the WIC list. To require SNAP recipients to make good food choices is just good policy," he said trying to make this sound like it was a good thing. "We ask all recipients to check our website for a list of approved foods so there is no confusion."

Julie had stood in grocery store lines with fistfuls of coupons while watching the person in front of her purchase gallons of sugary drinks, bags of candy, and exotic meats on a SNAP card. It infuriated her. No milk, no cereal, no peanut butter. No canned goods. A pile of crappy food. And she was excited to score a good coupon deal on shampoo. Sometimes she wondered why she didn't just get a SNAP card herself. Then she caught herself.

Julie had always wondered why SNAP cards weren't already in alignment with WIC benefits to begin with. *For heaven's sake*, she thought, *stores program into bar codes that cigarettes couldn't be bought with SNAP cards, one would think the same could be applied to chocolate bars.* But when the new administration did it, suddenly it was a "war on the poor."

Julie knew these protests for the "right to access food" would only get worse. *Since when did everything become a right?* Julie wondered.

The next news segment added to her concern. The local food bank, while it didn't accept SNAP cards, said it would make a policy to give out emergency food boxes that were in line with WIC food guidelines.

"Huh," Julie said out load. She realized that the local food bank was dependent on federal funding and they were making sure they were complying with the new rules before the Feds cut off their funding.

"And, so it begins," she repeated to herself.

Chapter 24

Decline into Darkness

Grocery store chains were criticizing the new SNAP policy. They had a lot of junk food on hand that sat dormant on shelves yet were out of milk and peanut butter. The news was spinning all the new policies as an affront on every "right" every American ever had.

Every "freebie" Americans ever had is more like it, thought Julie.

In the spring, rules for SNAP cards were changed. Eligibility standards were tightened. Audits of fraudulent card use were enacted—audits that hadn't been conducted in years. The amounts loaded onto cards began to slowly shrink. SNAP recipients had to work a job to qualify. Shoplifting in grocery stores skyrocketed. Health food stores, known for their pacifist beliefs, hired private, armed security guards.

The black market for SNAP cards had already been in place for years. A woman would take a fully loaded SNAP card, and meet with a drug dealer who would give her drugs for the amount of money the card was worth. Drug-addicted mothers bought their drugs that way. For the last two years, drug fraud wasn't being monitored or addressed—purposely, anyway. Anyone in Julie's line of work who raised red flag over the drug trade with SNAP cards was sanctioned. Karen had retired early. No one but Julie knew the real reason why.

Drug dealers and addicts knew that people in Julie's position could do nothing and took advantage of the situation. Since the value of the cards was dropping, the cost of drugs increased. An addict would need two fully loaded SNAP cards to purchase the same amount of drugs he or she could buy with one just a few months ago. Addicts were losing their mind. Overdoses were on the rise. Several on Julie's caseload reported overdoses in their low-income apartment buildings. Two of Julie's clients overdose late that spring. Julie upped her coupon game. She also noticed many more people in the grocery store lines holding coupons along with their SNAP cards.

***

Summer began, and Joel was home. He had three weeks with his dad beginning at the middle of June. Julie was a little concerned that a crisis would happen while Joel was with Steve, and she would not be able to get to him. She wanted to have Joel on bug out day. He was in danger if he was with Steve.

Over the past year since Julie made the trip to the cabin, Joel had made good on his promise to get his ham license. He didn't do much with it since he was in school, but he had it. Julie bought a basic pair of ham radios — Baofengs for about thirty-five dollars each — and regular walkie-talkie radios and stored them in the preps. She knew that they were weak in this department, but at least they had something. It was the day Joel needed to go to his dad's. Julie was nervous.

"Honey," she said, "you have to make sure to text me with your location if there's an emergency, okay?"

"I will, Mom. You worry too much," Joel dismissed.

"Well think about it. If something bad happens, where is your dad prepared to go? Does he have any emergency supplies?" Julie asked.

"Well, no, but he will take care of me. He's my dad," Joel said naively.

Julie was reminded that, at age thirteen now, Joel could be so grown up one moment, but still be a child the next. Of course parents take care of their children; Joel should expect nothing less. But, Steve was not prepared to take care of their son because he was blind to what was happening around him. Julie was angry but had no solution. Her only hope was if Steve had Joel, that Steve would call her for help. This would mean she would have to bail Steve out, but that was a small price to pay for getting Joel to safety. Julie was wound up tight the entire time Joel was with Steve. Things in Eugene changed quickly in the three weeks Joel was with Steve.

***

Floyd's phone rang. That didn't happen often.

"Floyd here," he answered.

"Dad! Hey, it's Seth. How are you?"

"Doing well, kiddo. This is a nice surprise. Where are you these days?"

"I'm in Chicago," Seth replied.

"Oh wow! How... uh... what are you doing there? Working?" Floyd asked, hoping.

"Well, I was. I was working at this great place. However, since our

137

asshole president pulled funding, the grant that funded my job was eliminated. So now I'm screwed," Seth complained.

"That's no good. Have you found anything else?" Floyd asked, already knowing the answer.

"No, that's the shitty thing. I got no notice, nothing. Just done. So umm...," Seth continued. It was the same story. It was a formula with Seth. Someone wronged him. He did no wrong. And those details may be true. Where he went off the rails is he expected someone else to help him.

"Son, I need you to find your own solution," Floyd said firmly, and with remorse. "I can't be the fallback solution every time things go south for you," Floyd explained as though he was talking to a teenager. "The federal cuts, I'm sure, are coming my way soon, too. I've got a pension and Social Security that are probably on the chopping block. Your mother has already been calling, too."

Floyd was not being fully honest. If Floyd lost the pension, his ex-wife did, too, and Floyd wasn't on the hook for it. However, the bitching campaign she would launch would be relentless. Floyd's Social Security was another story. That would be gone. He had a 401k, but if things really went to hell, he knew he would lose it all as the Feds and banks colluded to take everyone's savings. He had the cabin. That was it. He was not going to reveal that to Seth.

"Seth, tell you what. Do your best to find a job. Anything. When you do, call me. I'll give you a plan to think about for preparing for this sort of thing in the future," Floyd offered.

"My God, Dad. I don't need to be lectured on how to set up a bank account," Seth fumed. Then he hung up.

Floyd was going to give him pointers on how to arrange a bug out bag and location to get the heck out of Chicago when things became intolerable. But that wasn't the handout Seth wanted.

***

At Julie's work, things were at a boiling point. The entire focus of her agency's contracted services to the state of Oregon was "serving vulnerable families" in Eugene. That term pissed off Julie. It was "screwing poor single moms in Eugene," she fumed.

The office phones rang incessantly from about April through that summer. Desperate women needing housing services that were being cut. The agency Julie worked for was on a list of resources women could utilize if their direct state services dried up. The problem was that her agency was getting cut as well.

At home, Julie constantly watched the news. As the summer wore on, tensions grew in Eugene. Two things were happening. The round-the-clock riots continued, but the summer heat seemed to fuel their intensity. As the days grew longer, so did the riots. It didn't get cold at night either, so many times riots would go until dawn. The longer they lasted, the more violent they became. Several women were raped as they left their downtown Eugene offices. Business women simply going to their cars would be overwhelmed by large crowds, and pulled behind buildings for the unspeakable to happen. The third horrific rape happened at the end of June.

To make matters worse, the homeless population — with nothing better to do — joined the anarchists. Many anarchist groups paid homeless youth in drugs and food to boost their crowds. The homeless youth were happy to riot for free drugs and free whatever they could think of. As the University of Oregon's spring semester wound down, many college students who stayed in Eugene for the summer joined the riots. They were emboldened as they read headlines of protests at other college campuses against conservative speakers who had been invited to speak. News of major structure fires on other college campuses gave the rioters grander ideas of mischief and mayhem to enact. Police attempted to keep rioters to a dull rumble, but many times they had to call on fire engines to tamp out attempts to burn down buildings. It was simply a matter of time before a major structure fire would occur. Eugene was literally a tinderbox of tension and riots.

Julie watched in horror at the news. Interestingly, the only news she could find on the riots in Eugene were from the local stations. The channels from Portland made no mention of the riots, rapes, and arson happening almost daily in Eugene. Instead, news from Portland was riddled with press conferences from the governor and Portland mayor about the racist attitude of the new president and how his values are "not Oregon's values." There was no mention of their solution to the now-normal crime wave happening in Eugene. Julie wondered if riots were happening in Portland.

***

By mid-June, Julie's office manager turned off the incoming phone line.

The voicemail box filled up and no one ever replied. Their doors were closed except for Tuesday and Thursday mornings. By the beginning of July, Joel's time with his dad was almost over and Julie couldn't wait to have him back at the house. The idea of escaping to the cabin was becoming more and more real.

Oregon's governor was engaged in a pissing match with the Feds over illegal immigration. Early in his presidency, the president had cut federal funding for welfare to illegals for sanctuary states. Ninety percent of Julie's former clients were in America illegally.

The new president had a bigger weapon than just welfare for illegals. His administration had discretion on how to spend hundreds of billions of dollars of transportation money. All the requests from the sanctuary states on the Left Coast were quietly denied in early spring. The administration cited bureaucratic requirements that hadn't been met. Ironically, two major highway projects in Oregon that had been funded by the Feds missed huge benchmarks for state funding and infrastructure deadlines, although the state had agreed to them. Not only were the Feds denying future funding, but they wanted their money back on past funding, to the tune of billions of dollars.

This was the president's way of telling Oregon, California, and Washington states to quit breaking immigration laws. He knew just how to make it hurt. But no, Oregon's governor dug in her heels. She increased taxes by forty percent through an executive order, which hit everyone to make up for the shortfall. This destroyed Oregon's economy almost overnight. Unemployment tripled in a month.

"We say no to hate," was her response.

Her explanation for the executive order was simply and arrogant. "The president put us in this position, I need to provide for Oregonians. I am doing my job."

Tax revenues plummeted despite the executive order. The demand for state resources jumped. The tax increase ended up costing the state even more money, plus the federal transportation funds were gone. Oregon was even more broke than before and the repercussions were immediate. The funding streams had been cut off in May and June. Numerous businesses closed their doors the day after the governor's executive order. Julie walked around downtown and counted ten shuttered businesses that had just been open the day before. Large trucks were parked in no parking zones as vendors and shop owners moved items out. Julie heard two men conversing as they moved.

"We have to shut down. Everything we earn from now forward is revenue that puts us in the red to the state. No thanks."

By the end of June, the State of Oregon had missed payments to employees, vendors, and payments on bonds. The governor continued refusing to budge. She ordered all state agencies to stop making payments to the federal government on the mountain of money the state had borrowed. She made a statewide "State of the State" address that all networks carried. It was political theater.

The following day, as a direct response to her news conference, the president announced that all federal funding to Oregon would be suspended until the state resumed paying its debts. The president was treating Oregon like a business partner who owed him money. He had the leverage.

The day after that, California and Washington also stopped making payments to the Feds. It was a show of solidarity. The governors from all three states held a formal press conference a week later, declaring their campaign, *Resist!* They declared the three states would resist the "racist" and "immoral" acts of tyranny from the new president. They called on citizens in the three states to stand united and be prepared to weather some hard times.

"We're resilient and independent. I ask all Oregonians to join me in solidarity in demanding our president stop his policies of hate and make good on promises made."

In what quickly escalated into a pissing match, the president placed a full-page ad in all the major newspapers in California, Oregon, and Washington.

To the great West Coast states,

I ask two things of you. I ask that you follow the laws we have on the books. They are not unlike laws in every other country on our planet. The one law I ask you to uphold and enforce is this: if you are in this country illegally, leave or complete the process for being here legally. Anyone not here legally should not have the same rights and benefits as those who are here legally. Every single other country has similar laws. America is no different. I ask you to uphold laws that have been in place for decades. The second thing I ask of you is in response to one of your demands. You ask me to keep my promises of federal funding. The funding you demand is based upon need. There are forty-seven other states with similar needs who find no difficulty complying with federal law. Not only do they follow the laws I mentioned earlier, but they also are in full compliance with the agreements they have made with the government. In conclusion, I call upon you, great governors to follow the law and uphold your end of the bargain.

> *Let's talk soon,*
> *Your president and fellow American*

Julie couldn't turn away from the local and national news. What you didn't hear about on the national news were the city and county ordinances that were changing rapidly with the laws. While the riots had started out localized and mostly downtown, they quickly morphed into decentralized lawlessness. From what Julie could figure, it stemmed from two factions. Small groups of wannabe rioters would go into neighborhoods and loot small convenience stores, break windows, and terrorize anyone in their path. Several locals were assaulted by these renegade groups. Police couldn't do much since all their resources and manpower were downtown trying to stave off the major riots.

Eugene's mayor was under duress about the whole situation and held a press conference. *How many press conferences are we going to have this summer?* Julie mused.

> "I am asking citizens of Eugene to do the right thing. Those of you who are creating unrest, please put away your bullhorns, wooden bats, and signs. I ask that you meet with me and my staff to address the needs you demand. Your continued unrest in our city is reaching a boiling point. If you want—demand—solutions, then come to the table and let's find solutions. I, along with my staff, avail our resources and our listening ears to you. What is not a solution is your relentless assault on the citizens of Eugene."

"What a pansy," Julie muttered under her breath, "Since when is rape and pillaging 'unrest'? I have a better solution! Arrest all the SOBs and end it." Julie threw down the remote after clicking off the TV.

The next morning, Julie could smell that something was wrong as she stepped out of the house. It was putrid.

"What is that?" she said under her breath as she slowly scanned the neighborhood. Julie approached her car and a sense of horror slowly rose in her chest. Her car was smeared with feces.

"What the holy hell?!" Julie yelled.

She stopped in her tracks as her mind registered what she was seeing. Her car looked like it had been finger-painted with various shades of brown paints; if only that were the truth. Julie's eyes caught a glimpse of the car parked on the other side of her driveway and it had the same feces smeared on it. Julie slowly pivoted on her feet and horror rose in her a second time as she scanned the neighborhood. Every single car on her block was smeared with feces. Julie quickly bent over at the waist and vomited on her lawn.

***

As the summer progressed, Julie found herself regularly falling asleep with the same unanswered questions in her mind: *When do we bug out? At what point are things so bad that you have to leave? Is it when you lose your job? But the house is here, and roots are here. It's easier to find a job than to move. What is the difference between moving and bugging out, in that case? When will I know it's time to go? Should I sell the house and find a job somewhere else? Steve would take me to court and fight for custody. So, I should stay as long as I can because Steve is here, and the one financial asset I have — the house — is here. That brings me back to the original questions, when will I know it's time to bug out and go to Colorado? And when I'm there, how do I know when to come back?*

Julie's sleep was fitful and restless. Not only was her mind spinning, but knowing there were marauding rioters going through neighborhoods, every sound she heard during the night woke her. She kept a firearm, steel baseball bat, and fire extinguisher in every room.

Chapter 25

Unexpected Visitors

With Independence Day looming, media outlets speculated on what sorts of antics the rioters and looters could do and how everyone else could protect themselves. It was understood Independence Day would not be a time of fireworks and picnics this year; it would be rioting at a fevered pitch. Not only were citizens scared, but fire and medical resources were concerned. Several interviews with local fire chiefs indicated their concerns. In yet another press conference, the local fire chief stood at a podium with the mayor behind him.

"Citizens of Eugene, our number one goal for all Lane Country fire and city districts is your safety. The safety of your family and the safety of your homes. To those who would thwart our efforts to keep citizens safe, we implore you to stop. Our resources are tapped. The good men and women of our agencies want a safe and festive holiday for themselves and their families as well as yours. We ask all citizens, during this dry summer season, to follow the rules. Don't use illegal fireworks. Don't light uncontained campfires in undesignated areas. Have a water source nearby. Be safe."

The fire chief's offer of peace fell on deaf ears. It seemed to make things worse. Two nights after his press conference, two homes burned to the ground. It was quickly determined that the fires were started by Molotov cocktails that had been thrown into windows. Luckily, no one was home at either home. Tearful interviews with the homeowners were heartbreaking,

"Why would anyone do this? We have done nothing to these people!" one woman wailed as she stood in front of her smoldering home.

She implied what everyone suspected — the arson was caused by rioters. Even if caught, there would be no justice. Maybe a meeting with the mayor and a catered lunch, but no justice.

Right before the holiday, tensions were palpable. It was like waiting for a war and wondering who would be the first to fire a shot. Julie could feel the tension in her shoulders as she walked to her car after work. Tension at work and tensions in the city were taking on toll on everyone. She felt nervous just walking out of her building.

Government assisted housing was one of the rioters' main focuses. Why wouldn't they target her place of work? They hadn't answered the phone in weeks and were trying to close client files or refer them somewhere. In normal times, being bounced around the ridiculous cycle of trying to find housing could make anyone mad. But during these times? How would their madness make itself known? Arson? Worse? It was nerve-wracking to consider.

***

Julie had many of the outcomes spinning in her head as she focused on getting to her car quickly after work on a Friday at the end of June. The weekend couldn't come soon enough.

As she mulled these things over, she held her keys in her hand, prepared to use them as a weapon if need be. She had made it about halfway there when she felt it. A rock hit her in the left shoulder, hard. She took a quick glance over her left shoulder, and saw a group of four thugs who were laughing diabolically and walking directly toward her. It was two men and two women. Three of them had softball-sized rocks in their hands.

Julie rushed to her car and jumped in. She hit the lock button and turned the engine over right as a second rock hit the back windshield, making an instant spider web of cracks. She ducked as she placed her pistol on the passenger seat next to her. She would be ready if the thugs made it to the car.

Julie didn't hesitate by looking up. She sped out of the parking lot, hoping another rock wouldn't take out another window. About six blocks away, she pulled into a post office parking lot and parked. Taking a long breath, she called 9-1-1.

"If this is not a life-threatening emergency, please press one. Otherwise, stay on the line," the recording said.

Julie asked herself, *Is this a life-threatening emergency? Great question, it could have been. It isn't now, but almost was. Does that count?* She pressed one.

"Due to high call volume, the Eugene Police Department is unable to take your call now. You're very important to us and serving you is our highest priority. Please leave a message and clearly state your name and phone number. Also, please give a brief summary of what you are reporting so we can better serve you. Please include the nature of the report and where it occurred."

Julie gave the information through gritted teeth of anger and frustration knowing that the rock incident could have easily turned ugly, and her only recourse was to leave a voicemail.

"No one takes care of me better than me, I have to keep reminding myself, sadly," Julie muttered as she turned over the engine to head home. She felt her shoulder begin to throb. When she exited her vehicle at home, she saw patch of blood on the back of the driver's seat.

***

Julie used the damaged windshield as a reason to trade in her crappy car. She took out a loan, and bought a used 4x4 SUV with all-weather tires and a set of chains. The guy at the tire shop thought she was insane.

A few days after trading in her car, there was a knock at Julie's door. Julie peeked through the peephole with her hand on her firearm. *Carson's mother? Why is she here?* Julie wondered.

Slowly opening the door, Julie kept most of her body behind the door and only showed her face. In the not-too-distant past, Julie would have casually opened the door and invited Marcy in, but not these days.

"Hi, Marcy. Joel is at his dad's for a few more days," Julie said, hoping to say a quick goodbye so she could close and lock the door.

"I just wanted to drop off a few of Joel's belongings I found at our house," Marcy said. "We are moving the day after tomorrow and I wanted to make sure Joel's things were returned."

Julie opened the door a bit. "Moving? Where? What is going on?"

Carson's dad was a Eugene police officer with fifteen years of service. Government employees do not simply uproot and move on a whim. Years of service come with a guaranteed pension at the end. For someone to quit at fifteen years of service and kiss the ensuing pension goodbye, it meant something terrible was happening.

Marcy's eyes welled up with tears. Julie could tell it was all she could do to hold it together. Julie quickly opened the door all the way.

"Come in. My word, are you okay?"

Marcy was fully crying and trying unsuccessfully to stop. "No! I'm not okay. My husband has gone to work every day for the last six weeks

146

and gotten the shit beat out of him. He's been pepper sprayed so many times, it's a wonder he hasn't lost his sight. He's had God knows how many stitches put in from bottles being thrown at him, and he still goes to work. He's afraid, very afraid. All the officers are afraid. There is no end in sight for the violence."

"Oh my God, Marcy!" Julie exclaimed, feeling the throbbing from the welt on her left shoulder.

"We decided last week to move. No job, no matter how noble, is worth his life for stupid rioters. My last straw was when we got a death threat to our house. It threatened me and the kids... by name," Marcy whispered. She inhaled and caught her breath. "So... we're moving. There is a small county in Texas that Nate had applied to last year and he's fairly far in the application process. It's not guaranteed by any stretch, but it looks promising. We're headed to Texas. I wanted to bring Joel's clothes and a few of his videogames to you. I wish Carson could say goodbye in person, but we are leaving before Joel gets back."

Julie was speechless. She gave Marcy a long hug. It was a hug of comfort as Marcy softly cried. It was a final goodbye.

***

Finally, the news she knew was coming finally came: her agency would close its doors on the first of September. No one would have a job, but everyone would get a six-month severance package. That was something.

By the first of August, Julie was shopping her resume around. Her experience was in nonprofit government services. Suddenly, government wasn't hiring. Nonprofits were closing their doors. She wasn't surprised, but she was scared. She kept looking; she had no choice. No one was hiring.

Chapter 26

Bugging Out

Upon hearing about the Feds cutting all funding, Julie pulled out her bug out bag and prepared to depart. It was now a matter of when, not if.

Sure enough, the riots started about an hour after the president's announcement. The anarchists had been planning for this and had an extremely well-organized plan in place to start up the riots. It was ironic that so-called anarchists could follow directions so well, but they weren't anarchists, they were communists.

Like all the others before, the August riots originated in the downtown area of every large city in the Left Coast states. The same organizer who had lead them before was leading them again. They were paid to do this.

This time, the riots quickly went from the downtown areas into the neighborhoods. They were no longer directed at the government. Now they were seemingly random, although the organizers had planned them out well in advance.

Within about two days, it was apparent the police couldn't even begin to control the fevered riots. Soon, everyone who wanted free stuff started to riot. They chose places that were convenient and ripe for the most destruction. Stores, malls, grocery stores, and especially liquor stores. Nice office buildings were also targeted. Anything with stuff they wanted, or anything appearing to be rich was targeted.

For a full week, it was not safe for Julie or Joel to leave the house. At any given time, a large rioting crowd would be in a street somewhere in Eugene. The footage of scared children trapped in cars with their moms as rioters banged on them and held up Molotov cocktails was enough to keep Julie home.

The governor called in the National Guard, which were technically state units. But long ago, the Feds made these technically state units completely dependent on federal military support. The computers, logistics, and even personnel systems were under federal control. The Oregon National Guard, as tiny as it was, couldn't even call up Guardspersons as the governor called them; the Feds shut down the personnel system. The Feds controlled most of the fuel for the Oregon's Guard's vehicles. It was pathetic.

Oregon's governor refused to ask the Feds to release their controls over the Oregon National Guard. Instead, she blamed all the destruction on the president. He responded by saying, "Just call for help and I'll send it." She never called.

The rioting in Eugene was the least of the governor's concerns. The rioting in Portland was exponentially worse. Portland's mayor closed all freeways into the city. Portland is on the Columbia River, which is the border with Washington. Vancouver, Washington, the large city just north of Portland, closed the two bridges over the Columbia River to prevent the rioters from going back and forth and causing mayhem between the two cities.

Closing the bridges made it difficult for citizens trying to escape. Portland residents had two options. Go south toward Eugene, or go east toward rural Oregon. Most Portlanders fleeing chose to go south, only to find that Eugene was rioting like Portland, but on a smaller scale—if that was possible.

Julie's red flags went up when she watched the news footage of police barricades being erected on the I-5 and I-205 bridges. *That just made bugging out a whole lot harder*, she thought. Even though she would head east, the I-5 traffic would clog up quickly and people who would have gone north would now opt to go east.

The governor held another "State of the State" address at the end of August. She said all Oregonians should remain calm.

"The criminal actions of a few should not define who we are," she said with a syrupy smile. "We must stay safely locked in our homes, let the police do their jobs, and this too shall pass." The usual things a helpless politician says when he or she has no control over the situation.

As the governor was telling everyone that the mayhem would pass, Julie looked at the smoke rising from downtown Eugene. Police, fire, and emergency services were operating at full capacity. Hospitals were full. People were scared.

***

The next day, the federal response to the Left Coast governors was simple: you can have the non-military federal lands in your state back.

"We're denying federal aid," a White House spokesperson said, "but we're also forfeiting our claim to your lands. The federal government wants a collaborative relationship with the states, but we also recognize the right for each entity to exercise their rights."

The Feds basically filed for divorce from Oregon, California, and Washington, and were dividing up the property. Oregon's governor was the scorned ex.

With the stroke of the president's pen, federal lands in Oregon were handed back to the state. Oregon's governor now had the management of that land to deal with and right now, that was the least of her worries.

But that would change.

***

On the first of September, Julie's job was officially done. She hadn't found another job, of course. No one had. Julie could sense it. Her reasons for staying in Eugene were literally going up in smoke.

She hadn't been to work for three days because of the lawless riots. It was simply too unsafe, and her agency was a target for rioters because it was denying "access to housing."

By early afternoon, Julie noticed something when she looked out the window. The smoke was thicker, and lingering. It wasn't localized to a single spot like it had been up to this point—a building. That smoke had been black.

This time was different. In the distance, she saw gray smoke. It was different, and Julie couldn't put her finger on it. The forests. It was coming from the foothills. Julie squinted.

The foothills outside of Eugene were burning. Julie had to repeat in her head what she was seeing. It was too incredible to fathom. The forests *were burning*. All those mismanaged forests with tons of rotting timber were burning right before Julie's eyes. It wasn't in one spot, either. The smoke stretched from left to right in Julie's window view. It was a large and pervasive inferno.

Julie knew there was no way to put out the fires. They would burn until all the trees were gone—including trees in Eugene. They would burn until Eugene was gone. That was a thought she couldn't wrap her mind around and wasn't about to see firsthand.

She ran outside. The hills south of Eugene had billowing smoke swirling around them. She couldn't see flames, but that much smoke told her flames were there. Literally, where there's smoke there's fire. And there was an immense amount of smoke. She scanned her view to the southeast, more smoke. Smoke—east!

150

"JOEL!" she screamed. "Now! Grab your bug out stuff now! In the car in ten minutes. NOW!"

Julie backed the SUV up to the garage, flipped up the back door and loaded her bug out tubs into the vehicle. Joel came running out with three duffle bags and put them in the back seat.

"Mom, what else do you need?" Joel yelled.

"Grab the cooler and fill it up with food — not junk — from the fridge. Grab the cases of water from the basement," Julie called over her shoulder as she lifted a tub into the SUV.

They had discussed several times what they would do in a bug out situation. What would they grab if they had one minute? Ten minutes? No minutes?

In this case, the fires were a distance away, but Julie knew once they were out of the hills and leapt across the fields that Eugene would burn. In the summer's heat, the fields would go up like paper in a campfire.

Julie had already stacked up her ammo cans in the garage next to the tubs. She threw them into the SUV. She ran into the house and grabbed the guns. Rifles were loaded into rifle bags with locks on them. Her handgun was already on her.

"Mom, what else?" Joel called.

"Grab the firearms bin!" Julie replied.

He grabbed a box that had all the cleaning supplies and accessories for the all the firearms. The camping gear was already in the SUV. Food. Prepping supplies from the basement. What next?

Julie's neighbor rushed up the driveway. It was Marla, the one neighbor she liked. Marla and her husband, Larry, were nice. They seemed open minded, unlike most of her neighbors, and they liked Joel.

"Hey Julie! You look like you're leaving," Marla called out.

"Yes, you should too," Julie said as she squished things together.

"Hey, do you have a hitch on that SUV?" Marla asked.

"A hitch? Why? I don't know," Julie said as Marla got closer.

"Well, my dad left me a trailer last summer when he was here," Marla said rapidly. "I don't have a hitch on my car. I know this place is going up in flames and if you can use it, take it. Shame to let it burn," Marla said.

Who is this angel? Julie thought.

"Marla, are you serious?" Julie asked. She was in shock.

"Yes, let me see if we can do this," Marla looked at the back end of Julie's car. The SUV was so new to Julie still; she didn't know if it was

151

equipped for a hitch or even how to hook it up.

"Drive it down to my place, I'll have Larry hitch it up and show you how to do it. Hurry!" Marla said as she jogged back to her house.

Julie didn't waste time. Having a trailer on her SUV meant she could take more of the tubs in the basement. They wouldn't go to waste. It meant grabbing lower priority "comfort" items.

Julie saw the trailer. It was covered and fairly good-sized and not too big for her SUV to tow. It was perfect.

Larry explained quickly how to hitch the trailer. Julie listened as much as she could but knew she wasn't getting all the important details. Larry got it hooked up, brakes lights attached, and sent Julie off.

"Before I go, I want to thank you. Here's the key to my house. After I go, if there is anything that you can use, use it. Take what you can. I mean it," Julie implored.

She gave Larry and Marla a hug.

"I hope we can all come back to find just a few scorched spots on our homes. If not, God bless you both," Julie said with tears in her eyes. Not from the smoke. This was real. The shit was hitting the fan. The city was burning.

Marla held Julie a little while longer and whispered, "You take good care of yourself and that son of yours. Stay safe, you hear?" Marla's voice was soft and scratchy.

In that moment, neighbors who barely knew each other except for an occasional wave while at the mailboxes bonded. They would never forget that moment when their neighborhood, their homes, their lives, would never be the same again. Julie didn't even want to try to back the trailer up to the garage. She parked in front of the house and opened the door on the trailer. It was a small, secure room on wheels.

"Joel! Look! Let's load this bad boy up! Hurry!" Julie called.

In thirty minutes, the trailer was full. This meant that they could load things that she hadn't even considered part of their preparation. Joel threw clothes into suitcases. Blankets, towels, and sheets were thrown into the trailer. Julie grabbed kitchen supplies she didn't think they would be able to take. Gardening tools, cleaning supplies, a few pictures, some board games, extra blankets — luxury items.

"I need to find a lock for the hatch. Let's go look in the garage." Julie was ready to go.

Joel found a lock in the garage, rushed out, pushed the garage door button and met Julie at the trailer with the lock.

"Oh my word, one last thing! Run in the house, drawer to the right of the phone, notebook. Green cover, grab it," Julie instructed.

"Notebook?" Joel asked.

"Fuel stops along the way. We will need it," Julie called as she headed to the driver's door. "Lock the door with your house key. I gave mine to Marla."

As they headed out of town headed east, Julie fueled up. Gas was expensive — very expensive. She knew an increase in fuel prices would be part of bugging out, but so steep, so fast was jarring.

Her next stop was the ATM. As long as the machine spit out cash, she would empty her savings account.

Julie had withdrawn as much as she could from her 401K and pension before the August federal funding cut-off and put it in her savings account. Her last paycheck included her six months' severance pay. As they left the ATM, Julie looked over at Joel. She was bugging out with him. It was finally happening. She felt so thankful that Joel was with her.

Shit. She needed to call Steve.

She was moving along slowly in traffic headed east toward Oakridge. After going further toward Bend there was a fork. She could go south to Klamath Falls and head over the border east toward the Rockies. That would be brutal. Julie was hoping to go northeast toward eastern Oregon, touch Idaho then go south from there. Traffic moved at about twenty-five miles per hour. Cell service would get dicey soon. She needed to call him. She dialed his number. She switched on the speaker phone.

Ring.

Where would Steve go in this? Did Steve even take a moment to look around and see the fires? Surely, he was doing something to evacuate.

Ring.

The thoughts turned over in her mind. *Oh my word, would he go north to Mandy?*

Ring.

Where else could he go? His family was on the East Coast. There was no easy way to get there since so many others would have the same idea.

Ring.

"Hello, you've reached my voicemail. Leave me a message or text me."

She left a message. "Steve, I hope you're safe. Joel and I are safe; we are heading out. My car is loaded with supplies and we're headed to my dad's cabin in Smoky Flats. Cell phone service is iffy. Please text and let us

153

know you're safe. Take care of yourself."

Julie hung up and looked at Joel. Joel looked at her with a worried look on his face.

"Joel, he's okay. I'm sure," Julie assured.

"I don't know, Mom," Joel said with a quiver in his voice. "He doesn't have anything prepared at his house like we do... did... at our house."

"Did he ever tell you places he goes to visit friends?" Julie asked.

"He did go to Portland to visit Mandy. You know she's pregnant, right?"

Chapter 27

Domestic Immigration

"NO! What?" Julie tried hard not to screech. She was afraid she'd drive off the road.

"With your dad's… uh… hmm… uh…." Julie was searching for right words. Ex-wife, girlfriend? "Mandy?" she finally said.

"Yes, mom," Joel said. "Dad said I'd be having a brother or sister around the beginning of the year. I thought he had told you, Mom. I'm sorry!"

Joel was almost crying. Julie realized she was scaring him. She was scaring herself, too.

"Hon… hon… hon," she said reassuringly. She reached over, grasped Joel's knee and squeezed it to assure him that everything was alright. Her voice calmed down.

"This is a surprise for sure. You have no idea. But this is for your dad to figure out. I am sure he will travel to Portland if she is pregnant. We will have to wait for him to call us or text us. We've told him where we're going. It will make him feel better knowing you're safe. We've done what we can. I just can't imagine being pregnant in the middle of this," she let slip out. She tried to calm Joel. "It will be okay. It's okay. I mean it."

Julie knew that she and Joel would be okay. She didn't feel the same confidence about Steve and Mandy. He had gone from being unprepared to being the unprepared father of a newborn. In riots and wildfires.

***

As Julie approached Oakridge, she knew she needed to call her father while she still had cell service. When she stopped for gas, she gave some money to Joel to go to the Dairy Queen next door to get something cold and sweet. The smoke in the air had cleared as they left Eugene, but it was hot. Ice cream would be a nice treat. It might be a while before they could get any more.

Julie used her debit card. She knew she had a lot of money in her account. What she didn't know was how much longer she would have access to it before the banks shut down. Since Oregon was broke, it was only a matter of time before Oregon decided to collect those massive new taxes by ordering the banks to fork over everyone's money.

When Joel was in the Dairy Queen, Julie called her dad. He answered. Before he could even say hello, she blurted out, "Dad, it's Julie. It's time to bug out. I'm on the road."

"I am, too. Baltimore has bad riots and they are spreading. I think D.C. is next. If that happens, the military gets involved. I'm leaving first thing in the morning."

"Oh my God, you're serious?"

"Baltimore and the surrounding county where I live are sanctuary cities, my dear. They got a bunch of their funding cut just like you. Not the cut-off Oregon got, but a big reduction. It needed to happen. These riots are not the Feds' fault, it's the hired rioters who want a civil war. They're pretty close to getting it here. It's a warzone in downtown Baltimore. What's your plan?"

"I'm hoping we can find a camping place either in eastern Oregon or Idaho tonight," she said. "I want to get to the cabin late tomorrow night. It all depends on the roads, fuel, and a little luck. Please text me as you move along, too."

"I will. Hey, where is Joel?"

Julie could hear the worry in his voice. She had forgotten to tell him about Joel. "He's walking toward the car right now with two Dairy Queen Blizzards," Julie said with a smile on her face.

"Thank God."

Joel set the treats on the hood as he opened the passenger door.

"Joel, Grandpa is on the phone. Here. Talk to him. He'd love to hear your voice," Julie said as she handed the phone to him.

Julie got out of the car, got the ice cream, climbed back in, placed them in the cup holders, and started up the car. The AC blasted in her face and it felt so good. She took a spoonful of blizzard in her mouth, and tasted chocolate and smoke.

Julie listened as grandfather and grandson spoke. They would see each other soon.

Hopefully.

***

When they got to Bend, in central Oregon, she decided to go east toward Idaho. Going south took her through some desolate places and would put

156

them in California, which was just going from the skillet to the fire. Julie could sporadically get a radio station as she traveled. The news said that the border between California and Oregon was dicey. Both states had their federal funding pulled. Oregon didn't want to take in Californians and California didn't want to take in Oregonians. It was funny how quickly the solidarity between the Left Coast states was breaking down into pure self-interest.

Julie also realized that, while she was one of the first to bug out of Oregon, apparently thousands of other people were doing the same. She was in the first wave, but it was a big wave. That surprised her; she thought she was one of the few to jump in a car and leave. Apparently not. The road to Idaho it would be. Julie set her sights on Ontario, Oregon, and Roberta's campground. As she got closer, she picked up Idaho radio stations. Then she heard something shocking on the radio.

"Domestic immigration."

This was the new term being used to describe evacuees leaving states and entering others. She heard the term for the first time as she listened to an announcement from Idaho's governor.

He said, "Nonresidents can drive through Idaho. They cannot stay. Anyone evacuating to Idaho will not be given state resources. Idaho wants to help as much as we can, please understand, but Idaho absolutely cannot help everyone. We do not have resources for every evacuee from Oregon, Washington, and even California who needs it." The news said many of the states that bordered federally cut-off states were implementing similar domestic immigration policies.

Then another term emerged: Great State. This was the term being used for states that hadn't had been cut off from federal funding. It echoed the president's sentiment of wanting to make America a great nation again, like it once was. The cut-off states were being called Sanctuary States. So far, these were the Left Coast states and a few along the eastern seaboard, like New York. It got complicated when a state had sanctuary cities within it. It was chaos.

"Residents from Sanctuary States are welcome to travel through the Great States," the president said in a news conference as Julie drove, "In speaking to various governors, I can tell you this, every Great State will be implementing a domestic immigration plan. They have the sovereign right to do so."

Evacuees would not find help if they were looking for relocation services. Move on. Ironically, or perhaps appropriately, residents of Sanctuary States would not be given sanctuary in Great States.

Julie was amazed at the hard line of the Great States. They were saying they would not take on the financial burdens created by their neighbors. Who could blame them?

It wasn't as principled as that, however. Great States would lose their federal funding if they took in refugees from Sanctuary States. The choice was easy for Great States like Idaho: keep out the big-government people from the Left Coast and retain federal funding at the same time.

The radio station Julie was listening to aired interviews with evacuees.

"I can't believe I have no place to go!"

Another said, "Idaho, Nevada, and Arizona need to be neighborly and help these people!"

Liberals in those states even held protests in the capitols of those states. The protests turned violent, of course. But they were broken up by empowered police forces and immediate arrests. It felt like the very start of a civil war. At the same time, Oregon's governor held several press conferences. Predictably, she took the opposite approach of the Idaho governor. Her press conference sounded like a one-woman cheering squad.

"Thank you to all Oregonians who are pulling together to help during these trying times. Thank you for taking your neighbors in, putting out fires, helping law enforcement. That is the Oregon I know and love — that we all love. Please bear with us. Our emergency response ability has been stretched to capacity. We ask everyone to be calm. Stay indoors. Lock your doors. Law enforcement is working hard to quell the handful of lawbreakers. Our firefighting responders are doing their best to save buildings and homes in high density cities, for the maximum benefit to the most people. We ask that everyone stay calm. This is a temporary situation. I and my staff are committed to getting through this emergency very soon." She came within a hair of declaring martial law by encouraging citizens to stay home with their doors locked.

Gone was the rhetoric about resisting and stopping hate. Gone was bashing the president. The governor's speech communicated that she had bitten off more than she could chew, but she couldn't back down. She was losing, and it was obvious. Even to her.

Julie looked around. The freeway out of Oregon was full. People were not believing a damn word that woman was saying. They were getting out. Not staying home and locking their doors. No one was "pulling together." The time for that was gone.

Julie hoped she could stay at Roberta's that night. It was on the Oregon side of the border with Idaho. She filled up her tank in Oregon as she entered Ontario with her debit card. She couldn't believe it still worked.

She also wondered if her Oregon concealed handgun license was valid in Idaho. Then she chuckled. Of course Idaho wouldn't care.

She kept going the few miles from the gas station to Roberta's campground. It was late. Really late. Traffic was horrific. Julie pulled into the campground. She could see the office light on. Joel was sleeping in the passenger seat. After parking, she slid out of her seat and softly closed the door, hoping Joel would continue to sleep. She would need to wake him eventually, but didn't want to until it was necessary. The door creaked as she opened it.

"Roberta? You here? Hello!" Julie called out.

A door toward the back of the office opened.

"Who's there?" Roberta came out in sweats, flip flops, and a t-shirt.

"Roberta, you may not remember me. I am Julie. I'm from Eugene and came through last summer," Julie described.

"You're the lady with the beater camper. The trailer had barbed wire on it," Roberta remembered.

"Yes, that's me. I know it's late, but wondered if you had a spot for the night?" Julie knew a lot of people had traveled through before her. She wouldn't be the only one looking for a camping spot tonight.

"Oh, dear. Well, let me look at my books here. It's been crazy today, hon. You know about all the fires, right?" Roberta said and she slipped behind the counter and perched her reading glasses on her nose.

"I do, ma'am. That is why I need a spot tonight. My son and I are evacuating," Julie teared up a bit. She wasn't just traveling; she was evacuating. The gravity of the situation kept increasing. It was overwhelming.

"Oh my, well... hmm. Officially, we're full," Roberta said matter-of-factly.

"Oh no...," Julie groaned. She would need to travel further. The next campground was almost two hundred miles away. She probably didn't have enough gas.

"If anyone that looks official, with a uniform on or something, asks, then we're officially full," Roberta continued. "However, if you can pull your rig up next to the building, I'll let you pitch a tent in my yard, or sleep in your car."

"Roberta. Thank you. How do I thank you?" Julie asked.

"Well, pay me as though it were a full spot. I'm a business woman at the end of the day. The second way, make sure you get to where you need to get. I want you to be safe," Roberta said with a twinkle in her eye.

"Deal," Julie pulled cash out of her back pocket. "Thank you so much."

Julie decided to sleep in the car. It would be uncomfortable, but it sure beat pitching a tent at almost 1:00 a.m. She opened the door on Joel's side of the car and pulled the latch so his seat would recline. She threw a light jacket over him. It was summer but still cool at night in the high desert.

Joel stirred a bit and opened his eyes.

"Mom, where are we?" Joel said trying to sit up.

"Shh… we're at a campground. I don't want to pitch a tent right now, so let's just sleep in the car. Do you need anything? There's a bathroom over there," Julie pointed to the shower house.

Joel looked over the seat. "Not now," he answered and closed his eyes. Back off to sleep he went. He was blissfully removed from the new world of domestic immigration.

Julie locked his door and went around the back to check the trailer. The lock was holding. All was well. Doors were locked. She got back into the driver's side, pulled a sweatshirt over her head, reclined her seat and promptly fell asleep.

***

Bang, bang, bang!

Someone was banging on the driver's window, which was only a few inches from her face. Julie jolted awake.

"What?!" Julie yelled.

"Open the window!"

Julie didn't recognize the person, but she cracked the window about an inch.

"More!" It was a man.

"No! What the hell do you want?" Julie demanded.

"You're not supposed to park here!" he yelled.

"Talk to Roberta!" Julie yelled. She didn't know why they were both yelling. Joel sat up and watched.

"Who's Roberta?" he yelled.

That was Julie's clue. "Get the fuck away from my car!" Julie roared as she heaved her body toward the window.

The asshole was startled and jumped back. She unholstered her pistol for good measure.

"Fuck you!" he yelled and ran up the road.

She watched as he ran to take in all the details for a description.

"Jeez, Mom!" Joel exclaimed.

"What?" Julie asked. "He was a bad guy. Roberta owns this place. If someone doesn't know who she is, they don't belong here."

"Jeez, MOM!" Joel said even more emphatically. "You never drop F bombs."

"Joel, there are lots of things you are going to learn about me soon." Julie realized all the self-defense classes taught her to use a roaring voice with salty language. Language she tried not to use around Joel. But there were exceptions. Like when a man was trying to attack you at a campground.

Julie knew she needed to tell Roberta what just happened and opened the door to get out. She had her pistol in her hand. That guy might be lurking or, as Ash always said, "Criminals travel in packs."

She was reasonably sure the area was safe.

"Come on," she said to Joel. "You'll like Roberta."

***

"That son of a bitch," Roberta said squarely after hearing Julie's report. "Oh sorry, hon. I shouldn't say that in front of you," Roberta said, looking at Joel. "That sorry sack of garbage has been robbin' people in my campground all summer. The police don't come when we call. They're busy with a million other scumbags. A real spike in crime. It's gotten bad out here."

"Roberta, I gotta tell you. I don't see it getting better anytime soon. You need to protect yourself more. He isn't going to just go away. I think more like him will gravitate here if they know there's people to rob," Julie warned.

"You're right," Roberta said.

"Roberta, Eugene is burning. Portland is rioting. People will have no place to live. They will be evacuating for weeks and have no place to go. You're a great place for people like me who need to stop. But you're also a great place to rob people like me. You need to up your security and protect what you have. Any state police resources you might have had before yesterday are probably no longer here," Julie continued as she described the governor's press conference.

"Well, I was thinking I should hire a local guy to guard the place at night. That idiot who bugged you tonight has robbed quite a few people. I'm glad you were in your car. It's not so lucky for those who are in tents. But listenin' to what you're sayin,' I need to do more. I'll get on it," Roberta said.

Julie's eyes were drooping. She couldn't hold in her yawns any longer.

"Go back to sleep," Roberta said. "You can stay in my mobile home tonight. You need to feel safe to get to sleep, and you need to sleep to drive safely."

"Thanks," was all Julie could say. Within five minutes she and Joel were asleep on Roberta's couch.

Julie awoke at 6:30 a.m. She needed to get to the cabin. She quickly thanked Roberta and got Joel to her SUV and trailer. Nothing had been taken or damaged.

"You stay safe as you travel," Roberta said. "If you ever come back through, stop by, you hear?"

"We will," Julie said as she touched Joel's shoulder to head toward the door.

Would she ever come back through here? That was a very good question.

***

Julie and Joel got in the car. She turned on the radio and heard the new domestic immigration requirements in Idaho. The radio said occupants of cars with license plates from a Sanctuary State were required to show their ID. Their information would be taken down and entered into a database. They could stay for a maximum of five days to traverse Idaho and move on. As they were leaving Idaho, their information would be taken down again to make sure they left the state within their five-day visa. Yes, "visa," as in the kind of thing used to allow foreigners into a country. The Great States were treating the citizens of Sanctuary States as a foreign country.

She immediately called her dad. "Dad, you there?" Julie asked over a poor connection on her cell phone.

"I'm here." His voice came through faintly.

162

"Where are you?" Julie asked worried.

"No idea. Somewhere in Ohio," he answered. "Where are you?" he asked.

"Ontario, Oregon, right by the Idaho border. Dad, it's getting bad here," Julie told him all the news about how the new domestic immigration laws.

"How do states know if you're allowed to be there? I mean seriously, isn't this border patrol for states?" he said with frustration. "No one's ever done this in America."

She described the five-day visa and border checks. She didn't want to worry her dad, so she didn't tell him that anyone overstaying their five-day visa was subject to arrest, including citizen arrest. She and Joel would be hunted if they remained in Idaho for more than five days. Even if their car broke down or they ran out of gas.

"Is Oregon or Washington taking people in?"

"Good question. Haven't heard. But I don't think the broke, burning, and rioting states have a big problem with people wanting to come in," Julie said with a bit of the sarcasm that she learned from her dad. "I'm not seeing a whole lot of cars heading the opposite direction I'm headed. Certainly no out-of-state cars," Julie reported.

"God. What a nightmare."

"So, Dad, stupid question," Julie started. "What is the progress of the barn?"

Julie realized in all of the stress and uncertainty of the last six months, she hadn't thought to ask about the barn and if it was done.

"That's a good question considering what's going on, huh?" he chuckled. "It's done. I talked to Ned last week. As this was brewing, he realized the project could not get behind schedule. He hired an extra guy for a week to get it done before schedule knowing we would probably be coming soon."

"Thank God," Julie whispered. She had been preparing herself for a partially finished barn and the need to offer to help however she could to finish it before the winter set in. Temperatures would be dropping soon.

"Ned told me it will be hooked to electricity in the next few days. He has some plan to get it on a small solar panel system set up next summer. He's doing something like that to his house."

"That would be great. Wow."

Julie hadn't expected that. She wanted to get going. "I'm going to head to the border crossing." That sounded odd in America.

"Got it," he said. "Bye, Julie. I love you."

She got on Interstate 84 and saw the red tail lights of a traffic jam a mile from the border.

The line moved fairly quickly. She saw some police cars with their lights on. She got up to them and rolled down her window.

A baby-faced trooper easily ten years younger than her came up to her window. He saw the Oregon license plates and looked into Julie's car.

"Good morning, ma'am."

"Good morning, sir," she said, which sounded odd given that he was younger than her.

"Welcome to Idaho. Please limit your stay to five days. Drive safely," he said with a smile.

"Don't I need to...," she said, but then realized she shouldn't finish the sentence.

"Show some ID?" he asked. "No, ma'am, we don't have our system up this morning. We should have it up by later tonight. You're getting a free pass."

Julie smiled, rolled up her window, and slowly drove forward. Into a foreign country: Idaho.

***

Julie spotted it from the road. "Farm and Feed" read the sign on the store somewhere in Idaho. *Perfect,* Julie thought. She and Joel walked into the place, and the shelves were sparsely stocked. She looked around to see if there were any supplies at all that she could use. Julie saw a chicken waterer and feeder. The feeder looked like an upside bucket. She grabbed the last two.

At the end of the aisle she saw a small waterer, but only one. She needed more than one, but would take what she could get.

As she walked to the front of the store, Joel called out, "Hey Mom, look," He was waving a book.

Julie walked over to him. There was a small book rack of different animal husbandry how-to books.

"This is great! Good catch, Joel," Julie said with delight. "Hold your hands out flat."

She piled four books onto Joel's hand — one book each for general livestock, rabbits, chickens, and goats.

"Let's look around and see if there is anything else we can use," Julie suggested.

Julie found some livestock antibiotics, bird scratch, and feed. Joel found mud boots, tarps, and hatchets.

"Nice," Julie said when she looked at Joel's finds. "Let's go."

Julie approached the counter to see the sign stating that the store was only accepting cash. She had the cash. Julie had made a point to stop as often as she thought to at various ATMs to see if she could withdraw cash. For the last few stops, more ATMs were more inoperable than operating. The unfolding collapse in the big cities on the coast was starting to make its way into the rural communities.

"Do you have any chicks or pullets on hand to buy?" Julie asked. She chuckled to herself at how much she sounded like an old-time farm girl.

"I have about eight chicks left right now. This is not the typical breeding season, and the last shipment we had is almost sold out. I'll sell you what I have," the clerk explained.

Julie bought them, along with a heat lamp and feed. The clerk handed her a box the size of a shoe box that had soft cooing sounds emanating from it.

She looked at Joel. "I need you to start reading that book when we get loaded. I know a lot about chickens. I don't know much about newborn chicks. We need to keep them warm and alive. Also, odds are that half of them are roosters. Don't get attached to them. Some of those will be eaten soon. Okay? These aren't pets," Julie instructed. Joel nodded.

As they walked out to the SUV, Julie took in her surroundings. Everything looked fine. No panic. No flames or smoke. An occasional car rumbled by. A soft breeze whistled through the long grasses behind the feed store. The only indication that a collapse was happening was the "Cash only" sign on the counter and the sparsely stocked shelves. Such a stark contrast to the smoke-filled skies and violent riots Julie and Joel left just two days before. But the collapse of three neighboring states was reaching Idaho.

As Julie continued through Idaho listening to the radio, the new rules of the Great States were being updated constantly. People seeking to relocate to Great States were already trying to game the new domestic immigration rules. They were stealing license plates. Criminals who made fake IDs now had a new market.

The radio said Colorado had formally declared itself to be a Great State. That was good news and not much of a surprise. There were plenty of liberals in Colorado, but they were looking at the destruction on the Left Coast and not willing to cast their lot with the Sanctuary States. However, Denver was a sanctuary city and still hadn't decided its allegiance to either the Sanctuary States or Great States. Julie didn't give a crap about Denver.

Julie realized that when she got to Colorado she would have to get a valid Colorado ID to stay there permanently. She didn't have any documents proving that her father owned the cabin or that she had any connection to Colorado. She was getting increasingly scared that she'd be turned around and sent back to Oregon.

For about two hundred miles, she felt like she would throw up wondering if all her prepping was for nothing because she and Joel couldn't get to their safe place with the supplies they had prepared for. Because they didn't have ID. Something that simple.

Julie whizzed through Idaho. She could stay on the Interstate 84 and go through Utah and then Wyoming into Colorado, or take a smaller highway, Highway 30, and miss Utah. She decided not to chance an unnecessary border crossing.

She took Highway 30 from Idaho into Wyoming and then got on Interstate 80 to east through Wyoming. She realized that she could take an even smaller highway, Highway 789, and drop down into northwest Colorado, which was not too far from Smoky Flats. This provided two advantages. First, she'd be closer to Smoky Flats and not have to go through Denver, which was probably rioting. Second, the odds were that Colorado didn't have a sophisticated border crossing system operating on little Highway 789.

The first border to cross would be Wyoming. They ran into the same thing as the Idaho border crossing: a trooper who smiled and said their system wasn't up and running yet.

As she drove through Wyoming, the news came through. Great States were making concessions for people just like Julie. It was a sponsorship program, like the U.S. used to have for immigrants from other countries before any limitations on immigration were jettisoned.

The program was essentially that Sanctuary State people claiming to be joining family or friends in a Great State must name the people who would be their sponsor. Eventually, this would be done prior to entering the Great State, but they were scrambling to set up their systems.

In the interim, a Sanctuary Stater, as they were becoming known as, must apply for citizenship within five days of entering. The process would be streamlined and Great States were pulling volunteers to run the checks.

A Great State official or volunteer would contact the sponsor and verify they were indeed agreeing to sponsor the person. Sponsors agreed to be financially responsible for taking care of an incoming Sanctuary Stater. The official or volunteer would run a quick criminal history check. Sanctuary Staters were required to denounce their previous residency in writing, surrender any old Sanctuary State ID, and agree to not apply for welfare for five years. An incoming Sanctuary Stater must do all this within five days of entry into the Great State. Bottom line — within five days upon entering a Great State, you assimilate with family or friends who can help you, or you get out... or be subject to arrest.

The system, especially the interim system that relied on the honor system of people applying within five days of entry, wasn't perfect and its expedited nature would allow some people in who might not have sponsors or who might have criminal histories. However, Great State officials didn't want thousands of people waiting on their borders. That would lead to riots and Sanctuary Staters simply running into the Great State. An application, even a quick and imperfect one, was better than the alternative.

***

Julie called her dad again and explained the sponsorship system. "When we get to the Colorado border, who do we list as our sponsor?" Julie asked.

"I have good news," her father said. "I have an old Colorado driver's license with the cabin address on it, so I'm already a Colorado citizen." He chuckled, "And I have Maryland citizenship — I'm a dual citizen!"

"So, you can sponsor me and Joel!" she said with glee. The stress over the last several hours thinking how to get over that hurdle made her stomach knot up and her shoulders hurt. One simple call fixed that.

Chapter 28

Passport, Please

Colorado didn't have a border crossing because, well, America had never had border crossings among states. One exception might be between Oregon and California, where the most egregious infraction would be for an Oregonian to bring fruit into California. Julie's memories of crossing into California from Oregon made her laugh.

As Julie and Joel approached the Colorado border on Highway 789, which became Highway 13 on the Colorado side, she saw a single police car with its lights on. There weren't many vehicles crossing the border there.

It was her turn to talk to the Colorado trooper.

"Good evening," she said.

"Good evening, ma'am."

"I know the system," she said to speed things up. "I'm going to Smoky Flats to be with my father, who lives there and has Colorado ID."

"Well, okay, then," the trooper said, relieved that this would go quickly. "Be sure and apply for citizenship within five days. Drive safely." It seemed like all troopers said this.

"Yes, sir," she said. He waved her on. It was that simple.

The closest border station was the tiny town of Craig, Colorado, at the intersection of Highways 13 and 40. Julie and Joel stopped in the city hall there, which had a long line. They waited two hours, which was long, but not awful, and Julie told the volunteer, who was a retired man in the local Rotary Club, about her father and his Colorado ID. The volunteer asked Julie to call father, and then he talked to him, and asked the exact spelling of his name. The volunteer pulled up his name in the Colorado DMV records and verified his address was at Smoky Flats.

"It's beautiful there," the volunteer said. "You'll like it, ma'am."

The volunteer asked her father if he would sponsor Julie and Joel. He ran their criminal histories in a commercial database used by employers to see if prospective employees had a criminal record. Julie and Joel came up clean.

"Whew!" Julie joked. The volunteered laughed and then said, "You'd be surprised."

The volunteer handed Julie two forms for renouncing her Oregon citizenship, one for her and one for Joel as his guardian.

The last step was a printer that spit out a temporary Colorado ID card with their picture. It was a surprisingly efficient system.

Julie held up her Colorado ID and cried. It was done. The bug out was done. She was safely in Colorado. She just had to get to the cabin now.

***

Julie and Joel gassed up in Craig. Her debit card still worked there. They got on the road to Smoky Flats. While Julie sat in the car, she sent Steve a text. She hadn't heard from him at all.

Steve, where r u? We r safe in Craig, CO and heading to the cabin.

They stopped at a rest stop to sleep in the SUV. During a pit stop at a rest stop when Joel was out of the car, Julie called Steve. It went to voicemail, which she figured would happen. She left another message.

"Steve," she hissed. "You are worrying the shit out of me. That's not true. I don't give a shit about you. You're worrying the shit out of your son. I need to tell him where you are and that you are safe, that was the deal, remember? If you don't at least send me a text letting me know you're okay, I'll have to tell him that I don't know if you're safe. Then we have to wonder, then I have a kid who is messed up worrying about his thoughtless dad. Tell you what, text me by the end of the day, or I swear, I'll call Mandy to find out. We know that should be a fun call. Seriously, text today or call placed to Mandy. Bye."

Joel approached the window.

"Hi, honey," Julie was all smiles.

Two hours later, Julie received a text.

In PDX. I'm ok. Tell Joel.

Well that said so much, and yet so little.

Julie had managed to get a little more cash at the gas station, but it seemed pointless since prices were inflating quickly, even in the Great States. Better to stay in the car for the night.

"Let's hope we're out of here by noon tomorrow. You feeling okay?" Julie asked.

"Yes," Joel said evenly.

"I got a text from your dad earlier. Look," Julie showed Joel the text.

Joel's face lit up. He had been so quiet for most of the day. Julie realized she hadn't taken some time to talk to Joel about how he feels about all this upheaval. Obviously he was worried about his dad, and it showed.

"Joel. You know what I know. I haven't had any other contact with him other than this," Julie said. She didn't want him to think they had an "adult" conversation on the side and she was withholding information from him. This was all they both knew.

"I get it. He's in Portland with Mandy probably. Have we heard any news from Portland?"

"Honey, I think it's a lot like Eugene, just bigger," Julie said evenly. She didn't want to sugarcoat anything. The reality of what was happening in Oregon and around the country was out of hand and to explain it any differently than what it was would be dishonest.

"What could happen to Mandy?" Joel asked quietly.

"How do you mean? If she is pregnant, she will have a baby soon," Julie wasn't sure what he was asking.

"If Portland is burning like Eugene, what could happen to her? The baby? And even Dad if he stays there?"

Julie could sense that Joel had been thinking about this a lot.

"Honey, bad things. Seriously bad things. You and I need to pray that your dad gets to Mandy, and gets her out of Portland. I am hoping he hits the road like we have and takes her east. He has family there. Your dad can do what we're doing and leave." Julie painted one of the dozens of scenarios that could happen. It would be the scenario she hoped would happen.

She also knew Steve. He was a typical modern-day urban hipster male. He liked his hair care products, expensive shoes, man purses, and lattes. His idea of going outdoors was taking Joel to the park down the street. As far as Julie knew, he had never shot a firearm in his life. He had never gutted and cleaned a fish. Steve was a typical, progressive, urban man. He was kind, charming, and nice. Guns were scary and unnecessary. Being inclusive and loving conquered all conflict in Steve's world. He loved her through her inner demons; it was one of the qualities that made Julie fall in love with him. Now it irritated her to no end.

Julie also remembered something Joel said. Steve had not done any of the sorts of preparations Julie and Joel had. That told Julie the scenario she was "hoping" for probably wasn't going to happen.

"Mom. What will happen to the baby?" Joel asked. "That baby will be my little brother or sister."

Shit! She realized that she had only been thinking that baby was Steve and Mandy's offspring—not Joel's sibling. Joel was already getting attached to the idea of having a sibling.

The swear words that coursed through Julie's head were unrelenting. She was almost to the cabin. Refuge. Safety. Independence. Self-sustaining. Now Steve and his irresponsible behavior was ruining it. Joel was worried about his sibling in Portland. Julie realized she wasn't completely away from Oregon and never would be as long as Steve — and Joel's sibling — was there.

"Joel. You're right," Julie said after she shut down the stream of obscenities in her head. "There is nothing we can do for your dad, Mandy, or the baby. Your dad has my phone number. He knows how to reach us. If he calls, I'll find you so you can talk to him. I don't know what to tell you, but there is nothing I can do for him. He needs to fix this. He needs to get them out of Portland," Julie felt so helpless. Steve's "love conquers all" mentality would not be helpful in the hell he would be facing in Portland.

She also remembered her promise to her dad. Steve was not allowed at the cabin. She started thinking about a million potential problems. *Stop it,* she told herself. Onward. To Smoky Flats. To the cabin.

***

Julie turned up the road and saw the cabin. The sun was setting and the cabin windows were looking right at the sunset like eyes gazing at beauty. It was great to arrive. So good to be here. Julie could feel the tension and fatigue leave her shoulders as she pulled the keys out of the ignition.

Her father's vehicle wasn't there, but Julie recognized Ned's truck. She and Joel walked behind the cabin and there was the new barn. It was startling to see. Julie stopped in her tracks as she looked at it.

"Mom! Look! That is so cool!" Joel exclaimed. "I'm going to get the chicks to put in it!"

Joel had been taking gingerly care of the eight little critters. He had been doing so well that Julie really hadn't worried about them much. As Joel ran back to the car, the door to the barn slid and there was Ned.

"Oh, jeez! You startled me!" Ned exclaimed. "I knew you were coming, just didn't know when. I don't see people here often."

"I apologize. I should have called out. I am in awe of this. This looks great!" Julie said sweeping her hands at the barn.

"I was just about to head home since it's getting dark. We have a few minutes, want a tour?" Ned asked.

"Sure!"

Ned showed her the main room. It would house grown chickens and rabbits, hopefully. There was an area designated for pens, which would be needed for rabbits. There was a loft that a grown man would need to bend at the waist to be in, but would store hay, if they could get any. For sure, it would be storage of some kind. The side storage room had an old freezer in it.

"Someone was moving out of their cabin last spring, and left this behind. I grabbed it for you," Ned explained.

"No one wants a freezer?"

"Better way to say it, no one wants to haul a freezer out of here if they are moving," Ned said with a sly smile.

"Good point," Julie nodded.

The room with the freezer had a table that would be great to set the chicks up with their heat lamp. Ned helped Joel put together the setup while Julie watched. It was nice to watch Ned and Joel figure out the lamp and chat casually. It was relaxing. It was one of the few relaxing moments Julie had in days. Months. Years?

As they all left the new barn, Julie said, "Ned, I cannot thank you enough. I mean it."

"My pleasure. I am glad it got done on time. I was a little nervous. I'm going to head home. I know your dad should be here any day now. Let me know when he arrives?" Ned asked as he was turning to leave.

"Of course, again, thank you," Julie said.

"See ya later, Ned!" called Joel.

He smiled and waved as he turned over the truck's ignition. Julie watched him back down the driveway and head down the dusty road.

"Let's get what we need to sleep tonight. Get food in the fridge and freezer. Then let's sleep. And let's sleep in," Julie proposed to Joel.

"I am looking forward to sleeping in a bed," Joel said with a yawn.

"You got that right," Julie agreed.

Julie opened the doors and windows to air out the cabin. Then they unloaded until almost midnight. Julie knew that things were fairly secure here. If they left items in the trailer or SUV, the odds of theft were low. However, she also knew things were not as they were. People all over the county were doing strange things. She wanted to get as many things secure as soon as possible. The barn offered a great place to simply put things, then closed the door and lock it. It didn't take long.

When everything was securely stowed Joel said, "I need a shower. I stink."

It made Julie chuckle as she agreed. It took her a moment to think back a lifetime to three days ago when she had her last shower. Being at home in Eugene seemed like a decade ago, but it was only a few days.

Jeez, Julie thought. *This is messed up.*

Joel headed upstairs to one of the single beds. Julie decided she would sleep in the other one. Her dad would have the bedroom downstairs. Julie took a hot shower after saying goodnight to Joel. She stood there and let the water stream down her face as she faced the nozzle with her eyes closed. It was like a baptism into new life.

Chapter 29

Coming Home to Roost

The early morning light came through the upper stories of the cabin. Julie blinked and stayed still. She looked out the window and simply drank in the scenic pines; the stillness. It was the first time in four days she had been still.

Julie realized she had not relaxed since the moment when she stood in Eugene looking out the window at the horizon of gray smoke. She had been in full alert and defensive mode. She had almost shot a man at Roberta's campground. Sleeping in the car didn't help. Eating snacks from the car along the way for meals threw any semblance of a schedule into chaos.

"Today," Julie decided, "I will make a proper breakfast." She heaved a heavy sigh and closed her eyes again to simply relax.

Julie also knew she may not get the chance to again for a while.

Joel and Julie made biscuits and gravy. Julie had found an old chub of breakfast sausage in the freezer. Since the value of food and supplies was a premium, she decided to use it. She made a basic batch of biscuits. The gravy was simple. Sausage, flour, and hydrated powdered milk did the trick. It was not restaurant quality but it filled Julie and Joel's empty stomachs. They had been living off powdered drinks, granola bars, and leftover perishables they had grabbed from the kitchen in Eugene.

After breakfast, they spent the day organizing. Joel was amazed at all the supplies.

"You and Grandpa got so much done when you came! The barn! That is just sick," Joel said with glee.

The items in the barn were stacked either in the storage room or stacked with other bins in the cabin. Julie took in the chicken operation. Joel showed her how the heat lamp worked. It needed to keep the chickens warm. They needed constant feed and water. Soon, within just a few weeks, they would start getting their adult feathers. Joel said it would be easy to know which ones were roosters because they start crowing.

"You do know that I don't want a lot of roosters. Roosters will be dinners. I need one or two roosters to make more chicks," Julie tried to explain delicately.

"Mommmmm…" Joel rolled his eyes.

"This isn't 'the talk,' my dear. This is reality. Boy chickens and girl chickens make more chickens. Now, do you want to be in charge of this? If you are, there is no room for mess ups. I am depending on the eggs the hens will lay, and the meat the roosters will provide. Can I put you in charge of this or should I do it?" Julie was earnest. She knew taking on this operation required at least two if not more trips a day to the barn to make sure they were fed, water levels were plenty, and no predators were here. Trips to the barn when winter came would not be a simple walk outside in summer flips flops.

"I want to do it, Mom. But I've never done this. I don't want to mess up. Can you at least help me at first?" Joel asked honestly.

"Of course. I need to learn this too. Let's get these little ones grown up and laying together. Then go from there."

"So, Mom. Umm… when we need to make a chicken into a meal. How do we do that?" Joel asked with a scrunched-up nose.

"I'm not going to lie; I've never done it myself," Julie said. "But from what I've read, and we'll need to check the book, we can either wrench its neck or cut off its head with a hatchet. Next, we drain the blood from the carcass. Then we need to take the feathers off. They can be plucked or blanched in boiling water. That makes the feathers come off easier. I saw a YouTube video on it. We need a big pot. I don't know if we have one large enough. We'll have to see," Julie explained. "So, your aversion to butchering animals might need to be addressed. How you feeling about what I just described?"

"Well, yuck," Joel said. "You asked. But I took that one class that explained butchering large game. A chicken seems like nothing after watching videos of moose being butchered. I guess I just need to do it. It's pretty basic for most animals. You kill them, sometimes bleed them, take out the guts, then cut them up however you want."

"Oh my word!" Julie exclaimed. "I'm genuinely impressed! Seriously! I just had a good idea. Let's go fishing later and I'll show you how to clean a fish. It's just as you described except you don't need to bleed fish. It might be a good baby step. I can clean fish in my sleep. Chickens seem like a large fish to me. Larger game, you and I will need to stick together."

"Honey, seriously. I want you to think about the skills you learned in all those classes. Meat to eat will become a big deal. Food is already hard to get here on a good day just because we're far away from town. During a crisis, as you saw when we drove here, meat is as good as gold. So, think about squirrels, birds, and other game you think you can hunt

175

with the .22. Okay?" Julie asked. Joel nodded.

"I need to talk to Ned about rules for hunting," Julie said. "He was going to check and I never got the answer. But we'll find out. In the meantime, we are on private property, and we can hunt what we have here. However, you need to be mindful of where you're aiming. Take a walk around the property and get a clear idea of where other people's properties are. You cannot, and I mean absolutely cannot, ever hunt in a manner that a shot could be aimed and fired at a structure. I cannot stress that enough."

"Mom, I promise. I learned that over and over again in my classes," Joel reassured.

"Thank you, honey," Julie sighed. She reached over and hugged his shoulder. "Joel, I love you. We can do this."

As the sun started heading west later that day, Julie looked at Joel and said, "Let's go drown some bait."

"Mom, do we even have any bait?"

"You ask a good question. I think there is some really stinky roe in the fridge that is pretty old. Let's try that," Julie proposed. "But let's think about this," she continued. "We will run out of that eventually. Let's think about catching grasshoppers tomorrow. I also think we should try to dig up worms. It might be hard since it's mostly gravel around here. But let's look for damp soil spots to dig near the lake or as we walk there."

"How in the world do you catch grasshoppers, Mom?" Joel was incredulous.

"I was a pro when I was your age. I'll show you how to do it. Best time is in the middle of the day when the sun is overhead. I've caught many fish out of that lake with grasshoppers I've caught," Julie bragged. "Also, we should also go visit Ned tomorrow. We need to see if there are any catch limits in the lake since everything is in upheaval. Let's just catch one fish tonight, if we catch any. Okay?"

Joel agreed.

***

Joel and Julie sat quietly by the lake as the sun started to kiss the horizon. The air was getting a damp chill in it.

They had two poles propped up on sticks. Julie knew two ways to fish this lake. Off the bottom, where you put a weight on the end of the line, allowing the line to go to the bottom while the bait suspended above the weight having been attached to the line. The line was pulled tight and the pole propped on a stick. When the end of the line jerked hard or bent hard, a quick yank on the line hooked the fish to be reeled in.

Another way Julie knew was with a bobber. The bobber was a plastic ball suspended on the line and floated on the water with the rest of the baited line hanging below the bobber in the water. If the bobber took a sudden dive in the water, a quick yank on the line hooked the fish to be reeled in.

Earlier that day, Julie had found four poles in the closet. Two were completely tangled. *How in the world?* Julie mused as she looked at them. The other two were set up for fishing the bottom.

Joel sat next to one pole watching the end, Julie at the other. Julie was having many childhood memories flood back to her and she watched the end of the pole. Julie remembered as a little girl that she felt like such a grown up when she was allowed to fish off the bottom with a weighted line instead of a bobber. Bobbers were for little kids.

Julie remembered that if you concentrated too much on the end, the rippling waves behind the end of the pole created an optical illusion that made the pole look like it was floating away. These were silly memories. She relaxed as she replayed them in her mind.

Julie's thoughts wandered back to the events of the past few days. While she had managed to hear a lot of regional news, she didn't hear any news out of Eugene. It dawned on Julie. She had no idea what was happening currently in Eugene. *Had the fires been contained? How bad was the damage? Was her home ok? What the governor's promise that this whole mess was "temporary" true?* Her mind was suddenly not on fishing.

Julie found herself excusing away her memories as being more dramatic than the actual situation really was. But she also heard three days of radio stating that Portland and Eugene were burning uncontrollably and that citizens were being evacuated. She heard nothing saying it was okay to return.

Julie found herself almost arguing with herself. It was a fight between what she wanted to be true and what was probably true. The former was a much easier to imagine. The latter was rooted in reality.

Julie struggled with the idea that her home could be destroyed. What would happen then? It was insured. She would get something for it, but then what? Rebuild? Go back? Go back to what? She had house payments and car payments to make. She had no job in Eugene, and she doubted her workplace would be funded anytime soon so it could reopen.

Many nonprofits receiving government assistance to provide services would not be funded for years to come, if ever. Her job skills wouldn't be needed for a long time.

Jobs here? Julie just couldn't even fathom that thought. The closest town was two and a half miles away. In between the cabin and that town was nothing but ranchland and a handful of cabins. The town had a handful of businesses that sat on the state highway and provided roadside amenities to travelers going through the Rockies using the highway. There was a gas station with a mini-mart. A small restaurant. A county library. A post office. Jobs?

I'll be sure to get a paper to check the want ads, Julie joked to herself. She couldn't imagine looking up jobs online in the tiny town down the road.

She had nothing. Nothing. Tears burned up in her eyes. Should she go back to Eugene once this all blows over? *When would that be?* She worried. Julie's stomach was turning to knots. Very little fishing was happening. Julie just worried.

"Mom!" Joel's voice pulled Julie out of her worrisome thoughts. "Look!"

Joel pointed up the road. A car was rumbling toward them. Julie sat still. It wasn't unusual for a car to come by the lake while fishing. "Don't worry, Joel. Someone is just driving by," Julie replied.

"I think it's Grandpa!" Joel called.

Julie squinted. She looked hard at the driver. It didn't look like his car, but maybe he traded in the old for the new like Julie had.

A small sized SUV pulled up to them, and as soon as it stopped, she knew. Joel ran to the car as he sat in the front seat with a large smile on his face. Her dad was here. Safe.

"Grandpa!" Joel yelled as he ran to the car. Her father got out of the car and hugged Joel hard. He lifted Joel off his feet and gently swung him from side to side.

"Oh my word, it is so good to see you," he choked. "I have missed you. I've been so worried about you."

"I missed you, too, Grandpa."

"Young man, you got tall!" He placed Joel back on the grown.

"I'm so glad you're here," Joel said.

"Dad." Julie touched his shoulder. Father and daughter embraced for several moments.

"You made it. I'm so glad you made it. You're safe," he whispered in Julie's ear.

"I'm so glad you did, too. It is so good to see you, Dad, I'm glad you're safe, too."

"Well it looks like some fishing is happening. Any luck?"

"Not yet. I hope we can catch at least one," Joel said.

"Gotta be quiet. We have sun for about fifteen more minutes, so let's hope!" He sat down next to Joel. Everyone was quiet for the fish.

Discussion would happen later.

END OF BOOK ONE

Made in the USA
Columbia, SC
09 April 2018